The Unraveled

by M.C. Ray

Text Copyright © 2020 by M.C. Ray aka McSellin Ray II

M.C. Ray aka McSellin Ray II
www.jovenelray.com
Instagram: @UnveiledSeries
Twitter: @UnveiledSeries
Facebook: The Unveiled Series
Cover Art by JD&J Book Cover Design

The Unraveled / M.C. Ray aka McSellin Ray II – 1st ed
ISBN – 978-1-7363423-0-5

Thank you to Jared

Dedicated to my mother, Mary: the heart that beats for her children. She is the original Madja.

M.C. Ray

Chapter One

The sky was a brilliant blue. The purple hue that once emanated from the fallen veil would never grace the heavens again. Clouds soared overhead like the masts of giant ships, casting down spiraling snowflakes on the burned rooftops and crumbled stone of the city below. The cold, harsh wind knocked over small shrubs, sending them tumbling down the tarnished streets. The city of Keldrock had survived, but just barely, and at a great cost. Many an elf and human perished on the Day of Unveiling. From the window of my chamber in the palace, I watched the assemblage of black-clad elves carrying bodies to be buried in the rocky tombs that lay just below the mountain. From the heights of my chamber, I could see them trailing into the massive stone structures like a line of sugar ants carrying cubes to their anthill. The dead Dwala men and women had been gathered in the black ring's square and burned per the prince's orders, filling the air with the smell of roasting flesh.

It had been three months since a group of assassins attacked the Chamber of Light and murdered our protector, Shiloh. Although I hadn't left the purple ring—or even the palace for that matter—since the Day of Unveiling, I could sense that life continued on quietly below. I was sure that like me, the Dwala were in their homes, awaiting the judgment that would befall them from the courts, the lawmakers of our city.

I learned that the Guerr, the militia of Keldrock, returned about a fortnight after the Day of Unveiling, bringing with them a dozen or so captives who I assume had tried to attack these elven warriors at the veil's border. I was surprised that the Guerr took prisoners instead of ending the warriors of Wood Haven right on the spot. They were only prolonging the inevitable. The Guerr hadn't dealt a hard, swift sentence to these invaders, but I was almost certain the courts would.

I had barely seen my mother, whom I called Madja, my sister Mira, and had yet be updated on the status my Dwala friend Kala, or even my most loyal comrades, Segun and Rayloh, since everything had happened. I saw on occasion only my father because of his position on the council, mostly just to keep me updated on the status of my case against the royal family. I would sit and listen until he finally tired of talking to himself and left. My father had never put this much effort into our relationship before. Now it seemed he cared more than anything for my right to rule and viewed this case as no more than a spoiled brat's plea to a powerless birthright. Perhaps my father thought of me as an inevitable failure who would never evolve to be what he wanted me to be, but somehow I had become more than any of us could ever imagine. In two days I was to go before the courts where they would discuss the issues at hand: Who would be the new leader of our nation, and had I truly committed crimes against the crown?

Alag, prince of Keldrock, and the brat my father was keen on defying, kept his distance now. The few times I ventured from my chambers and ran into him, he simply nodded. The charming prince had apparently lost favor in me, even though I had no direct participation in anything that occurred between Shiloh and me in the Chamber of Light. Still, he could only see it that way. I felt that he would engineer my downfall himself if it meant that he would get the crown.

In the meantime, I dove back into the thing I loved most: books. I re-read many of my favorite stories and even picked up some new ones from the royals' extensive library. They had many volumes and novels, a more extensive collection than I had ever seen, even the library at the School of Talents. Some were old and worn, encased in leather and sealed in cases under lock and key, much like the sifting book that revealed the secrets to unleashing ancient elven powers, which I had lost in the fire at the Remni, the compound where I used to live.

The elves serving in the palace seemed to be aware of all the issues that went on in supposed secret. While some who waited upon me were extraordinarily kind and thorough in their care, others were cold and distant, their allegiance aligning with the prince's disdain. I enjoyed some of my favorite meals as well as a few exotic dishes and I donned the most elaborate and elegant of robes and nightgowns just to spend most of my days in my chambers, reading and watching the city from my window, as snowflakes floated down like angels banished to the troublesome quarrels of earth.

But nothing could distract me from the uncertain future. I'd wake in terrible tremors. The dreams, with each passing night, had become stronger, more lifelike. I could still see Sir Calo's chilling face and dark eyes as he lay still on the Remni's stone floor. I kept hearing the loud clap of his shaven head colliding with the marble. Over and over again, the same nightmare.

***

On the morning of my trial, my father arrived earlier than I expected, but I had already risen for the day. My body had lost its adapted rhythm of waking up at the time Master Tali required, and I had grown accustomed to sleeping in. Master Tali not only taught me at Shiloh's School of Talents but also selected me as her protégé to learn the art of sifting. The mornowl's call no longer rang through the skies signaling daybreak. It was said that without the call of the mornowl, our sun would not rise, and in some respect our sun hadn't risen, nor would it ever again. Without the veil, the sun looked cold and distant with winter, as the ice that coated the city streets. This winter, the harshest I'd ever seen. I could see the yellow garden's damaged dome, the repairs delayed due to the unpredictable weather. The destruction couldn't have happened at a worse time. The gardens were the elves' main source of food during the winter season, serving the city's two middle rings, and without that, the food rations were most likely deplorable. There were matters within the kingdom that would fall on the head of someone. Today I would find out if that someone would be me.

As we strode the walkways and covered bridges that connected the small intercity of the purple ring, the innermost ring, I pictured what it would be like around this time in the Remni if this tragedy had not occurred. The sprites and I would have been drinking hot chocolate by the fireplace after playing in the snow, tossing frost sparklers at one another until our noses were runny from the chill. I thought of Mira and me, cuddling under a blanket with bowls of vegetable soup while I read aloud tales of princesses in tall towers and brave warriors of distant lands.

It was such a simple wish, to wish that I would never have to grow up. The most disconcerting thing about coming of age isn't the ceremonies, the responsibilities, or even the newfound freedom, but the transformation that occurred without you noticing. I wondered if the caterpillar in its cocoon knew that it would awaken to find itself a different being altogether. Or maybe it didn't realize until it was too late, until its beautiful wings either lifted it into the skies or sent it tumbling to the ground.

Right now, I was falling and I didn't know if I would catch the breeze or be destroyed by the unforgiving trench. Some days I would stare at myself in the mirror and see a whole different being. My long strands of shimmering black hair had been turned, in response to the protector's light, to a silvery white—dazzling, but still not me. Some days, I would altogether avoid the mirror just to keep the pounding hypothetical of *what if this had never happened?* at bay.

My self-loathing would have to cease for the moment. Judgment day had arrived. The courts' chambers were magnificent. Even in my agitated state, I could appreciate the angles of this grand hall. A long bench wrapped around the walls, allowing each individual that sat behind it on one of the ornately detailed chairs to narrow in on the creature that came before them, deciding their guilt or their innocence based on the quivering of a lip or a twitch of an eyebrow.

The rows for the audience were filled to capacity with practically every elf I had ever seen, with the exception of the Guerr, whom I assumed had returned to their barracks and recommenced training. I spotted Madja and Mira amongst the attendees, their brows lowered to the floor. They knew I had come in and, more than anything, they probably wanted to run out into the aisle, grab my hand, and rush me away from this dreadful place. But they had to maintain their composure the best they could. I could see Madja's lips moving fast, her eyebrows furrowed, wrinkling her forehead as soft tears ran down her cheeks. She was praying.

"Where's Kala? Why isn't she with Mira and Madja?" I whispered to my father.

"She's not allowed in the purple ring. Only descendants of the nymphs are allowed past the gates. I'm sorry." I had forgotten that little known fact, but all in all, I knew he wasn't sorry. The words sprouted too easily from his lips.

I let my eyes wander through the rows of stern faces in search of the lads. They weren't here either. I hadn't heard word back from them and I refused to let my mind jump to the absolute worst of conclusions. The Guerr was successful in finding and capturing the warriors from Wood Haven. Segun and Rayloh had to have survived. Surely they would be here to see me. Surely their commanders would understand.

The courts were already in the chamber like wolves in sheep's clothing, robes of white draped around their bodies, while the lower officers that formed the council, in purple robes, held their noses high behind the bench. The four members of the courts sat behind the platform, two on each side of a grand throne that acted as the room's center marker. It didn't take me long to figure out who that throne was for.

"All arise for Prince Alag of the house of Estrellar, the grandson of Protector Shiloh."

The whole of the courtroom stood as his procession entered, some of the elves breaking out into applause as the remaining blood heir took his place. I kept my eyes straight ahead toward my jurors. Any dissonance from the stance of my peers would be just a meaningless distraction. Alag wore, surprisingly, unscarred armor, breastplates, and gauntlets. On his head, there was no crown—I assumed, since it was up for debate whether he should rule or not, it would be most humiliating for the prick to lose it in such a public manner, especially at the hands of a she-elf. An old elf I recognized from the lads' Guerr ceremony stood, his grey beard covering most of his face, drawing attention to his hard, impenetrable dark brown eyes. He held his palm forward, silencing the jeering drones that carried on behind me.

"The case brought before us today pertains to the state of our kingdom and whether a thief and a traitor lies in our midst—or if, in fact, the right to rule belongs to the one, Alya Lightstar." He looked at me, then motioned to Alag with the same hand that he extended to quiet the crowd once more. "Prince Alag will come before us, just as you will come, Protector Alya."

The crowd began to whisper, unsure of how to take this address. Even I was unnerved, considering that I had no wish to take the title, let alone the responsibility of defending these close-minded people who would probably rather see me hung from the gallows than wear the crown. To them, I was the cause of all of this unrest. The deaths that numbered were far too great, and now their anger was the only measure.

The old elf continued, "In the tradition of our ancestors, the accuser will address the courts first, then the defense. Prince Alag, you have the floor."

Alag stood, shimmering like one of the many painted likenesses of god-like elven warriors that graced the inner walls of the palace.

"Many years has my bloodline ruled the heads of elven kin born into this kingdom. Many have heard the legends of our great rulers, and the greatest of them all left this world on the Day of Unveiling: Protector Shiloh. I hope only to be as great as he. And if not for being on the battlefront, in the edgewoods, I would have been here to defend him—and our people—from the intruders. Today, I don the armor to symbolize my commitment to my people and in doing so, I want to stress that the right to rule belongs to me, despite my stolen birthright that shines bright above her brow, whitening her crown. I have come requesting the support of the courts that the accused understand the unlikelihood of such events. That Olörun's light did not simply pass from Protector Shiloh to Alya but was stolen. In any case, the next heir was to be me, so if the courts decide in my favor, then as my first act, I will pardon the she-elf of her treachery."

With that, Alag sat down. His speech was no more than a plethora of opinions with no substance behind them. This was who was to rule our people? His comments were self-involved, but the audience didn't seem to think so. The drones started up again without hesitation and I knew that other than my family, I was probably alone in this opinion. The prince had been taught well how to address his people, and even if he hadn't won the whole of them, his mercy upon my life if he took the throne pulled them to his side as well.

The old elf stood again, raising his palm for quiet. It took the crowd longer than he wanted to calm down, the intensity in his stare growing hard until their jabbering stopped.

"You may address the courts." His eyes bore down on me, his pupils driving hard into my conscious.

I stood up. The room grew still. The slaps of my slippers against the flats of my feet echoed throughout the chamber, bouncing off the ceiling and the high walls as I approached the platform.

"Well… I…" I started.

Before I could say more, my father spoke up. "I feel the need to press upon the courts, the officers of the council, and my kingdom, that Protector Alya has not been made aware of the law and all it encompasses, and it would be most efficient as well as honorable within our government that I represent her in this case." The whispers returned but I worried about none of that now. My father was speaking up on my behalf. We hadn't discussed this beforehand. Even though I barely listened to his words, for this I would have sparked to attention. I didn't quite understand his angle, but in all of this madness, I simply wanted to retreat from the judgment chambers. If my father could accomplish that, it was all the more reason to surrender my platform.

"Well?" The old elves that made up the courts peered down at me with requesting expressions. My father gently gripped my hand, urging me along. The seconds seemed to trickle by like drips from a leaky ceiling.

"Fine."

I turned swiftly and walked out of the judgment chambers, passing scrutinizing eyes. I nearly fainted as the doors slammed behind me. I couldn't stay in there any longer. I couldn't stand the murmurs that seemed to be shouting at me as I made the seemingly long trek to the back of the judgment hall and out to the lobby. I sat down on a stone bench, letting the bluster flow out of me in slow, long breaths. I ran my fingers along my neck, slowly tracing my throat down to my collarbone where the familiar feel of cold metal cooled my fingers.

The necklace I acquired so long ago in the black ring had somehow become a part of me. It was one of the few things I had left that reminded me of my old life, and I never took it off. I continued stroking it, running the tips of my fingers over the green orbs of the snake's eyes. It seemed like hours had passed. I could see the sun setting through the windows, which it did now much earlier than in the warmer months, and soon the rush of winds rattled the stained glass panels. It was odd, making a public spectacle of such an important matter. Before the Day of Unveiling, I had never been past the purple ring's gates, nor had Madja, and now it seemed everyone from the elven ironsmiths that resided in the blue ring to the common seamstress were in the audience. I buried my face in my hands until I heard the chamber's doors creak open.

"They'll see you now."

I looked up, allowing my cupped eyes to adjust from the blurriness caused by the pressure of my hands. I focused on the figure that summoned me. It was a guard. In fact, it was the very guard who had rudely urged me to take my seat among the sprites at the lads' Guerr ceremony, and the same one who discovered Nazda and me in the yellow garden's dome the day we ran away into the edgewoods. He didn't look me in my eyes. He just stared ahead, his fingers locked around the staff he carried.

"Your name, officer?" I asked.

"Kai. Kai Silvertail."

I stood up and followed him in, clenching my teeth as I passed the multitude of angry eyes that lined the aisle. I could feel the heat of their gazes poking at my skin. I wanted nothing more than to run into Madja's arms and escape from the burn.

My father stood before the bench, smiling. I didn't return his grin. I stood next to him, ready to receive the court's judgment. Alag had come down from his seat and stood on the other side of the aisle, adjacent to my father, looking forward. Just as I had taken my place in the center of the chamber did I hear the loud creak and the thud of the jurors' doors opening. The old elves emerged, followed by the members of the council.

"We have come to a decision. Per your suggestion, Lord Meoltan, it would be extremely difficult to decipher exactly what transpired in the Chamber of Light on the Day of Unveiling. Only two parties know what happened that day, and one has passed into the heavens. Still, witnesses can attest to Alya's bravery and her fight to protect our city. Although the Protector and the ruler of our nation have always happened to be one and the same, we have decided that Prince Alag will take his place as head of the nation and you, Alya, as his betrothed, will serve him as the Protector."

Whispers slowly began, mixing in with the sucking of teeth and the deep sighs of disappointed mistresses. I looked back at the guard, his eyes now on me, as if he expected me to say something—or possibly he was going to congratulate me on this news. I didn't know what he felt, but I knew that I had an opportunity not to be nudged in the direction that everyone thought had to be so. My advantage became apparent.

"While I'm sure that it took a great deal of time to reach that conclusion, I have another one that may rest well with the courts." I didn't have to raise my voice even slightly for all the commotion to end and for silence to take its place. "Whatever rumors or allegations befall me, I assure you I committed no intentional crime against the courts, the royal family, or my nation, and as the witnesses interviewed have pointed out, I staked my life to defend the Chamber of Light from the intruders. I can't help but think that we're entering a new age. I am the first she-elf to be named Protector, and the veil has fallen. I am needed whether my people choose to accept that or not."

The old elf began to scowl under his beard, but I wasn't finished. I knew I had to play my cards properly if my proposal was to go unchallenged. "I do, however, understand I have much to learn, and the courts have proven that they are more than capable of guarding the throne until the prince comes of age. I therefore suggest that the prince and I work in conjunction with each other without being married under the advisement of the courts."

Uproar grew in the crowd as the courts spoke amongst themselves, whispering in what seemed like less of a decision concerning my suggestion and more of whether or not I should be sentenced to death today or on the morrow. Soon the mighty hand of the old elf was raised and all quickly returned to calm.

"We have considered it. The prince has nearly reached the age to rule, a proper seventeen years. That much is true, but he is not the Protector, as history normally would have. That responsibility falls upon you, Protector Alya. Until you are old enough to rule, when your sixteenth year has passed, then will you and the prince take your rightful places on the throne." I knew this suggestion would work. The courts had been set in place as the temporary order of our city, and although we assumed their intentions were pure, not even the truest of hearts can resist power. "Still, the Protector and the royal line are one, and you are a she-elf. Therefore, you will be joined, but not until after your sixteenth year. That will allow time for the futures of our kingdom to become well acquainted and for you to learn your responsibilities. That is our final word."

In unison, the members of the courts stood up and exited the room, the thud of the door echoing against the marble columns. Guards rushed to our sides and escorted us out through the side doors while others stood in the aisle with their staffs outstretched, ensuring that none of the riled onlookers stepped out of line in an attempt to attack Alag and me. I couldn't help but cringe at the thought of marrying that brat of a he-elf. Immediately after crossing the threshold of the chamber doors, Alag departed, leaving me standing there with two guards to escort me back to the palace.

I took to my bed, feeling weak and overwhelmed. I had never felt so despised. I had prided myself on not being popular with the sprites in my year at school, but I had never been so openly taunted and ridiculed. I settled down slowly, letting the warm quilts and satin sheets wrap me in their warmth. Yet my body continued to shiver as hot tears ran down my cheeks onto my pillow. It was easier to sleep today, but my body trembled the whole night through, reminding me of the sadness and rejection that I would have to face in the morning once the news had reached the entire city.

Chapter Two

I didn't awake to the soft patter of snow against the windowpanes or the whistling sounds of the winter winds, but to the boisterous chants of angry voices. I looked out my window to find at the purple ring's gates a mob of Dwala from the lowest of the four rings with torches and staffs. The purple ring's guards had formed a blockade with their spears outstretched. The crowd wasn't violent, but they were angry. I stared at the group of about fifty or so as they slowly began to resolve to a single phrase which they chanted over and over again.

"Free our people! Free our people!"

I wondered what they could possibly be alluding to. To my knowledge, none of the Dwala within the city had been imprisoned, especially in the purple ring. Then I saw in the crowd someone familiar and recognized immediately of whom they spoke. I hurriedly hopped out of bed, stuffing my feet into my slippers, grabbed my housecoat, and sprinted down the hall and down the gigantic staircase. I struggled to open the heavy doors of the palace, the attendants scattered due to the unrest outside. I barely got them open wide enough to slip out before the wind forced them shut again.

The harsh current whipped at my face, numbing my nose and lips. My eyes moistened but it was way too chilly for tears to spill. After I made it about halfway to the gate, each step had become a small miracle. My strength and energy hadn't returned to me just yet after the past couple of days of strained eating, lack of sleep, and stress, but eventually I reached the gate. I was now able to see the individual flickers of the torch flames. In the front of the mob, I saw Yann, Shiloh's killer, with her black curls, this time a black ribbon working hard to tame her wild mane where the red one had failed. I assumed she had been killed atop the tower during the Unveiling, but here she stood. When she met my eyes, she didn't seem afraid. In fact, it seemed as if she expected me. She smirked, and while staring me daringly in the eyes, she continued chanting with the crowd. I didn't move any closer. My mind couldn't help but jump back to that moment in the Chamber of Light, when I was mere feet away from Yann, with no way to defend myself. The way she toyed with me like prey and the crazed look she had… She was Shiloh's killer, and that was reason enough to end her. It wouldn't happen again. I would be no one's prey.

"Guards! Arrest her!"

The words slipped from my mouth before I could order them in a more precise manner. I squared myself as a guard, more decorated than the others, looked at me, then to Yann, as he tried to figure out whether he was required to carry out this command. I hadn't shouted it as a command but more so a call to action that even as a common she-elf I would have shouted. But I wasn't a common she-elf anymore, and to the angry mob, I was no more than just another oppressor bearing down on them. The guard obviously decided to heed my words, so he grabbed Yann while his comrades continued to press against the boisterous crowd. I was still quite surprised at the amount of authority I had, and I knew I needed to use it to my advantage when dealing with such serious matters as an assassin like Yann. There had to be a reason why she'd come out into the open so publicly after committing such treachery.

"Search her, then hold her in one of the maid's cells until I meet with the prince and the courts to determine a date for her hearing."

The guard began patting her down, still just as confused as he was before. "Isn't it the law that only those of elven blood can pass these gates?" he questioned as he worked his way down her legs to her shins and ankles.

"That is no matter. She is permitted for reasons that shouldn't be discussed until I have made the proper arrangements." Just as he finished his search, Yann finally spoke.

"I request an audience with Alya, if so granted by you, Great Protector." Her comment was so drenched in sarcasm that the guard forcibly snatched her by the arm, the pressure from his fingers turning her light brown skin red.

"Choose your tone and words carefully, human," he sneered before turning to me. "Should I take her to the maid cells?" He had no problem exerting his authority and by the look of his uniform, which differed from the others at the gate, he had to be a highly ranked officer.

"Nazda told me that you were way more sensible than this, and even if that isn't true, I expected your weak trait of kindness to allow our conversing in private. I guess I was wrong on both fronts. The taste of power changes even the simplest of minds."

The guard let go of Yann's arm and raised his hand, bringing it down hard against her cheek. Before she had a chance to collect herself, he ensnared her in his grip once again. She smirked at the guard as a thin line of blood trickled from the corner of her mouth. Then she looked at me, winking.

"What will you have me do, Protector?"

I thought about it for a moment. I knew she had mentioned Nazda for a reason. Yann was manipulative, whether it was for the purpose of getting people to like her or fear her. For now, I was unsure of her plans, but I couldn't let her know I was nervous.

"I will oblige. Finish searching her, clean her up, and bring her to my chambers at once."

With that, I turned and headed back into the palace, allowing the warmth inside to encompass me. My fingers felt agitated, a burning sensation, as they thawed after being numbed from the cold. I rushed upstairs to my room and looked around for possible weapons, taking note of the lantern on my nightstand and the coatrack in the corner. I wouldn't be caught off guard again just to become one of Yann's meaningless playthings. I stood anxiously, staring out the large window at the commotion at the gates, until I received a knock at my door.

"Come in."

The guard, his hand still firmly gripped around Yann's arm, stepped into the room. Her face had been wiped clean; all that remained was a tiny split in the corner of her mouth from the rough reprimanding she had received.

"We won't be needing you anymore." Yann alluded to the guard without looking his way.

He looked to me and I nodded. He flung her into my chambers like the barkeeps would do when beggars slipped into their establishments to harass patrons for money. We stood for a moment. She smiled that same eerie smile that she always managed to summon onto her face no matter if the situation called for it. I had seen this expression too many times in the course of our short relationship, so I was prepared. I made sure my eyes remained unchanged, my mouth still.

"You're scared, aren't you? You can admit it." She began twisting the ends of her curly hair with her fingers in an innocent kind of way that misses do when they flirt with young he-elves. "I love your hair, by the way. The new color really brings out the fear in your eyes."

"State your business. Guards are waiting outside the door to take you away, so I would choose your words wisely."

"Oh my, how the fallen have risen. Who would have thought that an elven runaway would become the Protector? I'm sure that your people would want to know why you ran away, or have you forgotten your friends so easily? I mean, Niegi and

Nazda, they are so kind, but sometimes bad things can happen to good people." She giggled a little, sending chills down my spine.

"You wouldn't dare hurt your own." I puffed up, ensuring that I didn't display any signs of worry. "You have no power here. If I stop you from walking out of those doors—"

"You? Stop me? That wasn't an option I had even remotely considered. I've come for one reason and that is to free the ones you've captured. If this demand is not met, then I will have no choice but to attack the city."

"I'm not so worried. The Guerr have returned with your warriors. They didn't stand a chance against them or else we wouldn't be having this conversation." I smirked, trying to make my simper as intimidating as hers. It didn't work. She stared at me blankly, smiling. "Now is that all?"

"Oh no, there's more." Her tone was condescending. "You see, if my people are to see justice in your kin's eyes, then why don't we lay everything out for the judgment of your people. The death of the old elf is still unresolved."

"No, it's not. You and I both know that you murdered Shiloh, and as soon as we finish this banter, you'll never see the light of day again."

"I wasn't speaking of that ancient relic your people thought could protect you. I mean the one from the Remni." She pulled from her cleavage an old piece of parchment, soiled and stained from the elements. Even through its discoloration and the ink smears I could make out what it said. It was the wanted poster,

Nazda's face sketched to near perfection on that sheet. After Yann saw that I had recognized what it was, she stuffed it back into her bosom.

Nazda wouldn't have told her anything. She wouldn't betray me. I did leave her in the edgewoods, and who knows what tools of persuasion the company of Wood Haven may have used. I decided to play ignorant for the time being. "You can't possibly think that I had anything to do with that?"

"Oh, no. I think you had everything to do with it. You know I wouldn't hurt my own. That would be counterproductive, and I would lose the trust of Wood Haven—but you see, the elves know one human was there and if that person is found and has to face death, they might reveal more than you would want about your people's new Protector."

Now this Yann would do—turn Nazda over, claiming she was captured. She knew that when she came before me with this proposition that she had already won.

"So how do you suppose I announce their release?" I replied. "Should I just go before the courts and command that these enemies of Keldrock be released?"

Yann's grin grew wider. "You're fortunate you have me in this dealing because I'm going to make it easy on you. All you have to do is provide me the key to the prison cells tomorrow before sunrise at the yellow garden's dome—or whatever's left of it. You give me that and whatever secrets you have—as well as your friends—remain safe. Do we have an agreement?" She extended her hand.

I thought about it for a moment. All she wanted was their freedom; keeping them here wouldn't make any difference in any way other than that they would see death. Only one took Shiloh's life. Only one ended the veil. She was the one I wanted. She was the one I would get. I reached out, gripping her palm, until I heard the bones in her hand cry out in distress. She didn't show the smallest sign of agitation, but continued to eerily smile.

"Guard!" The headstrong officer cracked the door just wide enough to poke his head through. "Escort this wretch to the gate and ensure that she causes no more disruptions. The crowd should cease their chanting upon her return. I have her word." She rolled her eyes and left with the guard.

I took off my house robe and sunk onto the bed, letting my hair dangle off the edge. I let out a breath as I stared at my ceiling, painted with magical creatures dancing across it without a worry to be had. I wondered if they had encountered deranged assassins and fallen rulers in their kingdoms. Did the fairies ever become jealous of the angels and try to steal their halos, or did the centaurs ever become overwhelmed with power and insist that they knew what was best for the gentle fauns? I ran my hand over the scales of my necklace, allowing the rough creases of its pattern soothe my pounding head. I had just begun to relax when I received a knock at the door.

"I do not wish to be disturbed," I shouted. Still the visitor persisted, now banging on the strong oak frame. "A moment!" I yelled in annoyance.

I slowly arose, slipping back on my housecoat, and attempted to fix my hair so that upon receiving this visitor I didn't look as if I had just awoken for the day. I opened the door just as a heavy body collided with the floor, causing me to recoil in surprise. Blood pooled on the floor as I tried to make sense of the situation. I ran through the archway, over the body of the guard, treading through the red puddle.

"Help! Someone!" I shouted over the bannister as dazed servants and busy officials stopped in their tracks to look up at their new Protector screaming for help.

I looked around frantically, searching for the young assassin who was intent on killing whomever crossed her. I knew she had done this. The guard had pushed her, and the crazed Yann took yet another life. I stopped as my gaze landed on my chamber door. Her ivory dagger pierced the massive bulk of oak planks, just as it had pierced Sir Calo and now a palace guard. The blade was still fresh with his blood, tiny droplets forming at the junction where the ivory and metal met and dripping on the floor, landing in round, perfect orbs. Around the ivory handle was a black ribbon tied in a bow. I quickly wrapped my hand around the ivory handle and began pulling my hardest to pry it from the door, but it wouldn't budge.

"Halt." I snatched my hands to my sides as my father, along with a helmeted guard and Alag, galloped up the stairs.

"Alya! My daughter, are you all right?"

"I'm unharmed."

"What happened?" My father ran to the side of the fallen guard, turned him over onto his back, and opened his blood-stained robe to reveal a slit under his right breast. "The captain! It's the captain of the Guards of Candor! Did you see who did this?"

I hesitated before answering, turning and staring at the blade sticking out of my door. Did Yann know he was so highly ranked? Even I didn't know he was the captain of the Guards of Candor. It all happened so fast. Where had Yann gone? I had underestimated her again and so did the captain. His bronze skin was already beginning to lose its ebony luster as all life drained from his empty frame.

"I know that blade." That voice was familiar, and it annoyed me. The guard removed his helmet, tucking it under his arm. Silvertail. He continued his recollection. "Before being promoted to the upper rings, I was a simple post guard. While on patrol, I discovered a Dwala wandering about in the yellow gardens with…" He paused as his eyes moved toward me. I froze, waiting for him to finish his statement. "…an elven miss."

I hadn't realized I had been holding my breath the entire time he was talking. I let it out in small puffs, careful to not draw any attention to myself. He obviously hadn't made the connection right away as I had outside of the judgment chambers, and I didn't know why he would. Before becoming the Protector, I was no more than a spoiled elven miss like so many others in the yellow ring. But he had made the connection now. He recognized in me the once-dark-haired elfling in the yellow garden's dome who knew the Dwala girl with the shaved head and the blade with the ivory handle. He knew that I knew to whom it belonged.

"A Dwala did this. I'm sure of it. Quite possibly the same who killed Shiloh. The girl must have been a part of the coup."

"You seem to be well versed in the matters of this case," Alag muttered with a roll of his eyes. "We must ensure that our Protector stays safe. This blade was obviously meant for her and we wouldn't want anything bad to happen to her." He chuckled, then turned to Silvertail. "You are now head of the Guards of Candor in place of the deceased. Have your men bury their former captain and make the proper arrangements for a funeral after searching the grounds for the murderer. Then see about preparing a full investigation into the matter. I want you to find an answer to this riddle. Anyone you find responsible or in alliance with this transgressor or the band of invaders shall see the judgment halls and…" He paused, calming his rage before continuing, "…may Olörun's hand be kind upon their soul, because their body will belong to the lives they stole—or else my head be damned. You have my order."

Alag and my father retreated back down the stairs leaving Silvertail, the dead captain, and me in silence. I took a breath in and started to make my way to the staircase in an attempt to get as far away from this place as possible. I could hear Silvertail prying the ivory dagger from its hold with all his might.

"Protector." I stopped in my tracks but dared not look back. I didn't want to see him dangle what he and I both knew to be the truth in front of my face like a prize for a begging toddler. "I request an audience with you tonight at the captain's chambers. It's joined to the prison in the purple ring. I have a matter to discuss."

I thought about my answer, still standing in front of the newly appointed captain. A part of me thought that we wouldn't talk about it and that we would both go on in our highly ranked positions as nothing had happened and as if our past lives couldn't restrict us in the least. I was obviously mistaken.

"Very well. I will see you tonight."

Chapter Three

I paced about my chambers, contemplating what this conversation could possibly be about. I couldn't run away again. The edgewoods weren't safe and if I ran away again, guilt would speak louder than any excuse I could ever conjure. I would surely put my family and all associated with me in danger.

I put off my departure for the meeting with Silvertail for as long as I could before it would become suspicious for me to be wandering the streets. I slipped out through the servants' quarters, the servants being too busy with gossip and the cleaning of dinner plates to notice me. I caught the scent of warm biscuits cooling on a rack as I passed, bringing to mind a weakening feeling of nostalgia. I barely made it outside before I tumbled to the ground in a heap, finding it hard in that longing moment to go any further. The smell reminded me of home, of the Remni, of the simple things that I loved, a worry-free life I would never get back. After a few deep breaths, I was on my way to the prison to meet the new captain of the Guards of Candor.

The sky seemed darker, the air dryer, and the ground more unyielding—even for the winter—as I approached the prison. I heard the hiss of a cat and then its scurrying off through the snow-covered streets. Two brutish guards parted the doors as I entered the prison. The halls were lit with red-tinted lanterns, marking the path through iron-barred cells. The dungeon was eerie and reeked of waste and spoiled food as we made our way deeper and deeper. Rats scurried out of the way. It was suddenly clear why the cat's presence was allowed.

I heard the clatter of dinnerware hitting the ground, startling me from my weary trance. I grabbed one of the lanterns from the wall as I followed the echoes of the disturbance down the dimly lit corridor. Just as I turned the corner, I heard the slamming of iron. I raised the lantern to meet the eyes of Silvertail. I recoiled in surprise.

"Ah, Protector. I was beginning to think you weren't coming," he said as he returned a key to its place on a metal ring.

"Such a gloomy place it is."

"I agree, but I hope that once I settle in, it will feel like home." He chuckled. I cracked a nervous smile, but he could sense my uneasiness.

"You have nothing to be nervous about. I just wish to have a meeting of the minds. We will be working closely together, and I feel it would be best that we become better acquainted in order to achieve the most productive results." A loud clamor from outside interrupted his assurance. The cat, perhaps. "Come to my chambers where we can speak without any disturbances."

I had just begun to follow him when the lantern's light that bounced off the dirty prison walls caught in its glow a muddy face just beyond the iron bars. I raised the lantern to peer behind the rusted barriers. I saw the broken pieces of a dirty dish scattered across the floor as about a dozen or so girls squinted at the ground, trying to clasp the shards with their small fingers, pulling from the wreckage grains of rice and chunks of smashed vegetables. They were my age or younger, the youngest sitting in a corner, not bothering to squabble about the ground with her cellmates, and seeming no older than my sister Mira, who had seen but only nine years. The girls looked up for a moment, then immediately went back to scrounging at a hurried pace, assuming that the lantern's light would soon be extinguished once I followed my guide back to his hold.

"Will you join me, Protector?" I turned to see Silvertail standing at the end of the corridor, ready to lead me away.

I attempted to linger a little to share my torch's light, but it was no use. There were too many grains on the ground and I could tell that Silvertail was becoming increasingly irritated by my delay. With much regret, I followed him, unsure of what to make of what I had seen.

"Why are those girls being held in a place like this? I thought this was reserved for the worst of criminals. What could they possibly have done to deserve this?" I asked after we crossed the threshold of his chambers.

"They *are* the worst of criminals. They are traitors to Keldrock. These were the captives at the borders of the edgewoods. You have your elven elite, the Guerr, to thank for that. As well as Prince Alag."

I could feel my teeth clench from anger from the clear dismissal of the obvious—that these were no more than young girls, a threat to no one. Once we were settled in, Silvertail took off his jacket and hung it on an iron hook that protruded from the wall like a giant fish lure. On top of the rung, he placed the metal ring that held the two iron keys. Those were the keys to the prison, one of which I knew belonged to the girls' cell.

"*These* are the warriors from the edgewoods that the Guerr captured?" With my eyes widened to a strain, I beckoned his answer, almost demanding it.

He rolled his eyes, smirked, and walked behind the table that had strewn across it rolls of parchment, maps, a cup of mead, a bowl of ink, and the blade with the ivory handle that belonged to Nazda.

"Protector, they are traitors to our nation. There is no need to become riled. I don't know all of the details, being as I just came upon this position, but I'm assured that the Prince has put his seal on the matter. After all, he was in the edgewoods when the traitors attempted to attack."

"These are young children, the majority of which haven't even reached adolescence. They couldn't have harmed anyone."

"I take the same precautions that I would with anyone else. They are not to be underestimated, and if the wretches that attacked the Chamber of Light hadn't underestimated you, we wouldn't be having this conversation. I'm sure it was mere chance and a stroke of luck that you were able to defend the tower anyhow."

With one fell swoop, I had the ivory dagger in my hand. Before Silvertail could react, I had it up against his throat, the edge of the blade digging into his skin so precisely that one small move by either of us would produce blood.

"There's no need to prove yourself to me, Protector. I was merely stating what a many have tried to figure out." I slowly removed the knife from Silvertail's neck, and he cleared his throat. "I have called you here because I understand that there was an elven miss many moons ago whom I saw in the yellow gardens not too long after the dome was raised for the cold season." I tossed the dagger back on the tabletop.

Here it comes, I thought. My mind began racing, searching for excuses, but as I had concluded before, there was no lie great enough to cover this truth. He continued.

"I could see in your eyes you were threatened and that you were in harm's way, yet I left you alone with that wretched Dwala. It is quite obvious what happened." I thought to speak, but I decided to let him conjure up a possible conclusion so that I wouldn't have to do any more work than I had to. "She held you hostage after murdering Sir Calo and trapping his sister in the burning estate. She took you as leverage and made you hide from your family. I am very sorry I didn't do more. That I didn't see through the ruse. That I didn't answer your scream."

I swallowed hard as tears began to well in my eyes. Silvertail walked from around the table and placed a heavy palm on my shoulder. His fingernails were dirty; the tips black as coal.

He tried to console what he thought to be my breaking down at hearing a hurtful memory, when in reality it wasn't that at all but rather something I could hardly handle. I was floating, half of my body being pulled into the air while the other half was tethered to the earth, but now I wasn't falling. I was crashing, my body landing in a crumpled heap amongst the Remni's rubble, and the dead bodies of Sir Calo and his sister and Protector Shiloh, and all the other secrets I held.

The tears ran faster now until I couldn't hold myself up any longer. I dropped to my knees, then to my side, my fine cloak sinking into the moist dirt as strained sounds came from my throat. My hair was plastered against my face in a tangled bunch. The harder I tried to hold the sounds back, the louder they became. I had murdered. I was responsible for the death of two of my kin. Sir Calo might have been a horrible elitist pig that abused his power, but he hadn't taken a life. The death of his sister, who had played no part in any of this, made me feel all the worse. I was a fraud. I was no Protector, and I still couldn't fathom why Shiloh felt I was the one to carry the light. Maybe in his last moments he chose me as the closest vessel, praising me as worthy enough, when I was no different from those who had attacked the tower. I couldn't bear the thoughts banging against my mind any longer, tormenting me at night and in my dreams. I didn't want to open my eyes but when I finally did, I met the gaze of Silvertail, squatting on the ground next to me.

"Are you done? Should I send for your father? Or perhaps a nursemaid." I gathered myself, feeling ashamed. I dusted myself off, trying my best to shake the soil stains from my cloak. "I'll have you know that I've already put a plan in motion. We have the Dwala girl's description, and I figure that if we find her, we'll find the culprit to these horrendous murders. You wouldn't have happened to have gotten her name while you were being held captive?"

I looked at the keys that hung on the wall and then back to him, remembering my meeting with Yann. I paused before answering, scrunching my face as if I were trying my absolute hardest to conjure up some distant memory. Finally, I let out a breath in a faux defeat.

"No. She mentioned many names, but none were her own." I dramatically tucked my lip in my mouth, trying my best to appear as innocent as possible. "She is long gone, so there's no need to worry yourself on the matter. I am fine as well."

I thought to say he was wrong. That it was a misunderstanding and that Nazda had the truest spirit of any being that had ever been born within the city of Keldrock. I didn't want her to be put in any more danger. Especially since I had been the cause of all her present troubles. We were supposed to live out our days in the edgewoods together. She chose to serve a sentence with me, even though it wasn't hers to bear. She was alive and well, for now, and I had to keep it that way. I thought of my conversation with Yann. I needed the keys by tomorrow morning and there they were, dangling only a few feet from where I stood.

"I want you to feel safe." Silvertail's voice was deep, rumbling through his chest, and instead of making me comfortable, it made me wary and even more distrusting. He walked back around the table, staring at a delicate painting, a likeness of the murdered captain of the guard. "I think this should be buried with him. He felt awfully worthy to have this made and kept in his chambers." Silvertail laughed to himself, peering over his shoulder at me. "He obviously spent a many an hour down here, letting his eyes wander every crevice of this dark prison, as well as keeping a fully staffed guard on their toes. So many secrets these walls would tell if they could only speak. You know all secrets do come to light, Alya?"

This was the first time he had referred to me as Alya and I didn't like the way it sounded coming from his lips. It sounded condescending, and although time hadn't brought me far from spritehood, my experiences had, and I wouldn't be so easily manipulated. I wasn't the same miss from a many months before.

"Well, if anything comes to mind regarding this case, or you decide to confide in me about any other worries, I am at your disposal. You have the support of the Guards of Candor."

A loud scream came from the long black corridor. The shrill voice sent a rush of shivers down my spine, unraveling all of my senses. Silvertail brushed by me, almost knocking me over, and out into the dark stretch of hallway, not bothering to grab a lantern in his flight. I stared behind him and thought to follow but then remembered the keys, dangling like sweet fruit on a low limb, just waiting to be plucked. I looked over my shoulder. I couldn't see far down the dark corridor. I heard Silvertail's deep voice rumbling through the walls and figured he was reprimanding one of the girls for something or another. I stared at the keys and for a moment, in a cosmic dance with two options: Silvertail discovering me and causing all of my secrets to unfold was the first; the second was getting the only item that would keep Nazda safe from harm. Although I was almost certain that Yann wouldn't hurt another Dwala, one thing for sure was that she had a plan, and any casualty, in her eyes, was well worth its fulfillment. I had to make a decision. I had a small window of opportunity. There might not be another chance later. I grabbed the key ring from the hook.

Soon I heard footsteps outside of the door and I knew I had to move faster. The ring fumbled from my fingers, dropping to the floor, landing in the dirt with a thud. I swiftly picked them up.

"My apologies, Protector. The prisoners said they saw a snake, but after perusing the area I only found this." He opened his hand to reveal my necklace, in all its silver glory and detail. "I believe this belongs to you."

I took my necklace from him, quickly hooking it back into place. "They couldn't possibly have been afraid of this." I smiled at Silvertail, but he just looked at me with a blank stare.

"Yes, it is quite comical. For a moment, I thought I saw something slithering in the darkness as well, but when I grabbed a lantern from the wall, it was just the necklace. Strange accessory, it is. The detail is quite… realistic."

Unsure of what else to say after this incidental distraction, I decided it was time to take my leave.

"Thank you for your time, Captain, but I must be off now. Have a pleasant evening."

"Wait, Alya!" I shuddered as he said my name again. "A black ribbon was tied to the dagger. The one you almost took my head off with." he said with a smirk.

"Oh, I hadn't noticed. What of it? I hope you're not suggesting that I take it and use it in my hair." We both laughed a little. It was awkward, but to some extent I felt to ease tension between his ever-rolling mind and mine was to make him laugh. It was the only time his eyes didn't have that glazed look of *I know you know* in them.

"No, nothing of that sort, Protector. It's just that the girl on the wanted poster from those weeks ago, and the girl I witnessed in the yellow gardens, the owner of this blade, she would have had to have this ribbon if she was the murderer. My question is, why would a girl with a shaved head need a ribbon or have any use for it, for that matter?"

His attention to detail was impressive. "That is an interesting observation, which must be why the Prince appointed you head of the guard. As such, I feel you are the best person to answer that question." With that, I left, navigating the halls while rubbing the head of my necklace as the dry sniffles of terrified girls ushered me to the stairwell and out of the prison.

Chapter Four

The mornings were cold now. The grounds were slippery and covered in ice. I longed for the summer mornings when birds flew against the skies. That was the eerie part about the winter. The cold darkness produced nothing living. The wind with its incessant blowing uplifted branches, causing them to scratch against the ice, startling me as I made my way to the yellow gardens. I wished the houses and estates would stir. I wished that sprites were awake, playing on the side of the roads or wrestling in the snow. During this season, people didn't emerge from their houses until the sun was high in the sky, until most of the snow had melted from the paths.

The dome soon came into view, a familiar sight, and except for a few broken glass panels and ruptured beams, the structure was intact. Nothing remained of the doors except the frame. They were blown off their hinges. I pulled from a hidden pocket inside my coat a knife. I had stashed a few others within my garments—one in my sleeve, one hooked onto my belt that fashionably wrapped around my day dress, and a small one tucked safely in the bottom of my slipper. I couldn't let my guard down around Yann. I knew she couldn't be trusted.

I gazed into the yellow garden's dome. The explosion had destroyed the plots of fresh flowers and juicy fruits and vegetables. What few plants remained were either dying or deadened by the unforgiving weather that the damaged dome couldn't protect them from. I looked around, taking in the ruins where my sister Mira and I used to spend our days. I looked at our plot where our hydrangeas had grown. Planting them and caring for them had brought us closer. Somehow, two single stems stood proud and strong among the waste. I set the dagger on top of the flowerbed and pulled from my pocket the little pouch Mira gave me with its sapphire seeds and placed them on the soil, using two fingers to push them deep down into the dirt. I stilled myself, blocking out the world.

"*Creco!*" Through the dirt a sapling sprouted, producing a few leaves, and a flower bud of a rich blue.

It had been a while since I had sifted. I hadn't seen Master Tali over these long months and of course our training in this moment wasn't a top priority. And since the book had been destroyed in the Remni's fire, I wasn't sure if we'd be continuing. I had gained some strength from my past training with Master Tali; this seed exercise that once would have caused me great exhaustion cost me but a stifled breath now. Still, without practicing the words, my memory of them seemed to drift away until I had forgotten them, and the sentences I used to form without a moment's thought now required my complete focus. One word out of place, one accidental use of another in its stead, and that could be the end. So I had put all of that aside until this moment. Tears softly ran down my cheeks and tapped the soft soil that hadn't been damaged as much as the earth outside the dome.

It still produced life, soaking up the remnants of my sadness. I sat there over the sprouts as the darkness began to subside, the sun nearing its crest on the hill. I sniffed, wiping my eyes with my sleeves.

"It can't be all that terrible, Alya." I picked up the dagger from the flowerbed and stood, looking toward the dome's entrance. Nothing. No one. "Try looking up here." I lifted my head towards the ceiling to see Yann hanging upside down like an oversized opossum. She released the hold that her legs had on the support beam and twirled down to earth, landing on her toes like a delicate dancer. Her grace could only be matched to that of the Jalla, who were our top elven performers and a delight to witness. "Sorry to interrupt your self-loathing. I must admit, it was quite entertaining." Her hair held an orange ribbon today, the color of pumpkins. "Did you bring it?"

I glared at her, feeling like a puppet on strings, prancing within her grasp. I returned the knife to its place within my housecoat and from my pocket produced the two heavy iron keys I had managed to slip off of the key ring before Silvertail returned from the screaming prisoners. I had considered taking the whole key ring, but with it holding only two keys, I deemed it impossible for him to not notice and realize I was the last to be in his chambers with him and by extension, the thief who stole them. It was too easy a prize, so I couldn't make any room for mistakes. I used two fairly old keys, both belonging to my personal palace chambers, which I never locked when I was away because there was nothing in that room I cherished or had a desire to hide from whomever came along to snoop about. I tossed the keys at Yann's feet where they landed in the moist soil. She looked down at them and then looked at me, grinning, her smile summoning a devilish hue.

"I've kept my word, now tell me the whereabouts of my friends. They better be safe."

Yann picked up the keys, tucking them into a pouch on her side. "That wasn't the agreement, love. I said your friends would remain safe. And so they shall. But you know, there was something I didn't mention keeping safe, Alya. You seem pretty intelligent, so I'll give you a chance to answer that for yourself. Go on."

She strode to a nearby plot of vegetables that had been destroyed in the explosion, only the metal stakes in the ground remaining. I immediately slipped my hand inside of my housecoat, gripping the handle of the dagger. As she knelt into the plot, as if she was checking the dead plants, I searched for an escape route. I had no interest in this game and who knows what else—or whom else—Yann had up her sleeve. I was alone in this. I hadn't told anyone where I was going this morning and I immediately regretted it.

I turned just in time to step out of the path of a rusted stake shooting past me, just over my shoulder. It came so close that it sliced the skin above my shoulder blade, stinging like a heated needle. She was aiming for my heart. I knew the answer to the riddle. She hadn't promised to keep *me* safe. She stalked toward me, gripping two stakes in her hands while one, still dark and damp from the cold ground, stuck out from either side of her mouth, reminding me of when hounds discover an old bone and trot about proudly before burying it with their other worthless treasures.

I let the dagger in my sleeve slip into my left hand and pulled from my coat the second dagger into my right and lunged forward. We met in the air, swinging our weapons wildly, in deathly alignment with one another. I could tell she was becoming frustrated and tired, but for me, I had come into the fight scared and weary but proved to be a formidable opponent, which I could tell she hadn't anticipated. She lunged at me repeatedly, but I blocked every strike. I struck her to the ground and with one of my daggers, pinned her shirt collar to the cold earth. Just as I was about to condemn her with my final strike, a harsh blow took me from behind, knocking me off of Yann and into a pile of smashed fruit and garden plot labels.

My vision was blurry, but I could barely make out Yann reprimanding her warriors. She hadn't come alone. I should have known. She was cunning and she would account for every possible turn of events. My head was pounding severely, making it ever more difficult to stop my eyes from drooping. I was dizzy, the dome spinning around me.

The sound of a reprimanding slap kept me from drifting into oblivion as Yann sent one of her subordinates crumbling to the ground in a pitiful heap. I had never seen her so unhinged—even her curls had become unruly in her anger and had torn from their ribbon hold, tumbling around her face like tiny serpents preparing to attack.

"She could have ended me, and where were you? Next time, my hand will be heavier upon your brow. So heavy in fact, that I'll have your head. Pass me the blade."

My vision still danced in cloudy silhouettes and blotchy colors. When my vision finally came together, she was already upon me. I tried to get up, putting my entire weight on one of my legs in an urgent attempt to gain some ground, but she slammed me back to the ground, straddling me. I heard a tiny pop and an intense pain surged through my leg. I winced, then started shrieking involuntarily. My leg was bent to the side in an unnatural position. Yann reached behind my head as I cried out in pain. Her hand returned with a palm full of soil, which she shoved into my mouth. I was sobbing and gagging, the dirt clogging my airways, making it nearly impossible to breathe. My leg was being tormented from indescribable pain and I couldn't think clearly because I was panicking.

"Breathe through your nose," she told me. I quickly obeyed, taking in small breaths, but the dirt still made it hard to do even that. "You shouldn't die this way. No, suffocating is way too mundane a death for one as special as you." I started to move my hands, but she grabbed both of them and tucked them under her knees. I couldn't move. I was out of wits and it took all of my energy just for me to breathe. "I want to have fun. You're such a pretty spectacle. It would give me great grief if I ended someone so astonishingly beautiful as yourself—and with your new title, I'm sure you would agree that your death should be tragic, one that would make your people weep in dismay, no matter how many years have gone by. I want them to be fearful, not because you are dead, but because of how you died." She smiled that same wicked smile as before as she smoothed back a few strands of my hair from my forehead. "If we're going to do this, we'll do it correctly."

"I gave you what you wanted!" I pleaded, after managing to swallow some of the dirt packed into my mouth. "Please! Don't do this."

Yann tipped her head back, laughing hysterically. "You know how to put on a good show, Alya. I'm quite amused. You were about to finish me a few moments ago and now you're begging me not to do the same to you." She flipped the knife in her fingers, letting the dagger slip in and out between them. "Just like all the high elves of this city, full of hypocrisy. The difference is, I didn't beg. I think I shall kill you now, Alya. You've served your purpose. The daughters of Wood Haven will be released, the city will be left without a Protector, and all will be calm—but your pretty head, I want for myself."

"Why are you obsessing over me?" I cried out. That wiped the smile clean from her face, which was then quickly replaced with a horrible scowl. As fast as lightning, the knife came down on my head and I thought it was the end. A swift swipe of the blade, and her hand produced a bundle of my hair.

"What could I possibly be obsessing over? Your locks of shimmering silver?" She traced the tip of the blade over my mouth and nipped at the center of my bottom lip, cutting into it well enough to send a trickle of red down my chin. "Am I obsessing over your ruby red lips?" She brought her hand across my face, shoving my opposite cheek into the moistened ground. "Or is it the way your skin fills with life with a single touch, like dark waters. I'm not obsessing over you, elvish filth! I want the Protector. It was Shiloh before, but now that title belongs to you. I get what I want, Alya."

Yann picked up the knife and held it above her head like a newly birthed babe being presented to a congregation. She drew in a breath and as she raised the knife to its zenith, the red membrane of her inner nostrils, fiery in the faint morning light, flared with all her anger and aggression. I wasn't sure if I had grown numb to the pain or if the lower half of my leg had become a different part of me. I peered down at it, lying limp, my ankle twisted to the side, enough for me to see the small wooden handle of a dagger. Of course, the last of the hidden daggers. I looked at her dramatically basking in her moment of triumph and knew that my only hope for survival lay in a tiny knife no bigger than a whittler's blade. My leg was weak and pinned, but somehow I had to move—and fast. I peered up at her as she wrapped up her revelation.

I had to act now. I mustered all of my strength into my right arm. I was pinned under Yann and with her godlike strength, she could easily knock me back down to the ground—but she wouldn't expect to be unbalanced, and with that came my advantage. I had her beat concerning speed—not counting my legs, as well. Two advantages. I thought to myself. *Now!*

I heaved my lower arm up and her body tilted, tumbling backwards, buckling her heels and rolling over onto her back. I didn't give her any time to recover before grabbing the small dagger from my slipper. This time I was going to end this. I swept for her throat, but she moved too suddenly and from the strike, blood trickled from her eye. She screeched so loud that her two attendants retreated, backing away from their crazed leader. The sight was gruesome, and I stumbled back, out of her reach. Her attendants finally came to their senses and caught on that they had lost their captive and their leader was seriously injured. One shoved me with her foot as I was trying to stand, sending me sliding through the flower plots into a heap of broken pottery. My knee pulsed with pain, causing tears to pour from my eyes as the dagger slipped from my grip.

This had to be the end. I was out of wits, ideas, and now, weapons. I was to die by the hands of traitors. I waited for them to approach, bracing myself for another blow, but all that came were the sounds of panic. I turned to see a red bird, the size of a great horned eagle, swooping down onto the two assailants, digging its talons into their scalps and tearing at their faces and hair.

I took the opportunity to escape. My right leg couldn't be of benefit in this case. Standing would put too much weight on one leg, not to mention I wouldn't get far. I noticed an opening in one of the large glass panels. That was it. I had one more advantage that I hadn't bothered to notice, and one I had come to appreciate since my past dangerous encounters—I was resourceful. Quickly but cautiously, I turned over onto my hands and my good knee, careful to not to bear down on my right one, and made my way to the hole in the panel. I climbed through with ease, the large domesticated canines probably having chipped away at the frame to allow easier entry. I crawled fast, which was easier than I had anticipated on just one knee, with hands to help balance me and support my weight.

I crawled through scrubs and small bushes, frantically scurrying away from the dome. My hands were frozen numb and colorless. I started down a small hill towards one of the less traveled entrances into the blue ring and toppled over into a shallow pond. My body shuddered as the cold water soaked through my clothing, causing my teeth to chatter. I sat on my bottom, using my arms as little paddles to push me across the shallow pool.

I was near the shore when I heard splashing behind me. The water birds were gone for the winter and even the most unintelligent of fishermen wouldn't fish in a pond this shallow or this cold. I moved faster, hoping to make it to land to where I could crawl again, but the splashing continued and was coming nearer. I kept pushing until a hand gripped my mouth, capturing my scream for help before it could even pass my lips. I started swinging my arms crazily, trying to free myself from my captor, but the pain was intense and with the remainder of my energy expended, it was no use. My vision blurred as the sparkle of the shore, just a few feet away, faded into black.

Chapter Five

"Is it going to hurt?"

The whispers of hushed voices curled my ears. Thinking it was but a dream, I ignored their words and tried my hardest to awaken.

"Most likely, but only for a few moments. At least I hope. It's better in place than out."

I tried to identify the voices, they being nothing more than little lights behind my eyelids. My head throbbed with pain and sleep seemed to be the only thing that bought some peace.

"Brace yourself."

I felt a quick jerk on my knee and a loud pop. I awoke with a spine-chilling shriek, as pain lifted every hair on my body. A tiny hand rushed to my mouth, pushing so hard on my jaw that their tiny little fingers turned red from the pressure. I rolled over onto my side, waiting for the throbbing in my knee to subside.

"Just breathe. It's better now. Breathe."

The voices belonged to more than just little lights now, and I wasn't dreaming. It was my friend Kala and Rose, the sweet little girl Nazda looked after. I slowly propped myself up against an old sack, being careful to not put any pressure on my knee. I could feel the pain subsiding, but I hadn't come to trust it as entirely as I had before I was injured. Dust floated around in the sunlight, dancing off of the old wooden beams in the barn. I reached out for Kala and Rose all at once, pulling them close to me, burying their faces on either side of my head. Tears rolled down my cheeks as the realization set in that I was alive. I had walked into an ambush and had somehow survived. After calming my nerves, I questioned my saviors.

"What happened?"

I directed my question to Rose, who of the two probably had the least amount of information concerning my current situation, considering her age. But I was so happy to see such friendly faces that my mind hadn't regained its momentum.

"Your knee was dislocated. It had to be reset," Kala chimed in.

"Yes, I am painfully aware of that. I was alluding to what happened before I fainted?" I said with a snicker. "Last I can recall I was being fished out of a pond."

"Ah, yes. Well, I was on my way home when I discovered you wading in a weird fashion across a small pocket of water, quite a pitiful sight really, and I rushed over and hauled you out. I tried to stand you up, but you screeched in pain. I covered your mouth, but by that time you had already fainted. I carried you through the back streets to the barn. I knew you'd be safe here since you and Nazda took refuge here before the Unveiling."

I had underestimated the strength of Kala. To carry me all this way had to be incredibly difficult for a girl of similar stature as myself. But something about her answer puzzled me. How did she know that Nazda and I took refuge here? Kala smiled at me, her pearly teeth bringing out the beauty in her brown face.

"We have returned with bread and pork from the market. This should suffice."

Cadon and Meca, the two young runts Nazda also cared for, emerged from the hatch's opening, bringing with them the smell of salted meat and sweet grains. They had changed a lot in the months since I'd seen them last. Meca had lost the baby fat around his torso and had become incredibly thin. A man's chiseled features had begun to etch their way onto the boy's face. Cadon was just as strong as ever but had gained a series of muscles that stuck out from under scarred, patchy skin. He appeared to have taken on the role as leader and caretaker quite easily. Even little Rose seemed stronger and more resilient.

"It is great to see you boys. I see life finds you well," I said, but they didn't seem remotely interested. Meca simply smiled, nodding in my direction while Cadon altogether ignored my greeting.

They pulled out a discolored blanket from an old crate in the corner and shook it until it unfolded. They worked together to spread it out as neatly as possible on the barn floor. Meca set the pungent hunk of sow in the middle of the blanket while Cadon pulled out a pocketknife, sliced off half of the loaf of bread, and began grotesquely shoving it into his mouth, sending crumbs tumbling down his chin through the cracks in the floorboards to the stables downstairs.

"Half of the loaf was for Alya!" Rose shot at Cadon. "You know she doesn't eat meat." The young girl had discovered some bite about her as well during the months that passed.

"It must have slipped my mind," Cadon mumbled as the last bit of bread disappeared behind his curled lips.

"It's fine, Rose. I managed to haven't eaten my lunch yet. Hopefully my cheese has kept," Kala said. As she searched her pockets, my stomach growled, twisting at the thought of the bread Cadon greedily shoved down his throat. Kala's pockets produced nothing and she muttered, "I seemed to have misplaced it."

"It's fine," said Meca, standing erect, his broad shoulders blocking the dancing flakes in the light from the window. The few times I had gone to visit Nazda, I had never really heard Meca speak. His voice was higher than Cadon's but somehow managed to still the room. "Alya can have the rest of the bread. We will just wash down the salted pork with some melted ice. I'll bring some in and hopefully by the time our meal is done, a great deal will have turned to water."

"Sit down, Meca. The girls haven't eaten, and who are you to give away their portions?" Cadon said, obviously perturbed that his subordinate had overstepped his boundaries.

"I think it's a splendid idea and very selfless," Kala stated as she floated up to her feet, standing in between the two boys to ensure a fight did not ensue. "The mark of a great leader."

"A leader?" Cadon sputtered before kicking the pork bundle against the wall, laughing as he walked away, all while keeping his eyes locked with Kala's. He sat down at the hatch, letting his feet dangle thorough the opening.

"Never mind his nonsense," Rose said as she heaved the pig carcass back to the blanket. Meca climbed through the hatch with a bucket, careful not to bump, let alone graze Cadon.

I watched Rose carefully pick off small debris and gathered dust from the moist, bruised meat before announcing to everyone that it was time to eat. Meca climbed back through the opening with a sloshy mixture of ice and snow. Wary, I started to stand up. I began to move without worry, placing my full weight on my knee. I sat next to the bread as the others gathered around the bundle of pig. We all dug in except Kala, who claimed she wasn't hungry. I left not a crumb of the bread uneaten, even snatching up every bit that fell to the blanket, a vast difference from the lost appetite I'd had over the course of my time in the purple ring. Although I'd had limited encounters with dead animal, I noticed that the pig didn't look as fresh as meat should be. Parts of the ham where the pink had turned darker had gained little white spores, similar to the ones I had seen on old bread. We passed the bucket of water around, each of us taking full sips. I was careful not to mention Nazda and was slightly curious as to why Rose hadn't inquired from me as to her whereabouts.

After we ate, I lay out on the rickety floorboards, letting the sun's rays that broke through the high loft window warm my face, my hunger sated for the moment. I was still stunned that I had survived an ambush, that Yann still hadn't finished me and continued to let her strained ego overtake her objective in every moment. But this time I had outwitted her. This time I had won. I saw the blade pierce her eye and the trail of ruby red blood run from its socket. I could only imagine the pain she felt would only fuel her rage even more but I didn't have to worry about that. An injury that cruel could only lead to death. That was what I relied on.

"Such a pleasant day still. Wouldn't you agree, Alya?" Rose said as she lay down next to me, her little head of coal colored curls resting gently on my breast. I smiled to myself, closing my eyes as I delved into the sun's rays.

"Despite all that has passed, it surprises me that you still see the beauty in all of this." I opened my eyes and peered up at the window, watching the small wisps of cloud pass over in clear blue skies the color of the edgewood's winding streams. "But I do agree with you. It is quite beautiful."

"All is not lost, Alya. We have so much to look forward to. You'll see." Rose perked up, leaning up and over me so I could see her rosy face. "You should accompany us! The migration is only a few weeks from now. I'm sure you can—" Before I knew it, she was squirming, dangling by her collar like a duck in a butcher's shop. Cadon tossed her against the wall, anger swelling in his face.

"Hold your tongue, child," he snapped at Rose. I stood up in a fit of rage.

"Pay her no heed," Meca piped in, stepping between Cadon and me, his newfound confidence still catching me off guard. "It is but a play. A game between friends is all she speaks of."

As Meca tried to cover her words, Rose turned on her hands and knees and scrambled as fast as she could to my ankles, holding them tight. I could feel her shuddering, shaken up by Cadon's violent rebuke.

"Go on with Meca, Rose, the elf and I need to speak in private."

Rose by now was sniffling, holding back tears. She wasn't injured but I could sense that she was shocked at his reaction. She had spoken innocently, as most small children and elfling alike do, but obviously she said something she shouldn't have. Kala coddled Rose, helping her down the hatch to the ground floor of the barn. She locked eyes with Cadon before descending, but he didn't flinch—and with that, we were alone.

"She said what she shouldn't have?" I inquired with a forceful tone, demanding an answer.

"A game is all."

"Really. That was quite a strong reaction to a little girl simply recalling a snippet of her imagination. You tossed her clear across the room!"

Cadon walked to the hatch, peering down to ensure that no one was lingering within earshot.

"I was tired of her prattling on, not to mention I wasn't too fond of her tone when addressing me earlier."

"And who might you be?" I hissed at him, the stench of his pride so pungent that my senses could no longer bear the fumes.

He paused before answering, taking a breath in and letting it out, the vapors visible in the cold air.

"I am Nazda's legacy. The one left to protect them. Who are you to pass judgment on how I lead my company? You know nothing of our struggles, and haven't come close to treading in our footsteps, nor would you desire to. My father was blown to dust in the mines. My mother took the grief so hard that she went mad and took her own life. Meca's home caught fire during a night raid. The only thing that kept him from dying was his father's body on top of his. His father was almost burned entirely through, the fire almost reaching Meca, before the rains doused the embers. Meca wouldn't speak for months. Rose's parents were murdered in the blue ring. The Guards of Candor said it was a mugger, but our people rarely venture outside of the black ring. I suspect your people were the killers. Rose can't even remember what her mother looks like. Life was hard but I wanted to trust this city once. Like so many others before me, I believed Keldrock had the potential to be what all of those who lived within her walls ever wanted it to be. A home. A sanctuary. And just like every other lot handed to me and my people, it fell short. If Rose pretends to venture off into a distant land, to a place where food is plentiful and we are not stuck in poverty, then so be it—but one thing hasn't changed, and that is that you are an elf. You are the Protector. Now even more valuable to the powerful than you once were. It burdens me to hear Rose thinking of us somehow leaving this place, because it will never happen. We are stuck here and for as long as my duty is their wellbeing, I will entertain no such hopeful dreams. She has to grow up sometime."

Silence overcame the upstairs bunker where Cadon and I stood. I resolved to look at the ground as a single tear rolled down my cheek, splattering onto the wooden floor. Cadon had become hardened, more so than I had realized. Nazda was gone and it was my fault. Somehow I kept drawing the line back to me, and maybe it was because the blame was indeed mine.

"If there is anything I can do to—"

"You can leave. And now that Nazda holds no place here, there is no reason for you to return."

I hesitated, searching my mind for a response, but there was none. There was nothing I could do. I was in danger, and for their safety as well as my own, I shouldn't have been there in the first place. If certain things came to light, it would be all the more reason for people to be convinced that I was not to be trusted—or worse, that I was a traitor. Death would be my only suitor.

I walked out into the sun. Although the chill was somewhat harsh, it was warmer than normal. I walked across the spread between the barn and Mister Harmon's house to find Kala, Meca, and Rose building shelters out of snow. They looked up as if they had seen an apparition. They must have heard our hushed disgruntled voices. I smiled, nodding at them, and began making my way back to the purple ring. I had but reached the open gate of the black ring before I heard the patter of feet behind me—Kala, most likely. I turned to receive her only to find that Rose had trailed me.

"Why do you follow me?" I said as she approached, but she didn't slow down. She opened up her arms and wrapped them around my torso, burying her face in my stomach.

"Cadon is a liar."

I kneeled so I could wipe the tears from her face. "He's lying? About what?" I asked in a gentle tone.

She sniffed, clearing the mucus that had begun to run beneath her nose. "It's not my imagination. The migration is real. You will come, won't you? I won't go without you. Cadon is—"

"Rose!" I heard a voice call in the distance. Cadon stood a few hundred feet away, wrapped in a worn coat, his eyes daring and bold. The streets were empty here, the tall walls that held the gate blocking the sun's rays. Even though he was still some distance away, I could see the rage surging through his body. He began trudging in our direction.

I returned to Rose, speaking quickly in a hushed whisper. "I believe you, Rose. I do, but you can't speak of this anymore. No one will take you away. Not without me." She smiled, just as Cadon snatched her by her hair, almost holding her above the ground.

"You little snake, slithering about as you please." He shoved her away from me. He looked me in my face, his fierce eyes demanding an explanation.

"She wanted to bid me farewell. She has done no wrong."

Cadon smirked, a half-hearted smile for my half-hearted lie. "I will be sure of that." With that, he turned and walked behind Rose, who had begun running through the snow back to the barn. I stood worried, alone in the cold under the clouded still of the heavens.

Chapter Six

The foyer at the west end of the palace was empty, so I ascended the staircase without accompaniment of any guards, who oddly weren't at their usual posts. I opened my chamber doors to find a host of guards searching my room, inspecting my clothes and perusing my chests—reasoning enough as to why they weren't standing at the palace entrance. When they saw me, they stopped.

"There you are!" Madja exclaimed as she walked in behind me, wrapping me in her embrace. I was so happy to see her. Her hair was freshly done; she had it dyed at the ends the color of freshly stirred honey, which looked lovely against her long dark flowing locks. It reminded me of when the last golden rays of the sun were covered by the darkness of the night. "You shouldn't go wandering out into the city anymore, Alya. It's not proper for such of *our* ranking, especially during these trying times. And what happened to your hair?" She ran her hands over my head. Madja had obviously already taken to her new status as the mother of the Protector. Not only had she updated her appearance by adding dye to her hair, but also her wardrobe, which she formerly chose based on the current fashions of elvish ladies. That no longer appeased her social appetite, so overnight she had the artisans and seamstresses create her wildest fantasies, hoping to become a celebrated aspiration for the ladies of the elite that she had previously tried so hard to keep up with. "If the

Captain hadn't seen you leave early this morning, I would have been worried to death."

I eyed Silvertail in the corner of my room, flipping through a book with a cold look on his face. I watched him slip a piece of parchment in between the pages before returning it to its place on the shelf. I didn't know how much he knew, but he knew at the very least that I had left the palace this morning, even if he didn't know where I went. Still, why would he not look further after my departure? Why hadn't he followed me?

"I think we'll take our leave. Good day, Protector. And to you as well, Lady Alyawen," Silvertail said with a nod as he led his charge out of my chamber.

"Well, hurry and prepare yourself," Madja urged. "I have outlined a session with the housedame for you and your sister covering the etiquette of royalty. She instructed Princess Bellanor before she passed, peacefully may her soul rest, as well as Prince Alag. I think it would do you well to learn under her tutelage. I have learned a great deal myself in just a short time. Hurry! She arrives the hour after next. Prepare yourself." With that, Madja was off, the golden streaks at the ends of her hair lifting in the air ever so lightly as she exited. I closed the door behind her, locking it—something I never did.

My belongings had been moved around, tampered with, and it took me a moment to return to hooks the garments the guards had let fall to the floor during their search. After everything was back in place, I looked to the bookshelf where Silvertail had placed the book with the tiny piece of parchment. His height being greater than mine, he had put it on the end of one of the higher shelves, its black binding shining like hot oil. On tiptoes, I retrieved the book. *The Three Burdens* was emblazoned in red across the cover. I had never seen or read this book before nor noticed it on my shelf. I flipped through its pages, attempting to find the piece of parchment. The smell of the pages reminded me of rotting wood. It was an older book, that much I admired. As I flipped through, I noticed grand illustrations of a wilderness with poems alongside them. Drawings of what seemed to be giant insects floating across trees, devouring everything in their path, seemed frightening as I imagined the small ants the lads and I used to herd as children. It was a wild, seemingly dangerous, but exciting visual.

There was another page of nothing but large eyes in the night, and a black form. If I had to guess, it was some frightening apparition. The book fulfilled my longing for supernatural beings and creatures of myth, and I thought it odd that I had never seen it until now. At last I landed in between the pages where the parchment had been stuck. I pried it from the crease and unfolded it. It was a note. *Prison, Midnight* was etched across its folds. I shuddered at the thought of having to visit the prison again, that dark chasm of an earthly Hades. As much as it interested me, the book would have to wait for now. I brought my nose down to where my shoulder and pit met. I smelled of pond water and sweat. If I were not the Protector, I'm sure I wouldn't have made it past the purple ring's gates. The clothes my friends had dressed me in were obviously old and had been worn by many without a washing because a strong musk emanated from the garments. I shuddered at the thought, but then remembered that I should be thankful that I was alive. I ripped the pungent-smelling clothes from my body in haste in order to meet my mother's agenda. After putting on my house robe, I dashed to the bathing quarters to tidy myself up as much as I could.

***

It was strange that I thought of our visitor as some form of an actual teacher. Simply put, her job was to train me on the history, traditions, and behavior of royalty, as if my upper class upbringing wasn't worthy of the bluebloods of the purple ring. I loved going to lessons at the School of Talents, but since the Unveiling, school hadn't reopened—not that I would be allowed to attend anyway. I missed Master Tali and her wonderful lectures that triggered innovation and creativity, even the general lessons that I had to share with the mindless she-elves that cared for nothing but using their talents to impress headstrong lads and procuring the latest gossip.

"Your head must be held high, your shoulders back. A crown, although I have never had the pleasure of donning one myself, is heavy, much like the pride and respect it carries. You must maintain proper posture to summon its full effect." My instructor circled me like a vulture, evaluating my every move, critiquing the edges and curves of my body.

Her name was Mournadam. She was an older elf. Her nails were sharp, shimmering like crystals that hung so delicately from a chandelier. Her long, graying hair was braided into a bun, and although her chubby body was probably twisted in knots and nubs, she still held herself upright, not even resting on the cane she carried, which only seemed like a fashion accessory. Her eyes were tiny dots, buried in their sockets by her wrinkles. On her cheeks she wore a dusting of pink powder—a little more and she would have been the color of a newborn's bottom. Mournadam wore a plain gown, which I was surprised to see since even the lowliest of hand servants dressed exceedingly extravagant while on duty, valuing their positions as privileged since they waited on royalty and highly ranked delegates. Even the bath maids wore lovely gowns just to hand-wash rags for occupants of the palace.

"Much better. Now for the test. I heard from your mother you like to read, Alya. You don't mind that I call you Alya, do you?" She used the nurturing tone of a nanny, and it made me feel comfortable. I almost rocked my head off my shoulders with all my nodding, showing my complete adherence to whatever she requested. I wanted to please her and make her praise me just as a child seeks its mother's affection. I could see Mira practicing alongside me, straining to gain the same attention I was getting.

"We mustn't nod, young lady. Use your words. Now, what is your favorite book? Tell me."

I thought long and hard. I recalled a story I once read, then another, and soon I was mulling over five or six books while trying to answer her question in a timely fashion. Suddenly a thought came to mind and I figured it was just as good as any option I could present.

"Although I haven't had the chance to begin, I have recently acquired a book that I feel it is quite promising. I would have to say my current favorite would be *The Three Burdens*."

Mournadam's face drooped, causing her chin to ruffle, the skin on her neck wrinkling like a rooster's wattle.

"I myself have read that book many times. You're much too young to know and I'm sure that this can stay between us misses." She turned to Mira who had tired of extending her neck to its limits and was happy to finally be invited into our banter. I looked at our instructor, intrigued. "As the housedame to the royal family, I am one of many keepers of this house. An ornament that comes with royalty as they make their assent to the throne. As such, my responsibility is to educate. Few have been allowed to read the old scrolls and the ancient letters, but I have been blessed to be one of those few. As will you be, Alya. I have had the pleasure of adding to my collection of knowledge what lay beyond the veil. Tell me, do you know of the he-elf who sought the head of the Meric humans for peace between our nations?"

I thought for a moment, unsure of what elf she could be referring to. Then I remembered the story Master Tali told me, of the escorts that ventured outside of Keldrock with the traitor

Manu. Only one returned, battered and scarred, and managed to report to Shiloh and the courts, in his wounded state, of the Dwala representative's treachery.

"Yes, I know of the he-elf. What of him?"

Mournadam switched her cane to her other hand and held it at her side, refusing to give in to bad posture.

"Well, on his travels, the he-elf made a journal of the path, so that Shiloh could lead his people through the wilderness without loss or turmoil. Beyond the edgewoods, there are more than just trees and shrubs, my ladies. There are things in the foliage that are even stranger than a lady Protector," she said with a wink. "*The Three Burdens* is his account. Many secrets lie in this book, and only a few copies have been made and are kept safe from those who might want to leave the confines of the city. However, the author became a changed being and no one knows if these accounts are in fact true or just his mind warped from his extended voyage in the jungles. His words are wrapped in riddles, and some of the illustrations could easily have been exaggerated. It is strange still…." She shifted to the side, looking like a plump hen perching on a pedestal, the pride of her height above her spectators giving her confidence. "It is strange that such a scarce relic be found in your collection. Thank Olörun that it was, because it is a worthy read. Still, it is strange."

"What happened to the he-elf? Does he still live?" Mira inquired, her eyes full of wonder.

"I don't believe so. Many accounts claim his whereabouts. Some say he was driven mad and ended his life while others claim he died in a peaceful sleep. Some even claim he was murdered."

I couldn't believe that in my room were the answers to whatever threat the veil protected us from. I suddenly came back down from this high that years of gossip and storytelling had caused my instructor to inflict upon interested pupils. I couldn't put too much stock into what she said.

"Well, then." I said, rising to my feet, signaling the end of this tall tale and my first etiquette lesson. As I turned to exit, I asked Mournadam, "What do you believe? For all we know, this book could just be an entertaining collection of poems and pictures meant to keep children in bed at night rather than daring to wander the edgewoods."

"I don't wonder about such things. The veil held its place in the skies since I was a little miss. I was born under its protection and have never even seen the outside of the city's walls. I ask you, Protector, would the veil have ever been raised unless we knew for certain that something lay on the other side of these walls more terrifying than any power that lies within? One must know for certain. Since that veil has fallen, I suspect we will be seeing if the book rings true or not. My bones have been giving me grief, and that I can say hasn't happened since my granddaughter went into labor with my great-grandson. Something is coming." She smiled. "Now for tonight, I want you both to place a big book atop your head and practice walking with proper posture. Until the next time."

She turned and trailed away, the tapping of her cane growing quieter as she made her way to the hall's doors. She was an odd lady, yet she was intriguing.

***

The washroom was empty, giving me the time and capacity to observe its beauty from all angles. Although the Remni's bathing quarters were beautiful in their own right, the washrooms of the palace were exquisite beyond compare. There was a large fountain of gold; in its center, a great statue of an owl that ran water all day over tiny fish called peelers that picked your skin free of dead flakes in mere minutes. They shimmered like pink gems as they swam over blue pebbles, knocking into each other to get to the next offering of food.

I let my robe slip to the floor. I wasn't worried about being intruded upon. The bath maids had an adjacent den where they sat until they were needed. I thought of how I met Kala, her sitting in the bath maid's chair as I soaked in the tub, my skin wrinkling like dried prunes.

My life had changed so much and I had little to show for it. The new trinkets, the new attire, even the new claim to power were nothing without my friends. I sat in luxury while Nazda was an exile in the edgewoods. The lads were still being held in the soldier barracks, when after serving in an Unveiling, they were supposed to be released to return home and never have to serve again.

I dug my toes into the smooth pebbles. They were cold, holding the chill of the water. After the peelers went on their way, their food source depleted, I strode to one of the bathing tubs, careful not to slip on the shiny, polished floor. I slid into the water timidly, learning the hard way on my first time being introduced to peelers that they pick your skin's entire hard dead shell, leaving nothing but the softness underneath. The water wasn't scalding, but was hotter than I would have liked, so I released the pump's valve to allow for cool water to flow. After a few flushes, the temperature was more tolerable, and I allowed my body to relax. I dropped orange fairy blossom leaves into my bath, watching them float about like little canoes. I was exhausted, but the bath seemed to ease away all the stress of the day along with any energy I had left. I found myself drifting into slumber. I tried to fight it, but soon my eyelids felt like heavy gates bearing down on my conscious mind, and sleep overtook me.

He stared up at me, his eyes bulging. I could see the bones in his thin face, his forehead almost skeletal, the most prominent of all his features. He had that grim smile etched across his face, like a hyena in the night. Then the flames warped around, engulfing us.

"Alya!"

I awoke in a fit, sending water splashing over the sides of the tub. Madja backed away, careful to not let any of the bath water dampen her garments. I calmed down, realizing it was but a dream. I still hadn't escaped the nightmarish Sir Calo, the look of his face from that night, and the flames climbing the drapes only to demolish the Remni.

I pulled myself out of the water and reached for a towel, which Madja happily handed to me. I dried myself while she pricked and pruned at herself in the large mirror, plucking loose strands of hair from her new color scheme.

"The prince, as well as the courts and their families, are supposed to be joining us for dinner this evening. I hear he brings grand news and this dinner will serve as a joining of the peace between the three parties that rule our kingdom. It's quite humble of him, dear. Wouldn't you agree?"

Other than in passing, Alag and I rarely even exchanged a glance. Suffice to say that he was probably quite upset to find that his throne was to be split in half and his birthright taken from him. We hadn't had a meeting since the trial and it seemed that he had no intention of initiating one. It was surprising to say the least that he would want to meet over dinner.

"I will be ready in a few moments."

I grabbed my robe and returned to my quarters to find a maid waiting. Apparently Madja thought I would need some assistance in getting ready for dinner, being that I hadn't taken any recent opportunity to be involved in our family gatherings. Even my relationship with Mira had been strained. The maid twisted my hair into one long braid down my back, looping through it a piece of sapphire colored string. I had many dresses so I figured I could find one that would match.

Tonight's dinner was held in the Crystal Parlor. It was a beautiful room where everything was glassy, crystal, and transparent. The entirety of the decor, from the chairs, table, and chalices to the bowls, plates, cutlery, and floors were crystal. Even the drapes that hung from the large windows were composed of tiny crystalline fragments strung together moving ever so delicately. As the light passed through them, little cuts of color sparkled with every turn.

Alag's servants were there early making arrangements for his table placement. My sister, who locked herself away in her room most days, was already seated at the table, watching her feet swing back and forth through the transparent tabletop. It seemed Mira enjoyed the Crystal Parlor as much as I did. Madja appeared, taking her seat next to me, followed by my father, who then sat next to Mira, and soon the royal procession began. A slew of the highly ranked Guards of Candor marched in hurriedly, lining the walls behind the servants, barely giving them enough time to move out of the way before being trampled. Our family sat towards the end leaving an open space at the head of the table for Alag. I wasn't too keen on that idea, but I had to understand where he was coming from, and after all that happened, I felt to some extent guilty, even though I wasn't solely to blame. I hoped this small concession would let him to know that his royal heritage wasn't being stripped away by me being chosen as Protector.

Within moments of the guards' procession, Alag arrived with his personal attendant close at hand. As he approached the table, he examined each of our smiling faces. I saw out of the corner of my eye that even Mira had stopped her kicking and was now grinning at the prince—excessively so. Alag's good looks had seized her attention, causing her to behave like an airheaded school miss. His attendant started to pull the chair out, sliding it ever so easily on the crystal floor, when the prince's hand shot up in a motion for him to halt. His palm was smooth and free of creases, having not seen even an hour of labor. The attendant with quick feet pattered to the other end of the table, Alag following behind at an even pace. They settled at the opposite head with ten spaces on both sides from where my family sat. His servants rushed to make up for their error, moving his setting to the other end of the table. Mira frowned with puzzled eyes and returned her gaze back through the crystal tabletop down at her feet.

Once seated, Alag whispered something to his attendant and soon the meal commenced. I watched as kitchen aides waited on him, taking the time to collect his wine choice, specific delicacies, and which of the dishes brought to the table would be worthy of his palate, while my family and I weren't even offered water. I could feel my skin crawl and even under the thin material of my dress, I was deplorably hot. I couldn't take it any longer.

This brat deserved a lesson, no matter how he felt about me and our current dilemma.

I stood up, shoving my chair back. I had forgotten in that instant how maneuverable they were, due to the lightweight crystal design, but I didn't care. Fortunately enough, the guards stopped it before it would even come close to shattering one of the delicate walls behind them. I swept over the empty chairs that were supposed to hold the members of the courts, who had yet to arrive. As I was almost upon Alag, his attendant blocked my path. He was a scrawny elf, his build reminding me of the scholars that studied in the blue ring or little lads that have yet to inherit their father's brawn. His hair had an immense amount of wax smeared over it, making it shine as if oil had been struck in the center of his temple. His narrow face was riddled with bumps and a few scabs that he had picked off before they had a chance to heal. From his quick reaction, I knew he was experienced in his dealings.

"I must require you to take your seat, Protector." The guards remained in their places, faced with the same predicament of the day before at the purple ring's gates: whether I was powerful enough to end them, or whether my ending was within their power.

"I need to speak to the prince, and it would behoove you to step aside." I started to go around the attendant, but he stepped clear in my path. He eyed the guards, and soon, two stepped forward, standing next to the two of us to stop whatever altercation was about to ensue.

"Protector. What can I do for you that cannot wait until later? I'm sure your father has briefed you on the formalities of dinner etiquette, so I ask you kindly, to cease your harassment and have a seat." Alag didn't even look at me when speaking, only adding fuel to the fire that was building inside of me.

I stared in utter awe as the word *harassment* echoed in my head like an annoying gnat. How dare he use such an incendiary phrase? We were equals, as was decided by the courts, and he was doing very little, if anything, to help acclimate me to the inner workings of city politics. I could no longer contain myself.

"You spoiled, obnoxious prick! I'll have you know—" Before I could go any further, a large cymbal sounded, echoing against the crystal of the elaborate chandeliers that hung from the glass ceiling and the strands twirling in the windows, causing them to tinkle like wind chimes.

"You idiot!" the attendant snapped at the chamberlain.

"My apologies, sir." The chamberlain recoiled, shying away like a newborn pup. Silence claimed the room as the chimes stilled.

"Well?" the attendant ventured, requesting reasoning behind this interruption.

"What can I do for you, my lord?" the chamberlain asked in confusion.

"Get on with it, simpleton!" the attendant snapped.

The chamberlain regained his composure and cleared his throat. He didn't seem too bright.

"By way of the attendants of each respective house, I regret to report that the entire order of the courts and their families will not be attending dinner this evening. They have taken ill and apologize to their prince…" He took his bow toward Alag, who nodded in return. "…and their Protector," he continued, taking his bow toward me before exiting the room.

I found it odd that all at once, the entire order of the courts had fallen ill. What were the chances that four of the city's highest ranked officials and their families would all have to report their absence to dinner, a dinner that was arranged for the meeting of the minds that formed the powers of our city?

Prince Alag stood and addressed me. "I would love to stay and entertain your insults, Alya, but being as the courts won't be in attendance, the purpose behind this meal cannot be fulfilled. I will take my leave. Good night to you and your family, Meoltan."

My father simply hung his head, refusing to even look at Alag. Although I still had many things to say to the prince, I thought it best to lay it to rest for the moment. He didn't give me any time to debate his departure before he left the table with attendant and guards following close behind.

I returned to my seat, one of the guards being kind enough to return it back to its place. The kitchen servants brought out our food, but no one seemed enthusiastic about the meal. Madja didn't even try to engage us in meaningless conversation as we ate. Nothing was the same and I was sure it never would be. I was so angry that I could barely finish my dinner. This catastrophe of a night was as opportune a time as any to take an early leave.

I stood up and turned to leave, waiting to be lectured by Madja or badgered by Mira, but none of this came to pass. It seemed that we had lost our normal rhythm. I didn't bother to return to my chambers to grab a winter covering or even a light shawl—I needed to get some air as soon as possible. I didn't believe that even the chill of the night could make me feel as cold, distant, and dark as I felt watching my life change for the worse, and after meeting up with the captain of the guard, I was sure it would only get ever colder.

Chapter Seven

The winds didn't blow tonight, that I was thankful for. The darkness was a stilled hush, but I didn't find peace in it. My heart pounded in a rushed rhythm and I wondered how long I could keep living like this. More and more secrets were building on top of lies and it seemed that the next day I could easily be imprisoned, dissociated, or even suffer a fate worse than death itself. It couldn't be healthy to keep on like this. Nevertheless, the thoughts fell upon me like waves upon the sand, pulling me out to sea. It seemed like all the beauty had left my world. I pushed these thoughts out of my head as I approached the entrance of the prison.

"Protector!"

I nearly jumped out of my skin before I turned to see Silvertail approaching with two large brutish prison keeps following close behind him with gigantic hammers fit for an ogre.

"I wasn't expecting you this early."

"Good evening, Captain. I thought it better to visit earlier, having started my day at such an early hour." I didn't feel like sharing my actual reasoning with someone I hardly knew.

Before engaging in any further conversation, he turned to his prison keeps. For men so large and strong, they were timid, not embracing the presence their full height and weight rendered.

They sunk down, lowering their necks as if to be roped like herded cattle when being spoken to by their captain.

"You may continue work in the morning," Silvertail said to them. "The iron door must be raised within the next fortnight. I suspect we'll have some prisoners soon." He turned to me as his prison keeps took their leave, laying their hammers outside of the prison entrance before trudging off to their homes—or judging from their boorish appearance and sluggish behavior, one of the local pubs in the middle rings for the night.

When the captain and I entered the prison, it smelled of ashes and old cinders. The lanterns, quietly burning their wicks, were sprayed with a dark residue of what could only be described as a combination of tar and paint. Something had happened here, and as we rounded the corner of the corridor, what I had anticipated was confirmed.

The bars of the cell were bent and turned every which way like trees after a rainstorm. The same black residue that was sprayed across the lanterns was dotted on the metal bars. The little girls were gone, and in their place was a dark mark, like an angry scar on the floor. It reminded me of when the lads and I would get stuck in a thunderstorm in the edgewoods and would have to wait for it to cease. On our way back to the city, we would see where lightning struck in the form of great burning scars on the ground or against a cracked tree.

"Odd, isn't it, the markings and the black splatter? I've never seen anything like it. It seems they have some form of a new weapon. Something more destructive than fire."

We paused for a moment, staring at the black ring on the floor that emulated what smoke would look like if it was suddenly frozen and plastered on a canvas.

"Who could have done something like this?"

Silvertail turned, continuing down the shadowy corridor.

"I have an inkling."

Once in his chambers, we sat at his grand table, where he picked up some scarred, splintered wood. I examined the other pieces he had laid out, noticing one with a hinge and another with a lever.

"Do you recognize this, Protector?" he asked, holding up the piece in his hand.

"I can't say that I do, Captain. It's just a piece of wood—from the looks of the rest of it, I'd assume a small door."

He tossed the wood on the table with a smile, affirming my answer. "Exactly. It's the remnants to a small door, a hatch to be exact. Do you know which hatch?"

I widened my eyes in a puzzled expression, irritated that we were playing a guessing game. Still, I gave it some effort and the answer seemed to summon itself.

"From the Chamber of Light. The hatch. The explosion. From the Day of Unveiling."

This time Silvertail almost clapped with excitement. It was strange to see so much emotion from him when he's normally stoic. "Exactly! Luckily this time, the prison was empty when the explosion happened, and much damage wasn't done. I think it was meant to scare us. To shake up the city's defense. This one was much bigger. Much more dangerous."

"Couldn't the explosion have been used to free the prisoners from their cell? It seems quite logical."

From the table he picked up a heavy lock, rusted with age. "I would have also made that assumption Alya, but the explosion would have killed whoever was within a few yards of it. I suppose that is what they want us to believe. Perhaps not." He placed something in the center of the table. "It was somehow undisturbed from the explosion, but it was unhitched from its hold. It was unlocked." It was the lock to the prison cell.

I could feel my heart sinking and a nauseous feeling ran from my throat down to my stomach.

"I decided to try my key, fearful that a duplicate had been made in my ignorance, perhaps while the previous captain of the Guards of Candor, peacefully may his soul rest, was in authority." Silvertail set down the heavy lock. "When I tried my key, it didn't work. I realized then that my keys had been stolen…and a pair was left in their stead."

I swallowed with difficulty, the gulp straining my dry throat. The very air seemed to be sucked from my lungs. There was no way of telling how far he had investigated into the matter of things. He knew I had left the purple ring early this morning. This afternoon, he was searching my room. One hunch, another inkling would have led him to try the key to my door, and I had to assume he had.

"Do you have a suspicion… Do you think you know who might have switched them or who the keys belong to?" From there I held my breath. I was walking the edge of a knife.

I waited for him to smile, that expression that implored me to tell him what he already knew. I imagined admitting to him that I had swapped the keys, that I had killed Shiloh in order to take the city, that I was a traitor to my kin. But that scenario was not to be.

"I have no idea," the captain confessed. "I assume they were taken when I was away searching your room." He slouched over the table, drawing in a deep breath and letting it out with an air of longing. I let mine out as well and much relief came with it. "I've been watching you, Protector," he said. "I can't say that I fully trusted you, so I watched you. Examined your movements. It's hard to believe that you didn't have a motive in the Chamber of Light and with all the accusations; it's hard not to put stock into the idea. When I saw you leave the purple ring early this morn, I decided this would be the best time to search your room, and the prince, eager to know your whereabouts, allowed us to do so."

Clearly ashamed, he wouldn't look at me as he spoke. Still, why would Alag want to know of my whereabouts? His affection for me was nonexistent and he intentionally avoided me at all costs. What interest could he have with my whereabouts?

Silvertail continued, "In a hurry, I left the keys. I'd imagine that sometime during my absence, the keys were traded, and the prisoners freed. I would understand if you'd have me relieved of my duties, but I thought I should share this with you now that you have all of my trust. I should have never doubted you."

I couldn't believe my ears. He still couldn't look at me. Silvertail, for all his wisdom, believed himself to be more so to blame than I. While relieved, I couldn't help but feel that familiar guilt hollowing my soul, making me emptier and emptier inside. Still, who could he believe the infiltrators to be? I needed to know so that I could bury at least one secret.

"So how are you going to go about finding who the keys belong to?"

He straightened then turned around to face a map, which had replaced the mural of the deceased captain. It was a map of the city, from the edgewoods and the great stone bridge to the farming fields and mountain ways.

"I considered commanding that all latches be checked in the homes of the black ring, but that might not be the best plan of action, because you see, only one of elven blood could pass into the purple ring without permission. It is law. There would be very little need being as they're not allowed to work in the palace or the homes of officials. For all visitors, regardless of race, the guards keep on record." He pointed to a large stack of parchment. The top of the first page read today's date. "Only ones of elven descent passed through the gate this morning and by afternoon, their whereabouts were all confirmed, as well as yours, for I had seen you leave the purple ring and return."

I couldn't see where he was going with this detailed report or if he was leading me anywhere at all. It is possible that he didn't have a clue to whom they belonged, and just wanted to elaborate on the lengths he went to in his evaluation to prove to me that he was worthy of his position.

"What of it then?" I blurted out in frustration.

"I promise, Protector. There is only but a little more to share and it is pertinent that you understand my efforts fully before I divulge my suspect." He sniffed, sucking in the running mucus that was summoned by the constant chill in his quarters. "No one, other than you, left the purple ring before the prison break, which leads me to believe that someone inside assisted the infiltrator. Someone who wants you dead."

I could feel the color returning to my face as he uttered those words. Of course someone wanted me dead. In fact, if it wasn't for the rogue fowl, I would have been dead.

He went on. "The keys, I suspect, are simple old spares and it would be nearly impossible to check every door of the purple ring without causing offense and more damage to my reputation. And if the keys belong to not a door, chamber, or lock in the purple ring, that could be quite dire. What then would I order? That the black ring, the Guerr barracks, or the whole city is to be searched? That would cause uproar, possibly a rebellion. It would be wiser to cut our losses and fill the gaps in our scenario."

He pushed himself off of the table, now standing fully erect. He looked into my eyes for the first time. I had never noticed how average he was. He was of normal build, not much in brawn, and his face, for his age, reminded me of a young lad's. I met his imploring gaze and knew immediately where he kept his swells of emotion, where his intimidation lay and his secrets dwelled. His eyes would tell what his mouth couldn't. I nearly could have uttered his conclusion from his stare.

"I suspect that the prince may want you dead."

A gust of wind made its way through the captain's chamber, sending a chill down my spine, followed by the thud of armored feet running through the corridors, getting louder and louder as they approached. Soon, they were upon us and a young guard, nearly out of breath, collapsed into the chamber, gasping for air. He held up his hand as if he had something urgent to say but the cold sprint had stolen his breath. Silvertail helped him up, leaning him against the wall, as the guard collected himself.

"My captain. Protector. By Olörun's hand you are alive." He was relieved, unbothered by our puzzled looks. "I bring grave news to you."

My imagination took over, conjuring the worst thoughts possible. Anger, sadness, and longing swelled within me as the thought of Yann hurting my family gripped my mind. I couldn't wait any longer. I had to know. Before I knew it, I had the guard pinned against the wall, my hand around his throat, clenching whatever breath his body had recovered.

"Protector. Please." Silvertail scrambled to the aid of the guard, attempting to pry my hand away, but I was determined. It wouldn't release until I had drained the news from his lips.

"Speak!" I commanded.

With one loud spraying gasp, he sputtered the message. It came out like a gagged whisper that was barely audible even though the room was quiet. "The courts."

I let him go as he struggled to gather himself once again. I sunk back down, my rage fleeing me as fast as it came, leaving me with only surprise. I didn't know what had come over me. The necklace hung heavy against my neck, its cold metal the only thing I felt, as clarity returned to me. I stroked the head of the snake as the guard stumbled back up to his feet.

"My apologies, sir. I'm not well," I managed to say as the guard glanced at me with forgiving eyes, half smiling as he rubbed his throat. He turned to the captain, continuing with his report.

"The order of the courts are dead."

Chapter Eight

Silvertail, along with the breathless guard, hurriedly escorted me back to the palace, their bodies lined against the deceiving darkness. I couldn't believe the guard's words. I admit that I thought it odd that the courts as well as their families had taken ill at the same time and couldn't report to dinner. I surmised that they wanted to avoid me altogether, like Alag, and thought a sick notice would do well in formality, but all of them passing at once was a strange phenomenon.

"Plague!" shouted a council member I recognized from the Remni, his eyes consumed in fear. "Another plague."

The foyer to the palace's west gate was crowded with lingering officials. I spotted Madja and Mira sitting on a bench with Sir Fuerto, father of my best friend Rayloh. Father had arranged for Rayloh and Segun's family to come live with the rest of us in the purple ring since the Remni was destroyed instead of taking residence in one of the other estates in the yellow ring. Sir Fuerto's face was dry and his beard coarse, which was more noticeable due to the lengthy time we'd spent apart. I could look at him and tell he wasn't the same. His wife had passed long ago and now Rayloh, his only son, had been taken from him by the Guerr. He was alone and nothing I could do could ease the despair he felt.

"Well then, what are you going to do?" the squawking council member directed toward me, placing his hands on his bony hips like a flamingo in the surf. "What are we to do? Some sickness has wiped out four houses before the sun has set."

People chorused in agreement, tightening in around me with fearful expressions. I started up the center stairway to rise above the panic. The guard I had thrust against the wall demanded their attention with a blow of his patrol horn. He nodded at me, presenting the floor as now my own.

"I understand you may be afraid or unsure of what to make of this." The crowd buzzed with whispers as soon as the words left my lips. "There's no need to panic," I insisted.

Just as the guard was about to give his patrol horn another blow, Alag arrived with a clap of the chamberlain's cymbal as his call to order. The room stilled, everyone dropping to their knees in reverence as Alag entered the foyer. He passed over them as they all held their place in silence. The Guards of Candor swept in and lined the walls, blocking exit or entry. The prince ascended the stairway, stopping on the same step as I. He stared at me for a moment, smiling before turning to his subjects, who had slowly risen to their feet.

"It is my belief that something has gone awry, but I will work hard to reach a resolve. We cannot afford to worry as the elite of this city. We are still safe within these walls." He raised his hands high, as if directing an orchestra. "Now return to your homes and let not your minds be burdened with trouble."

In a bat of a lash, the once disgruntled crowd turned and left, with only a few whispers riding the air, mainly about how noble and handsome Alag was. Although he disgusted me with his bigoted ideals, it was quite wondrous how he confidently commanded the attention of the people. He possessed a certain energy, an aura that would make even his enemies be still.

Alag left as quickly as he had entered, the guards trailing out behind him. The foyer was empty except for Mira, Madja and Sir Fuerto. He stood up, smoothing out the wrinkles from his cloak. As he came past the stairway, he glanced up at me. In his eyes, hurt gleamed along with blame. I just stared at him, wishing I could bring comfort to whatever he was feeling. The he-elf who once made me squeal with adolescent lust was now a hollow corpse of sadness. With that he left.

Madja and Mira didn't bother escorting me to my chambers for the night. They simply went their own way, not even giving me the slightest nod or bid of farewell. It bothered me to admit that even my relationship with them had changed for good. I settled in my bed, pulling up the blankets over my cold limbs. The necklace was still around my neck, its coils tight against my skin. I treasured it as one of the only things that survived from the Remni's destruction, but it somehow was becoming more to me. I thought of how my fingers would run over its detailing, quenching my troubles with every stroke. I tucked it in my blouse and rolled over, ready to welcome sleep after the long day I had, when a loud thud startled me.

I looked over the side of my bed, my movement causing whatever lay next to me to be disturbed from its settlement. In the faint light of the dimly lit moon and the starless sky, I spotted the old leather book. *The Three Burdens*. I hadn't remembered to question Silvertail about the journal, not that I would have had a chance since the terrible news we received interrupted our private meeting. I wondered whether truth lay in it at all. If Silvertail slipped this journal to me, there had to be a reason. I tucked it in my pillowcase. Immediately nostalgia took me as I remembered how I used to stuff the sifting book into the casing along with anything else I wanted to keep secret. Secrets back then used to be easily tucked away in pillowcases and oak chests.

***

Now was as good a time as any to begin reading the journal. I had fond memories of hard school days and coming home to dive into the tales of adventure that kept me so entertained. I pulled *The Three Burdens* from my pillowcase and sat on the windowsill, feeling the cool glass through the thin sheet of dark, draping material that hung from the ceiling. I cracked the leather binding. A distinct crinkling sound was made as the leather gave in, and the scent of the pages filled the air. I began.

At the arbomai rojal your journey begins, where the grass is green with even winds. But beyond the elves, an evil sleeps, awakened by your prancing feet.

But like the light you must glide and on the winds you must ride.

Whoever took the time to write out these words was quite imaginative. I thought about the housedame Mournadam's words, how the passages recorded in these pages were the true accounts of the last of the party to leave Keldrock and return. I continued with the passage. On its page was a sketching of a large tree with twisting branches and leaves that seemed to curl in animation. It stood in the center of a field, surrounded by gorgeous flowers with gigantic petals and tall stems. Giant bees hovered across their budding pistils collecting pollen. I couldn't help but feel like I'd seen the tree before. Its trunk was enormous, the bark appearing red. I felt the beautiful markings of the illustration but as I passed over the tree, the texture of the artwork changed. The body of the tree was pasty like the paint on a canvas.

I took a break from my admiration to open the curtains, wanting now the sun to cover the room. The day was glorious and promising, even with all that had passed the night before. I sat back down to continue my reading when the tree took on new features. With the sun's kiss, the tree trunk glowed a sparkling red that bested even the fieriness of rubies. It was a wonder how such a secret could only be revealed through the sunlight. I looked out at the giant orb of blinding light, squinting my eyes as long as possible to entertain its shine. While Madja always advised Mira and me not to look directly at the sun, I couldn't help but want to stare at it. I looked across the palace courtyard and out to the lower rings until my eyes fell upon the tower of the School of Talents within the blue ring. I saw how the sun kissed the marble steps and the gold accents of the surviving estates of the yellow ring. The glass that was shattered in the yellow garden's dome shimmered like morning dewdrops on cobblestone. My eyes rounded back to the purple ring and noticed that even the prison seemed less murky and foreboding. I examined the flowerless prison lot, occupied only by an archer stringing his bow. Even from a great distance, I admired its slender wood and silver endings gleaming in the sunlight, bringing fond memories of the bow I once had. In fact, it was too similar. Then a sparkle caught my eyes. It was like a spider's web kissed by the forest rain, drops of water beading shining against the sun like silver at the ends of the bow.

I made sure to return the journal to its proper hiding place before throwing on a shirt, trousers, and boots. I walked leisurely to the prison, growing more and more convinced that the bow I saw was mine, the one that came to me in the black ring's market that I later found out once belonged to Shiloh. Since the Unveiling, it had been missing and it didn't even cross my mind that someone could have simply found it or even was using it in sport. I was convinced the warriors of Wood Haven took it in their retreat or Alag, in his jealous rage, reclaimed his grandfather's talisman as his own with no intent of ever returning it.

I rounded the front of the prison where the large brutish guards, with drunken faces, struggled to work on the metal door. Without acknowledging the guards, I followed the dark dirt path, wet from the melting snow, where sealed barrels and scrap weapons, most likely used for training, were tucked in pockets of the prison wall.

The prison lot was even more barren up close. Even the training dummies scattered about the yard were dead in their imitation. What was left of the snow and ice clung to these oversized mannequins created from cloth and stone. I walked on to the archer's arena, where large targets of hay bales painted red and black were stacked against the iron gates of the prison lot. To my surprise I found Silvertail aiming an arrow from a short distance at a red circle painted on one of the rounds of hay. It reminded me of when I used to practice my aim with a target painted on a tree in the yellow gardens. I watched as he balanced the bow against his trembling finger, struggling to keep the arrow against the string. He tugged his arrow back, pulling it much farther than he should have. The arrow soared right to the ground, lodging itself into the cold soil. I couldn't help but giggle, feeling that I had done infinitely better on my first try.

He turned around, startled and embarrassed to see me watching. "Protector!" He bowed, the sweat from his forehead dripping to the ground. "I wasn't expecting you. I hope you didn't see too much. For my sake and yours," he said with a laugh as he tugged the arrow from its hold and tapped it against his britches, loosening any clinging soil.

"No, I'm afraid I suffered the entire shot, or the attempt at least. No need to fret. I was quite the buffoon myself when I first learned to shoot."

He looked surprised. "Wow. I didn't know maidens were trained up in such things." He laughed to himself. Although his statement was one I would rebut, I had said too much, realizing my lessons with Master Tali were to always remain secret. "How did you spot me anyway?"

I was almost embarrassed to say. "From my window." I could see a mature smile crawling from his lips. "I was reading when the glint from the metal at the ends of my bow caught my attention."

"Your bow?" he said boldly in shock. "I figured the arrow and quiver belonged to one of the Dwala that attacked the city, but I realized a relic like this must have been made from elfish hands. How did you come upon it?"

"Do you believe the truth is not on my tongue, Captain?"

His eyes widened. "No, Protector, I simply meant—"

"Alya!"

"Pardon me?"

"Alya," I said a little softer. "Call me Alya. Now that we trust one another, I think we can be on better terms, even when addressing one another."

He smiled, the hairs in his beard making scratching sounds as he wiped the scruff of his chin. "Well, Alya. While I am no champion at archery, I am quite the swordsman and a decent spearman as well. Since arrows can be scarce at times, I think it wise that one learns." He handed me the bow before retrieving for me the quiver of arrows that sat against one of the nearby targets. "Since you seem to be an archer, maybe you could teach me."

Just like that, a bond was made, and when he said my name, it didn't sound wrong to me anymore. It seemed we had a lot more in common than I had realized. Silvertail seemed different than the others of the Guards who were bent on ordering others around and the petty squabbles of city folk. He really cared about the welfare of Keldrock. From then on, we met every other day against the rising sun sparring, shooting and throwing our weaponry. He was truly skilled at the blade and didn't bother introducing me, as Master Tali had, with a large root or stick. When he had night watch, I would join him, walking the city under the night sky and dim stars that had just begun to make their return from their winter sleep. I had to admit I missed their light. We would speak of our childhood, our families, even some things that most keep reserved in the deepest realms of their memories.

Silvertail never knew his father, who had abandoned his mother before he was born. His mother died while he was very young, no more than half a score. Being orphaned and a common elf of the blue ring, Silvertail sought the warriors of the Guerr. Having always had a calling for combat, he thought it would be the perfect opportunity for him. He knew somehow that his destiny lay beyond those heavy metal gates on the opposite end of the blue ring. He trained for an entire year, pushing himself beyond his limits while working to feed and clothe himself. When it finally came time for him to present himself, he snuck into the courtyard of the School of Talents, and when given his turn demonstrated his skill with weaponry. A student whose house had given him work revealed in front of all that he was an orphan, not belonging to a house, and he was dismissed against the quiet judging glances of his kin, he being lesser than their own sons in their eyes.

In an effort to redeem himself, he went to other end of the city, where the Guards of Candor had settled for the evening, drinking and gambling. He strode in, watching them around the fire, the merriment and the camaraderie of what could be for him a family. And so he sought the head of that patrol, and after serving for years as a simple barkeep and servant, he rose to be an officer of the Guards of Candor and by chance, the captain.

Our stories were so different. Still, both of us defied the odds. It's funny how someone can become your inspiration and your hero in such a short amount of time. I never knew what it would be like to have an older brother. I had brothers—or the like at least—through my best friends Segun and Rayloh, but Silvertail was older, wiser, and although I was the Protector, it seemed that he wanted nothing more than my welfare. So we spent our days like this, I like his shadow. No one questioned it, assuming that we were working diligently to solve the state of the city, which we would allot time to discuss. The months swept away like seconds against the clock, and soon the last of the winter snow was melted well before the sun crested the mountain and it seemed that the trouble was pacified for the moment. Guards were posted in every crowded area, but Yann didn't appear. With my contribution, I made sure Silvertail was aware of every exit and entrance I had come to know. Even the groves were searched and a post set up amongst the trees. I didn't know if Yann and the occupants of the edgewoods had given up, but somehow, in the short months that passed, I had forgotten the danger.

***

One spring day, I awoke to a loud clash of a cymbal resounding like claps of thunder. Startled, I peered around, wondering if my dream had conjured the sound or if I was hearing this in reality. Another resounding noise confirmed the latter. I grabbed my housecoat and opened the door a crack to see the klutz of a chamberlain counting to himself as he tried to track the spacing between his cymbal claps. I grabbed the edges of the cymbals before he could bring them together again. He looked up and smiled, most of his teeth missing from his heavy infatuation with rum tobacco and sugared syrup.

"The honorable Prince Alag wishes you to join him for a meeting, the details of which can be found in this notice." I watched him pat the sides of his overcoat, before finally reaching in his pocket and producing a small fold of parchment sealed with the narrow head of a golden fox: the royal seal.

After thanking the guard, I returned to my bed, watching the early sun's rays stretch across my bed sheets. I couldn't believe that Alag wanted to have a meeting with me. We hadn't really acknowledged each other since his address on the stairs the night we found out the courts had passed. He had an angle. He had been trained in the art of charm and deception. He was a prince after all, whose job was to lead his people through any series of events. However, he wasn't counting on needing me. That much was certain, so maybe he had come around to what would be the most favorable of options: a truce.

I had but just returned from the washroom when I discovered Madja searching through my closet. Word had traveled quickly.

"No. None of this will do."

She tossed her hair over her shoulder, now dyed an airy auburn color. The few elves and Dwala I had seen with red hair had freckles to match and Madja didn't miss this detail. It was odd seeing her with tiny little orange pecks on her face trickling around the tip of her nose, nostrils, and cheekbones. The imitation didn't have quite the same effect as normal freckles, hers reminding me of tiny red gnat bites.

"When is it darling? When is the meeting?"

"A full course from today."

"Splendid." She clasped her hands together as toddlers do when they are extremely happy. "I will summon a seamstress and have her bring her finest garments for us to eye. As for the meeting, I have requested Mournadam to prep you this afternoon.

This is the first time in a while you and the prince will have an audience, and I want everything to run smoothly."

"Do you love father?" It slipped out like a leak in a dam. "I mean, did you love him? When you first met?"

Madja stopped in her place, her excited movements suddenly stilled. I couldn't tell if she was angry, saddened or simply reminiscing. She turned with a half-smile in my direction, then stared down at the floor, her eyes glistening as each thought passed.

"Does this have to do with your betrothal? To the prince?" I couldn't really affirm that this was the only reasoning behind my inquiry but it had some part to play, I had to admit.

"Yes. It is quite a burden to bear with the events that have passed."

She settled on the bed and patted it, requesting I sit next to her. I could see flashes of how she used to be. Now she seemed like less of a doppelganger of the petty elf ladies and more my mother, the one I remembered and loved so dearly.

"I understand your reservations," she started. "I can't say that I didn't have them as well. My father was a widower, you see, a former lieutenant in the Guerr who had fought valiantly during the first Unveiling. He passed before my Kei and our groundskeeper, a foolish elf, requested my hand for his son. Your father."

She giggled to herself and I could tell that this was a happy memory, something she looked back on as a pinnacle in their relationship.

"And you were accepting of this?"

"I didn't have a say. My upkeep fell to the keeper of my father's house, and with no sons to inherit his will, his fortune would vanish if I didn't marry." She shook her head. "But that was a long time ago. Your father and I were young, and his ambition intrigued me. He was optimistic in those days, vibrant and hard working. But like so many, he was seduced by the lust of power. I don't think I could really blame him. He was, after all, the son of a groundskeeper with a chance to change his course for the better."

The half-smile faded from her face, replaced with sorrowful eyes. I could tell she didn't wish to carry on, but I wanted to know more of this story.

"But did you love him?"

She gathered herself, returning to a smile, lifting herself from the bed.

"It was a different time, Alya. You're marrying a prince."

"I understand, but what of love if I don't get to choose who I marry? I didn't ask for this."

She floated across the room to the mirror where she began grooming herself, arranging the hair that had wisped to the side of her face to the back of her head again.

"Alya, love will find you in time. I assure you that the prince will be everything you ever dreamed of. Give you a life of royalty. He's no mere groundskeep—"

We stared at each other for a moment. I could see her eyes welling and I knew she didn't want this explosion of unresolved emotion to happen in front of me, that she would give anything to reverse time and simply have pat my cheek and told me it was going to be alright instead of divulging a past that she had kept hidden for so long. She rushed for the door, letting it close loudly behind her with a thud.

My father had changed, the sickness of greed and power growing within him as I grew from elfling to miss. Madja understood but I didn't. I didn't have a choice, but she did. She didn't say it and didn't have to. She never loved my father. Even before his hunger for power grew fierce, she didn't love him. She hardly knew him. I pondered this as I dressed for the day. Mournadam didn't like when I was late.

Chapter Nine

"Proper protocol is necessary in such meetings. You are a she, as am I, and we are not to interrupt the lords. They are leaders and we are the heart that beats quietly behind them, keeping healthy the body of our nation."

It almost sounded beautiful, the way she poetically recited the roles of she-elves. Mournadam viewed the path of elven misses as not simple servants to our male counterparts but as the backbone of civilization. It still made me sick to think that I was expected to surrender my wants and desires to serve a lord and his house. I, who was now Protector, and defended our city during the Unveiling, was expected to stoop lower because of what lay beneath my bosom and within the crevices of my thighs. I sat still, accepting what she said for the sake of appeasing Alag. If we were to move forward in a spirit of goodwill, one of us would have to yield. For the sake of those I loved and those who put their trust in me, I accepted the task.

As Mournadam continued to lecture, I caught wind of her scent, a combination of honey peppermint and wild chives. It was an unusual mix for one so ancient. It was a decadent potion, seductive and enticing, and was known throughout our lands to arouse the spirits of young lads. I took in a large whiff as she continued her spiel, pouring out nonsense like a leaky well pump.

"If you must speak, wait until the room has come to a still, or if it is requested of those attending by the conductor, that is the prince, that you offer your opinion. If either of these circumstances occur, ask permission before beginning your statement."

I scoffed at this absurdity. "Is there not a protocol for the one who holds the responsibility as Protector? I feel that honor precedes any rule against my nature."

"Be careful, young one. Remember what precedence stands against you. You proved your truth enough to be pardoned by the courts, but the hearts that beat for tradition are not so easily changed."

The housedame was a minion that had been brainwashed to never question what she knew other than that it was right and it must be followed. We continued on with our lesson but I couldn't help but let my mind wander. I had proven my case with the courts, but I was naïve to believe a civilization could change with this one decision. I had to marry someone who believed I stole his birthright. I had to spend the rest of my life with someone who despised me just as much as I despised him, and who possibly wanted me dead.

***

By the day of the meeting, I was fully prepared and well versed on the statutes of royal etiquette. The last time I had walked beneath the judgment chambers' elaborate ceilings of ornate gold and marble was when I awaited trial for alleged crimes against the kingdom. It is strange how life can change so drastically and what would have happened if my father hadn't offered to speak on my behalf. Now I strode by the heavy drapes of black that hung over the windows honoring the deceased members of the courts. Something was definitely coming. No matter the good that had passed over these few months, and no matter how hard I tried to deceive myself, I couldn't ignore the obvious.

The meeting was to be held in the hidden arena, a room tightly secured behind the judgment chamber. The real discussion happened in this room, where the courts retreated before deeming their verdicts. A large table sat in the center with a throne chair wrapped around it. Upon my arrival, an usher presented me with the agenda then showed me to my seat. I quickly realized that the audience I was supposed to have with Alag was no more than a council meeting. I wasn't angered, convincing myself that I should have expected his lordship to remain strong-willed, his heart hardened and still unwilling to speak with me alone. Still, this was somewhat of a surprise.

I was seated at the head of the table that was closest to the doors. The two chairs next to me were empty. I glanced around, spotting Silvertail against one of the walls along with his guards at their posts. I didn't bother speaking to the members of the council that were dotted about the room in their stately robes, eyeing me with either distaste or in an admirable awe, debating whether or not to speak to me. I took my mind off of these petty matters and anxiously read the agenda.

State of the City

-

-

-

Celebration of the Fawn

-

-

Captain's Report

-

-

-

Shiloh's School of Talents

As I skimmed down the parchment, pausing to read the few items that seemed somewhat interesting, I discovered that it consisted of nothing more than meaningless points. Nothing of the courts, their deaths, or even the appointing of replacements for their positions was listed, not to mention the warriors of Wood Haven.

"You're quite fortunate, I must say. This meeting should be briefer than those previously held." I looked to who was standing by my side, surprised that one of the council members finally had gathered either enough nerve or enough cause to converse with me, but it wasn't a council member at all.

"It's great to see you, Master!" I was delighted to receive Master Tali standing before me in all her radiance. She was still just as beautiful; her brown skin and dark braised hair signature to that which I had always known of my favorite teacher. It had been months since I had seen her, and my affectionate outburst caused some judgmental eyes to shift my direction, but I wasn't fazed. I squeezed her tight before noticing a heavy bulge hanging from her side. She plopped it by her seat with a heavy thud before continuing.

"It's great to see you as well, Alya. The light looks favorable on you."

She ran her fingers through my hair. Sometimes I forgot that the once dark locks of my hair were now replaced with a bright flamboyant shade that can only be found in pure starlight— a mark I was granted to carry until my reign as Protector ceased. Master Tali settled in the seat next to me and soon we were informing each other of what we had been up to during the months apart.

Master Tali now spent her days assisting any way she could with the city's upkeep, and even invited a few pupils, whose were nearing the age of their Kei, for private talent instruction. It was an easy outlet and form of income since the school had closed and nothing more than the basics of their talents would need to be taught in order for these misses to win a lord. As we chatted, servers made their way around, distributing bronze-rimmed glasses to guests that were filled halfway with a mixture of spirits and apple grape ale, a slightly cheaper version of the spiced wines that were a delicacy for the elite.

Alag finally made his entrance along with his wormy attendant, and the council minions, no matter their opinion of the royal brat, clapped, lining up to exchange greetings with him. I thought it best altogether to avoid his glance. Master Tali leaned into my ear with a mischievous smile.

"He is handsome. You must agree. And you two were lovely at your Kei."

I laughed, shaking my head and scrunching my face in disapproval. Whatever feelings I didn't acknowledge that night, I knew what I felt now, and that was complete and utter disgust. Master Tali let out a girlish laugh before changing the subject.

"Have you been practicing your studies in my absence?" I had almost forgotten about the wonder of sifting. With the book destroyed and with all that had come to pass, the ancient words had slipped away from my mind like a summer breeze upon the heat of the day.

"I'm afraid I haven't. I actually spend most of my days..." I hesitated, unsure if I should tell her of my sparring sessions with Silvertail or my struggles with Alag, the deaths of the courts, or even my deadly encounters with Yann. I didn't know if she would view me the same or if she would in fact call upon her decision to tutor me privately as a costly mistake.

A clash of the chamberlain's cymbals ended the conversation and for that I was thankful. The council members, with their toyed-over beverages, settled in their places. I took note, also, of the School of Talents coordinator and masters. The seat to my right remained empty. It seemed intentional the way the snobbish council members avoided me, and although I remained fearless, it admittedly caused me some offense.

"My apologies for my tardiness, my liege."

My father's voice almost made my heart sink into my stomach. It seemed that no matter what program or order I attended during my time in the purple ring, he would be there. To my right he placed himself, bowing towards Alag and smiling at Master Tali and me.

"First order, I would like to welcome our esteemed Protector Alya Lightstar from the House of Meoltan Lightstar," the prince addressed.

There was no welcoming round of applause or even the slightest smirk from these elderly, narrow-minded he-elves that my father so desperately strove to please. He was the youngest of their order, and from what I had seen during my many months behind the purple ring's gates, he offered nothing new or innovative to this group of traditionalists. He seemed to be more than willing to carry on whatever views they had reserved from their ancestors than to advise reformation.

"Now, for the state of the city. For those of you who were not made aware, the former captain of the Guards has now passed," Alag calmly stated, staring at me as he did. It came to no surprise that he had no intention of revealing the detailed truth of what happened that day just outside my personal chambers. Maybe it was better this way, considering that it would cause more outrage and panic than actual planning. Still, I thought the council would prove most useful in such matters, considering we no longer had the courts to depend upon. I held my tongue and decided to see how everything would pan out.

"His replacement, thanks to many dedicated hours under the tutelage of the honored deceased, is Sir—and now Captain—Kai Silvertail." Alag paused a moment for the council to turn in their chairs or look up from their sparkling drinks and smile at Silvertail, who simply nodded. It was entertaining to see him acting so formal. Then again, he wasn't the emotional type by any means. "Captain Silvertail has done a wondrous job at improving the state of our city. He has created new posts for his guards, instituted mandatory re-education as far as training is concerned, and has quieted the reign of terror upon the city caused by the Unveiling." The council muttered amongst each other before breaking out into a hushed applause.

The agenda was extensive, and from what Master Tali told me, it was hard to believe that there was a previous program that could be any longer than this. Soon it fell upon the final line of the agenda, which I believed was the reason behind the attendance of the school Coordinator and the Master.

"I believe it is best for the young to reopen the school," the timid coordinator started, his hands trembling. There was a small hump in his back and the tips of his ears drooped next to his lobes like a frightened feline's. His face was clean-shaven unlike most of the elders who donned beards touting their lengthy lives. "Not much exists any more to distract them from the wrong that happens in our world. Most of them have lost loved ones in the siege of the city. Perhaps it best that we allow some form of purpose back into their lives."

The prince brushed his chin, rubbing it with two of his sharpened fingers. "I understand your feelings, Coordinator. I myself found that schooling, although separate from Shiloh, calmed even the most jangled of nerves. Still, I hardly think that now is the time for us to reinstate Shiloh's School of Talents. Our city is safe for now, but who knows what threats may come. For the moment being, until the veil is raised, we should focus our attentions in the home."

"But within the homes is not certain comfort. The invaders burned most of ours to rubble." Angry eyes shot to my end of the table. I didn't forget the first rule of protocol: you must ask to speak. Master Tali seemed to have forgotten or was never instructed otherwise because she continued, "If the school isn't reinstated, then who will train those who will help defend us in the future?"

Alag didn't seem remotely unnerved. In fact, he appeared to be amused. "Master Tali, it was and still is the belief of myself and the courts—the pillars of Keldrock, peacefully may their souls rest—as well as the whole of this council that the threat has been flushed due to our extensive measures. I have informed you of the captain's work. And the veil—"

"—will never rise again. We need to take action before the enemy does." Gasps erupted around the room as angry he-elves struggled to remain in their seats. The smell of spirits and anger filled the air.

"That is quite enough, Tali. Emotion is a thorn in the side of those that belong to your nature and I'd hate for you to sputter when you should recoil." A few chuckles came from the prince's most loyal minions.

Master Tali shifted her enraged glance from him to me. "Well?" she questioned.

Her eyes became enlarged and the blacks of her pupils bored into me. I knew why she called upon me. I was the Protector, that much I recognized, but she had misplaced her trust. In front of all, she was made a spectacle, and her words ignored. Although I wanted nothing more to aid her in her argument, I knew that any word I offered would hinder my strategy and any good that would come. I leaned in close to her, trying my hardest to be as quiet and comforting in tone as I could be.

"I think you should go." She looked at me, her eyes surprised and then accepting, realizing what she felt to be a betrayal. "I believe it would be best for—"

Her hand, like a flash of lightning, was raised, cutting into my words like the blade of a knife. The same gesture she would use when nonsense was thrown around at lessons or when she had when she had enough of a student's disruptiveness. She had never silenced me before. Master Tali threw her chair back, brushing past the guards at the doors, and soon the only remnants of presence were the small chuckles from the throats of Alag's admirers.

I shot him a look of dismay, but he didn't notice. He had made his mocking for the day and for now his appetite was sated. All that was left to be taught were the misses, the lads having been drafted to serve in the Unveiling. To Alag, she-elves weren't worth much other than wives and servants. Master Tali, of all, valued the talents of the young misses she taught not for the sake of entertainment or assisting in the house but to innovate change. I couldn't blame her for being angered at their refusal to reopen the school or upset at me for not speaking up. I had let her down and in more ways than one, I had let myself down.

For another half hour, we sat and discussed alternatives to reinstating the school and its curriculums. One of the masters of the older sprites suggested a restructuring program that was nothing more than an outlet for baking, gardening, and hard labor that paid hires were compensated for.

"The resources we'll save from the workers will go toward rebuilding the city," he said, "and stores for weapons. Our chief architect has been troubled and some work will gladly bring him back to life. Especially if his pockets, as well as those who aid him, are full."

I couldn't believe what selfish rubbish I was hearing. They couldn't possibly consider removing the Dwala workers from their posts. I thought of Kala and the other servants of the Remni. I thought of how some took up these occupations to care for their families and their sick. I couldn't hold my tongue any longer. I knew I had to say something. Just before the defiance escaped my lips, a terrible tremble which I can only compare to a powerful earthquake surged through the room.

The glasses of ales and spirits toppled over, spilling over the sides of the table onto the red-carpeted floor. Silver trays held by the servants banged against the marble as servers lost their footing. The old scribes looked at each other in both disbelief and questioning, as if one of their brethren had somehow known the source of this disturbance. Silvertail and the few members of the guard in the arena led the council out through the judgment chambers from whence we came. I followed suit, trying to keep calm. My father grabbed my hand and although I wasn't too keen on him holding me, we had little time for dramatics. We were just about to cross the threshold of the hidden arena when I noticed Master Tali's bag on the floor where she had left it. I wanted to stop to grab it, but it was out of reach and not worth my life to stop and get it. We quickly strode through the rattling halls, the curtains shaken from their places and hanging limply from their loose holds. The lobby outside of the judgment chamber where I had awaited the courts' decision a many months ago was now littered with debris. The once-beautiful stained-glass windows were broken, pieces strewn across the floor in a colorful mess.

"This way!" Silvertail ordered.

I watched two of Silvertail's elites usher Alag ahead of the procession, dodging toppled marble and glass as they departed. My father continued holding my hand, pulling me in the direction of my assigned guards, but it didn't make sense. None of it did. The explosion had to have been close by, but nothing was severely damaged where we stood with the exception of a few broken windows and pieces of ceiling. I shook loose of my father's grip and raced to Silvertail, who was directing people down the stairs and onto the main floor where another one of his guards received them.

"Shouldn't we remain here?" I suggested. He considered it for a moment as his eyes continued to race around, examining the startled council members. Some began to wander to the windows noticing something peculiar beyond the main road as rain pattered down outside. Across the way, I spotted from whence the explosion came. Smoke rose from the Chamber of Light as flames engulfed the crumbling rubble. From our distance, I could see the building wavering, swaying amidst the rain and flashes of lighting.

"It was but a lightning strike that caused the rumble," a mouthy council member shouted, attempting to be the first to deliver the news to his shaken comrades. I stared out into the sheets of water that poured from the heavens, as smoke lifted to the skies, masking the crumbling building. I looked down at the dying flames and noticed a flaw in the council member's logic.

"Look there on the ground." I pointed out into the storm where tiny red and orange flickers slowly extinguished under the heavy shower. "The explosion happened at the base. If it was lightning, the smoke would be rising from the zenith."

Why the Chamber of Light? Silvertail and I looked at each other, both hoping that the results weren't what we knew to have happened in the past. A high pitched shrill broke our contemplation, and with bold beating wings, a great bird, dark as night with violent red eyes, swooped in through the broken window and landed on the marble floor just as a flash of lighting splintered across the sky. He held his great wings open, shaking them ever so lightly, creating small puddles around him. With his neck outstretched, he made another call, high and piercing but still welcoming to the ear. From his talons he rolled over a leather cylinder, capped and sealed with wax. I could see the seal of the Guerr on the casing. Silvertail rushed to it just as the bird disappeared into the hard rains and crackling skies. He picked up the cylinder quickly and with a knife from his side chipped away at the wax, loosening the cap and letting it fall to the floor.

"From the czar of the Guerr," he explained as he pulled a piece of parchment from its hold. I watched his eyes grow wider as he read. He looked up from the message, swallowing before he allowed the words to escape his lips. "The school… Shiloh's school has been destroyed." The council members grunted and gasped in surprise as Silvertail let the note fall to the floor. "The czar said it was some sort of… explosion."

A slow rumbling laugh bellowed from the throat of the mouthy council member who paced towards Silvertail and me with his arms wrapped around his back in a lecturing form.

"Another lash of the lightning's blow. No matter. Why make a deal of this?"

It was almost as if the universe answered his question directly. Like the strike of a viper as it corners its prey or the buildup of force behind a river dam, followed by the final release of power that plummets to earth, destroying all that lies in its path. I felt the surge before, the quiet before the eruption.

The first thing I heard was a high-pitched screaming, whether from pain or panic, I could not tell. Smoke filled the halls, blinding my sight, and choking me. All I could hear was the loud screaming but it wasn't screaming. My ears were pinched, a loud ringing surging through my eardrums, a sound I could only compare to the screech of the flying rodents that flew from the mountains at night. I lifted my head up from the floor, my body aching all over. I tried to get up but couldn't. I squinted my eyes, trying to make sense of the situation, attempting to decipher the undetectable force that sent me flying against the wall of the lobby. The large heavy doors of the judgment chamber, intricately carved from the finest of woods, were now twisted and torn from their hinges. My nose caught the scent of something burning, and I was thankful I couldn't see the charred corpses. Silvertail. I immediately regretted my thought. He couldn't be one of the dead.

"Silvertail!" I shouted through the dark clouds that filled the lobby, growing ever so thick as the storm outside grew fiercer.

I began to belly crawl, pulling with all my strength. As I crawled, I brushed what I first thought to be a heavy sack, but I could make out enough of the identity of the mouthy council member, his face nearly destroyed from the blast. I vomited, letting it spill over onto the shards of glass and stone that lay strewn about the floor. The smell was unbearable, my eyes watering as more bile spewed from my throat.

I gathered myself and continued calling out Silvertail's name. My voice sounded distant like a whisper from another world. I began to panic. I squeezed my ears, trying to make my hearing return, and then I began screaming. The high-pitched ringing left my mind and soon I was left with soft sounds and screams. Screams of torture. I began sobbing uncontrollably, feeling my consciousness slipping into madness and despair. I could see the flames filling the building and the fiery twist of bright orange and dark red piercing the dark grey smog.

"Alya!" I sparingly made out, quieting my sobbing.

"Here! I'm here," I tried to shout, but smoke had claimed my lungs and in turn my voice.

By now I could barely speak. My nose burned and my throat clenched in desperation. I could feel my face dripping with sweat as the flames crept closer and closer. They began to warp and dim. I was losing my mind. Then I could see him coming to my rescue with his curly hair, his adolescent figure, and his beautiful brown eyes. Then everything went black.

Chapter Ten

"Rayloh!" I shouted, not fully awake or aware of where I was.

"Alya! Open your eyes." I recognized Madja's voice.

I squeezed my eyelids tight before letting them part. I was in my bedroom. Two lanterns flickered on the walls above my bed. Concerned faces stared down at me, some scarred with recently cleaned cuts and bruises while others were smudged with grime. For a moment, I thought my life had ended or that I was still asleep from the night before, conjuring up all the fire and madness that had passed in the form of a nightmare. I knew that wasn't so. The scent of burning flesh I now knew too well.

"Where's Rayloh?" I asked Madja, her nightgown flowing down past her feet like a flower's drooping petals over the side of my bed.

"My dear, you know where he is," she urged as she candidly smiled at me and the other observers in the room. "He's in the Guerr barracks, where he's been for months."

"That's a lie!" I shouted, causing Madja to flinch in surprise. "I heard his voice. I saw him. He saved me. He saved me from the fire." I knew I sounded mad by the expression on her face.

Madja softly touched my hand, trying to calm me. "My sprite," she said softly, her words kind but firm, "Rayloh wasn't there." She reached out to one of the observers, beckoning him into my line of sight. "Your father carried you to safety."

I couldn't believe what she was telling me. I knew I saw him. I saw Rayloh. My father was a worm who, had it not been for the sake of prestige, would have let me burn. I knowingly accredit my very existence to his drive for his own self-interests in my newly deputized position. I looked about and finally took inventory of who had come to take note of my health. A medic, probably one who served alongside Sir Calo, held in his bony hands gauze that he used to wrap my hands and knees. Silvertail was present as well along with two of his elites and Mira who lay on one of my chairs asleep. Her eyelids were large and puffy. I knew she had been crying. I was surprised my parents would allow such a scene for a young sprite; I myself had seen much that in hindsight I wish my eyes were blinded to. It had been months since any harm had been dealt to our city. Lightning wasn't the cause of these catastrophes, but I knew that's what Alag and the council would claim.

A spark of considerable thought flickered behind my eyes. That's what the invaders would want to happen. These attacks had been strategically planned. Whatever magic they hailed from, I could not tell, but I knew I had seen it before. I remembered the hatch opening in the Chamber of Light atop the high tower, and the splintered wood and twisted metal, imitated today by the judgment chamber's doors. I remembered the damage, the sound of shattering glass and planks cracking as smoke rose to the sky from the yellow garden's dome on the Day of Unveiling. I just couldn't think of a reason why the city had been attacked again—but deep within my soul, I knew there was one.

I had to speak up but I knew with all that had happened and my assumed hysteria that they would call my notions mad. I had to speak to someone I trusted.

"Captain, I must speak to you in private." Silvertail looked caught off guard by the request, an odd reaction for one who was normally so well aware.

"I think it best that you rest for the night," my father piped in. "You've been through much and no doubt your mind has been riddled with trouble. Blessedly I was there to save you." I knew I hadn't burst with thanks at my father saving me, and I meant not to. The satisfaction it would bring him would be too depressing.

"I need to speak with him tonight!" My tone was direct and I could see my father boiling with a rage that I recognized from my past but he had restricted for the sake of remaining within my good graces. I knew his game.

"No harm in waiting until the morn. I think we'd all be better off after a restful night's sleep," Silvertail responded, neutralizing the tension. "My charge is dismissed to their posts," he said, turning to his elites, "and I will return to my hold. I think I might spar in the moonlight. It'll serve me well." He winked at me and I got the message. *Meet at the prison yard.*

***

My bedside visitors filtered out, Madja carrying a sleepy Mira. Only the medic remained behind to check my bandages and to exchange the pus-filled gauzes for the night. I watched the shadows of my bedposts shorten and lengthen in the flickering lantern light as I waited out until the wee hours to slip out of the palace. I bent and straightened my legs and stretched my arms. They were sore but most of my strength had returned thanks to the full day's rest. A bowl of lemur roots sat in a clay bowl on my nightstand along with a pitcher of chilled water. I poured a glass, guzzling it down like sweet nectar. My throat purred in delight having been burned by smog and cinders.

From my window I could see the full moon in all its magnificence. I remembered the Remni's nurse, an old spirit of the Dwala clan who nurtured Segun, Rayloh, and me in our toddlerhood, who used to tell us stories of the moon. She seemed obsessed with it, how she would go on and on with tales of how it controlled the waves, the pull of the earth, and the minds of some animals ignorant enough to wander their eyes upon its majesty while it was full. Even some beings react to the moon's strange power, lashing out in ways that would seem unnatural, she would say. That is until the sun returned to rid the spell. *Strange things happen under a full moon.* I stared up at the moon, gazing into its wonderful light. It was quite a spectacle and it surprised me that such legends existed about the moon and those whose gazes lingered for longer than they should. I thought to defy it by letting my eyes remain upon the moon's surface, but I thought well not to. A legend is a legend until it's proven true and I thought it more a game to honor it even though it was just as well a fright.

Instead, I let my eyes wander to the prison yard, searching for any movement in the darkness. The prison walls blocked out most of the moon's light, casting shadows on the sparring dummies below. I knew that Silvertail would signal me, although how, I did not know. So I waited, watching my reflection thin and ghostlike in the window.

After another two hours, a burst of bright flame caught my attention. I watched it swoop and swirl like a buzzing bee and I knew that it was Silvertail, waving his torch at my window. Just as quickly as the swirling flame had appeared, it vanished without a trace.

I jumped from my window seat and threw on my slippers, not bothering to change into some breeches or something more appropriate for a lady meeting the captain of the Guards. I had no time to stall with such trifles. I raced through the halls and down the stairs, only stopping once to allow the night maids to continue on their way, leaving me undetected. The maid quarters were dark and smelled of lemon snappers. I walked slowly, attempting not to brush against anything and wake up any of the housekeepers. My eyes soon adjusted to the darkness and I made out the door's latch. I quietly and slowly pushed it up, opening the door just enough to slip out into the night. The sweet chirp of crickets filled the air, and lightning bugs floated about blinking every so often. The fresh scent of oak and spring grass still wet from the storm rains brought comfort on this terrible day.

I paced myself, tucking in the shadows and looking over my shoulder whenever I got to a clearing. Soon I came upon the main road where I had to be particularly careful. I took off my slippers, remembering the clapping they made. All it would take was for one of the servants to walk past a window or a head official to wake for a late-night morsel and I would be had. I could see the prison wall up ahead, long and still in the night. I decided to run, the moonlight being most prominent on the main road like a large mist. I took in a few large gulps of air. I didn't feel safe even with the new posts added or the watchful eyes of Silvertail over the past few months. I could hear my heart thumping so loudly in fact that I thought it was liable to thump right out of my chest. I took in one more large gulp of air, allowing the exchange of force to flow through my body like an electrical current.

Then I shot like prey from its burrow having been discovered by a hunter and left with no choice but to flee. My heart thumped faster as my lungs filled and collapsed, pushing my body to its limits. Within seconds, the prison wall came into view, my goal nearly within my grasp. I had just rounded the outside wall when I heard the newly placed heavy metal doors of the prison open and two figures step out into the moonlight. I instantly dropped to the ground, rolling into a ditch, splashing into water from the rain that had run off the prison roof.

"What was that?" I heard a voice whisper, sounding just as paranoid as I felt. I struggled to catch my breath and stay quiet at the same time. I heard the crunch of pebbles under heavy feet coming in my direction. I could feel small salamanders that had sunk into the cool mud sticking to my legs and wiggling in the crevices of my toes.

"It is nothing, my lord. You are but the only one who would pick such odd hours to address the feeblest of matters. Especially in such times as these." I heard the feet retreat to their previous place and was instantly relieved.

"You are right, Captain. I would hope that others aren't lurking about at this hour. It is your duty to hold the city's grounds, especially these."

"These grounds are well protected, my lord. No need to be concerned."

"I sure hope so, Kai. And remember, anything you're told that would aid the joint houses of Estrellar and Lightstar is to be brought to my attention. I'd hate to come to the conclusion at the next council meeting that you aren't capable of your new position."

I could hear Silvertail lightly chuckle, refusing to yield to the intimidation. I listened intently, trying to make out the voice, but all I could hear were whispers not remotely close enough to stem recognition.

"I'm not at all worried, Meoltan," Silvertail continued. I gasped but quickly silenced myself.

"I swear on Olörun that something is out there."

"Perhaps it is your mind trying to find its way back to its host. As I said before, a night's rest will do everyone some good. Some more than others. I bid you a goodnight." I heard a disconcerting scoff and then footsteps trailing off into the distance until they were no more.

"You can come out now, Alya."

I sat up, peeking over the low mound of the ditch. Silvertail was quite clever and I wasn't surprised that my presence didn't get past him. I picked up my shoes which lay mostly dry on the mound and returned them to my feet. The salamanders between my toes instinctively removed themselves while the ones stuck in my hair gradually fell to the ground as I stood up.

"What were you doing with my father?" I inquired. I could hear the accusing tone in my voice.

"Easy, newt," Silvertail said with a laugh. "I didn't invite him, if that's what you're suggesting." He looked around and I did too, wondering if he were hearing something that I hadn't noticed. "Let's go inside."

We retreated to his quarters, the aroma of green lemon turtle tea filling his office. He had prepared two places with cups and thin crackers.

"Sit. Eat. I know you're hungry and we're not discussing anything until I see you eat something."

He was wrong. I wasn't hungry. I couldn't force down any of the lemur roots that I had left on my nightstand, but in order to appease him, I quickly scarfed down four crackers. They were delicious I had to admit, with goat cheese layered on each one. He poured each of us a cup of tea and then settled down on his side of the table.

"So, about my father. What was he doing here?"

Silvertail took a sip of his tea and swished it around in his mouth before speaking, leaving me hanging for his answer.

"He wanted to know if you had told me anything that he should know about. He's apparently caught wind of our training sessions and wanted to know if any of your secrets were confessed to me during those sessions." He took another sip of tea. "I told him his inkling was misplaced."

I sighed heavily. I wasn't surprised. "I wouldn't say his inquiries are misplaced. Just premature."

He leaned back, finishing up his tea, before gently laying the empty cup down on the table. He stared intently at me before finally responding to my comment.

"Alya, your safety is important, and I can't promise I won't act on anything that you tell me today, but one thing I can guarantee is that your name shall be disassociated from any report or action I take and that you have nothing to fear from me. You have my word."

I nodded, acknowledging his promise, but there was so much to divulge. I hadn't thought about which parts to tell him, which to leave out, and which would cause more questioning. At this point, I had a lot to lose but I had even more to lose if I stayed quiet. I could feel my throat squeezing together and it took me three or four gulps to swallow the saliva that had gathered in my mouth. I took a sip of tea, swishing its sweet and sour tang in my mouth, just as Silvertail had. I took a deep breath and began. I kept my eyes on the walls as I skipped around in my divulging about my encounter with the Wood Haven warriors, the attack on the tower, the death of the captain, and the threat from Yann. I told him of the altercation at the yellow garden's dome, and my theories surrounding the deaths of the courts and how I believed they might have been poisoned.

"I know there's much that you are wondering about, events that don't connect or add up, but I ask that you refrain. I have divulged all I can."

He crossed his arms, his eyes rolled to the ceiling in contemplation. I thought I could trust him, but it seemed he was at war with his own morals. I watched him fumble through his mind, weighing his options. Abruptly he stood, nearly causing me to topple over off of my stool onto the floor. He went to the map that hung from the wall. From the edge of its cloth, he pulled a key that was tucked in the seam.

"Shut the door quickly." I jumped from my seat, doing as I was told.

The corridor was dark and abandoned but I didn't ask why he would have me close the door. He pulled from under his desk a small chest barely big enough to hold a pound of rice or a few stones. He laid it on his table and with the key slowly opened it.

He pulled from it a small sack clanking with what I suspected to be money. He tossed it aside and pulled from the bottom of the chest a creased piece of parchment. He unfolded it and placed it on the table, smoothing it out before me. I examined it, the drawn-out lines, the listing of names, possible scenarios, and in the center Alag's name was large and bolded. I knew then exactly why it was hidden.

"An overthrow against the government is being orchestrated and I believe there to be some alliance formed between the invaders, those who you've informed me to be the Wood Haven warriors, and the last of the bloodline of Shiloh." He pointed to the time signatures jotted on the parchment as he went on. "The Prince has the greed of humans marked upon him." He pointed to the top corner. "When the city was invaded, nothing was stolen from the purple ring or any other for that matter. They killed many but in an attempt to solely destroy Shiloh." He cleared his throat. I knew he was just as hesitant about divulging his secrets as I was. I poured him another cup of tea which he pushed aside. "I've also recorded every attack in the city since I've become captain and all are mainly centered in the two upper rings, mainly the purple ring."

"And why would that lead you to believe the invaders were aided by the prince?"

He cleared his throat again, but this time decided he would take a sip of his tea before continuing.

"The purple ring has the most heavily guarded gates in Keldrock. It always has. For those barbarians to cross the purple ring's borders undetected, something had to go awry. Alag is the only power that hasn't had his life threatened. You, Shiloh, the courts, the captain of the Guards, and now the council have all been attacked, and you all are powers in the city to some degree. He is the only one who remains unscathed. He is the most likely to have wanted Shiloh dead and would have the most to gain."

"But I wasn't a part of the calculation. I wasn't supposed to be in the Chamber of Light that day. The light wasn't supposed to choose me."

"Exactly and…" Silvertail paused. "Check the door. What I'm about to say is treason and if anyone should know of this, it would prove dire for you and me both."

I opened the door, checking down the hall, ensuring that no one was there. Not even the scurrying of rodents was heard. "We are alone," I said as I shut the door once again.

"Rumors say that the prince never left the city during the Unveiling but remained here, hidden like a rabbit in its hole. No one knows for sure, and bribery or the steel of the blade has probably silenced those that do know." He looked up from his parchment at me. "You saw how his armor that he claimed had seen war shimmered like new? You saw the prisoners they brought here to await trial for high treason against the crown. Something is awry and I would almost stake my life to believe that the prince has all to do with it. He was unscathed this morning, ignoring the call of my guards and leaving the lobby. I'm also willing to bet that he was the one who rigged the judgment chamber."

I settled on my stool, discomforted at my disbelief in how I had never suspected anyone of such betrayal. I had seen the good in Alag, but I had also seen the bad. I had also seen what power and lust can do to people, bringing to mind the newfound amicableness of my father and the predatory nature of Sir Calo.

"It is my policy to exchange a secret for another, so I have told you everything I know regarding the current state of things. You have my word that your secrets are kept as long as mine are held in the same token." He extended his hand with a crack of a smile and I shook it firmly, a pact now formed.

"How do we find out the truth about the edgewoods? To know what really happened on the Day of Unveiling?"

He looked at me, smiling. "Your playmates from the Remni, if I'm not mistaken, are a part of the Guerr and guarded the veil's border once it fell. With your position, we might just be able to talk to them. There's no way the prince can hold the tongue of the Guerr. Especially if he doesn't suspect our visit to be concerning him."

I thought about it for a moment. It was somewhat a brilliant idea as well as completely dangerous. To inquire about the true nature of things involving Alag and the day of Unveiling could put me and those I loved in more danger, especially if we are overheard by anyone who fought alongside him, if it came to light that his truth was just that. We needed something more urgent, a matter that would provoke us to interview Segun, Rayloh, or any other of the enlisted of their accounts. I peered at Silvertail's parchment. Written on it was every place where attacks had occurred. He had noted areas of the city that had been badly damaged and where people died. He even drew out a small simulation of all the rings. I realized then what our cause was.

"The only leader in the city that hasn't been attacked, other than the prince, is the czar of the Guerr. It could be a coincidence, considering their positioning, but if the prince didn't go to the edgewoods, it could be all the more reason for us to investigate. The stench of a rat lingers—and I think it's high time we sniff it out. Even if his blood is blue."

"Very well. On the morn we go. There's no time to waste."

"Agreed."

I nodded with angst. Silvertail chuckled and I had to admit I felt quite foolish playing detective alongside one whose job it was to actually formulate these schemes. With that we retreated down the hall.

Clouds had filled the sky. I could hear the rumble of thunder in the distance and as I had many nights before, I wondered what lay beyond our city walls. Would it be such a bad thought to leave our keep in Keldrock and make our way out into this new world?

An agonizing scream interrupted my dance with the beauty of the night. Silvertail formed a sword from air and tossed it to me. For himself, he formed a two-edged spear blade. His talent, which I had never thought to ask about, was quite valuable.

"Watch your back, Protector." It felt immensely satisfying that he trusted my skill enough to protect myself. I focused my energy, erasing all fear as I hurried behind him on tiptoes.

Hushed grunts with sharp hisses were heard piercing the quiet as we made our way around the backside of the prison. The clouds moved apart overhead, releasing bright moonlight upon a prone individual. Behind the gate was another figure. They wore a hooded mask of what seemed to be in the likeness of some terrible animal with eye sockets like walnuts and feathers around its beak flaming about its head. It bore no resemblance to the masks of the warriors of Woodhaven, yet the way the creature lingered before darting off, I could only assume this enemy were one of their ilk. Silvertail rushed to the injured individual who was breathing heavily like a dying animal waiting for its hunter to finish it off.

"Alya!" He turned to me with pained eyes. "Come now! Hurry."

I stepped forward, peering over the crouching figure of Silvertail as he lifted the head of the injured body. Master Tali's face came into the light, her long black braided hair streaming across the grass like vipers ready to snap. I gasped at this terrible surprise.

"Why is she out and in the purple ring as much?" I yelped.

"Quiet!" said Silvertail in a harsh whisper. "She's alright. Just knocked out. We don't want to draw attention. If suspicion is created amongst us, there will be all the more reason to silence you. She took up residency here about a month ago. The prince's orders."

He rose quickly, hoisting the body over his shoulder. He burst through into the confines of her abode not too far from where we stood, toppling over clay jars filled with powders and herbs that were kept on the wall to the side of the door. With a loud series of clinks and spins, they settled unharmed. He gently laid the wounded she-elf on the futon in the middle of the room. I rushed to the kitchen and dipped a cloth lying on the counter into a container of water sitting on the floor. I then placed the rag against her head to see the upper half of her body raised against the arm of the futon, with Silvertail's hand cupped around hers.

"Are you alright, Master?" he beckoned. She looked at him with glassy eyes. She appeared confused and dazed. A lump had begun to rise on her head.

"What happened, Kai? Where is she? Tell me she's safe!"

She leapt from her slumped position and stumbled outside into the moonlight, screaming. I could make out these words easily. I could hear them loud and clear and it made my heart sink.

"Where's my sister?" I cried. "Where is Mira?"

Chapter Eleven

"What happened, Tali?" Madja urged in a tone that was both stern and demanding. She didn't seem the least bit concerned with maintaining the air of glamour she had carried for so long around the palace.

We all had gathered in the Crystal Parlor: my family, the unharmed of the council, the servants, royal attendants, and elites in our nightgowns and house robes. Alag even decided to make an appearance and made a show of expressing his sincere concern. Madja ignored it all and focused her entire attention on the last person to be with her daughter: Master Tali.

"I am not sure. I was cleaning my house—specifically the floors—when I heard a knock at the door to only receive your daughter Mira. She was concerned for… I mean, not to get anyone into any trouble but…" She looked at me with apologetic eyes. "She was worried for Alya. She said she had spotted her sneaking out of the palace and followed her. I being concerned went out to settle whatever worries Mira had when we were attacked and… That's when I awoke in my home." The room was hushed as everyone considered Master Tali's account.

Madja didn't seem even remotely satisfied with this answer. She continued to stare at Master Tali with all the anguish that a glare could summon. Her hair was back to a dark black. I wondered if the color of her hair changed with her mood. It didn't take the palette of her crown for me to realize that Madja's temperament was worse than I had ever seen it. I wondered whether I made her worry like this when I ran away and what Mira had done to comfort her. Madja valued us more than anyone and anything. I had started the lot of this and now another loved one had been taken away. I had destroyed our home, our lives, and really, although it took this happening for me to realize it, all we had was each other. Even father played some contribution to Madja's happiness, no matter what problems they had.

She continued to stare at Master Tali across the transparent table as tears welled in her eyes. I thought to interrupt the deadly quiet as the others in the room looked at each other with sideways glances, not even brave enough to clear their throats. Just as my father raised his hand to pardon the tension, Madja shot up from her seat and if a guard had not caught her chair, it would have shattered the wall. She marched from the parlor like a spirit of mourning, quietly sobbing, her hair and night drape flowing behind her.

I looked at Master Tali then to Silvertail, their eyes full of sorrow and empathy. I could feel something. In fact, I could feel a lot of things, but mainly the familiar guilt. I caught wind of Alag consoling my father with a pat on the shoulder. He whispered something that I couldn't make out and then exited the parlor.

"Come with me," I commanded Silvertail.

I rushed from the Crystal Parlor, ignoring the outstretched hands of council members' wives and servants expressing their regrets. I saw Alag turn left at the end of the corridor past the elaborate study that reminded me so much of the one at the Remni that the lads and I deemed our little sanctuary. I rounded the corner and called out to him.

"I need to speak with you, my lord." I humbled myself far beyond what I felt was required even for the private agreement I had made to myself to be the forthcoming person in creating a relationship with Alag. I even noticed Silvertail raise an eyebrow as if he were witnessing some strange phenomenon, but this wasn't about me. This was about rescuing my sister and bringing her back home.

"I've told you, Protector, that I—"

"I know you're busy with city affairs," I interrupted. "And I know my family's loss is minute compared with the tasks on your plate, but I request your council."

He looked me up and down, smirking. He seemed to be enjoying my humiliation and was going to milk it a little longer. He scratched his chin, eyeing his attendant who gave him the same playful smirk in return.

"I think it wise to talk." A voice echoed at the turn of the corridor from whence we had all come, elegant and powerful in all its majesty. "I think it well that a conversation be had."

Master Tali sauntered in our direction, stopping at the threshold of the study. She opened it and entered. I turned to Alag who seemed to be the least concerned with facilitating any kind of partnership between the two of us. He looked at his attendant who simply stared back, unsure of what expression of flattery or disdain to use to gain ground with his lordship. Then Alag did something I didn't expect. He continued looking at me as he approached, that cocky smile wrenched in between his cheek bones like a grotesquely painted doll face that only translated horror to young children instead of intense happiness. He stopped just short of where I stood. I could sense his whole presence, an almost physical feeling, even though not a portion of our bodies touched.

"After you."

I turned in partial disbelief, not even bothering to address his arrogance. I quickly crossed the threshold of the study with him close behind and found Master Tali settled in on one of the couches, letting the rag she had tangled in her hands that I used to wipe her head fall to her side. I sat across from her on one of the footrests. The interior of the study was a little more elaborate than the one in the Remni, but it was close enough to give me a comfortable feeling of home. Alag leaned against the wall as if to advertise his indifference. I looked to see if Silvertail and Alag's annoying attendant would be joining us but all I received was the click of the door as it closed.

"I thought you chose to stay out of government affairs, Nan Tali," said Alag.

My eyes grew big as I looked to Master Tali who smiled in a way that people do when they're annoyed but want to keep the conversation from reaching a turn for the worse.

"This isn't about power, Alag. It's about—"

"You shall address me as Prince. Prince Alag, or not at all."

A frown drenched the face of Master Tali. I knew too well that she didn't like insubordination, no matter from whom it came. I had never known Master Tali to have any relatives, let alone ones of royal lineages. In fact, I never knew her to have any family. What a secret to keep from everyone, even me. The truth is, the sprites in my rotation—probably passing down information through the older elflings who had gotten it from their respective households—had whispered about her. Even I was intrigued. Some said that since she belonged to no house and was under no lord, that she was a barren and therefore deemed useless in the home, explaining her solitary lifestyle. One rumor that had never passed any elven child's lips was that she might be the relation of royalty. After hearing about her tutelage under the old Master of Shiloh, I had drawn the conclusion that she was either an orphan or was barren.

"I didn't know you were related to Prince Alag," I said. "Why not tell anyone? Why not tell me?" I remembered how she stared at me with such disappointment for not speaking against Alag at the council meeting, when she had a more intimate relationship with him than any of us.

"That is none of your business, Protector," Alag answered for her.

"I am the eldest daughter of Shiloh the Protector and sister to Princess Bellanor. My sister passed many years ago and for a time, although a burden it was on my being, I looked after her runt of a son."

Alag rushed toward her, leaning over the armrest of the couch. I would have thought that he was going to strike her, but he only leaned in close to her sharply, gritting his teeth, just a hair from the bridge of her nose, and said, "I will not have you insult me like some common peasant when you turned your back on your family."

The room became still. She either deemed the argument unworthy to indulge or accepted Alag's words as truth because she turned away, breaking her locked stare with Alag. He then turned to me. "What would you have me do about your sister?" He regained his posture and grace like pure white geese after a quarrel.

I glanced over to Master Tali and she nodded, urging me to speak. I knew there was only one option and that was the road I had to take. "I have to get my sister back. I am requesting the resources of the kingdom, specifically the members of the Guerr. I want to venture into the edgewoods."

Alag scoffed. "You feel that your loss demands the whole of my army? Your request is denied."

"Please, Prince Alag! I beg you. Has your heart been so hardened that you would not lend me but a few of the elite of our city? They have ventured into the haunted wood and have conquered it."

"Don't question me of my caring, Protector. I've lost my grandfather and mother in my short life and not once have I wasted the talents or the lives of the Guerr on meaningless vengeance. Some loss must be endured, but you are safe. Your mother and father are safe. Be grateful. My answer is no."

He turned for the door and I could feel my heart sink down to my feet. A lump the size of a cherry formed in my throat. I didn't even bother attempting to suppress my tears. This couldn't be it. I couldn't go alone. I had faced Yann and barely survived, not to mention there would be a whole slew of her followers in the edgewoods. I needed help and my sister needed me.

"They are my army just as much as they are yours," I declared just as he turned the knob to exit the study. He didn't turn around. He just stood there. I knew I was playing with fire, challenging Alag's authority. From what I could tell, control was something he valued more than anything.

When he finally turned to face me, an unfamiliar combination of amusement, anger, and dignity-preserving expressions were oozing from his trembling mouth. He stepped in my direction. "Without my seal, who would follow you on this foolish mission?"

"I would." I hadn't heard the smooth click of the door opening as Silvertail stepped inside. "I've heard how Alya, riding atop a black-haired beast, stopped the invaders, and how she defended our city." He strode past Alag and placed a hand on my shoulder. "I will follow a leader so brave anywhere." I felt another hand slide into my grip, holding it tight.

"As will I," Master Tali said. She, along with Silvertail and me, represented an impassible wall that stood to defy whatever ruling Alag could decree.

Alag looked at the three of us in with more pity than indignation. "I find your persistence entertaining. Let the record show!" he said aloud. He paused, looking behind him, not having realized that his attendant wasn't in our company. "Where is that blasted simpleton? Very well," he continued, turning back toward us and clearing his throat. "Let the record state that you chose this on your own. Since I believe your mission is folly and I am an honorable heir, I will allow you to request the company of the Guerr, but not by mandatory involvement. They must join in this quest willingly."

"You have my word," I quickly agreed.

With that he left the room. I grabbed Silvertail and held him tight, burying my face in his stately uniform. I felt his large hands patting it in a comforting manner.

"Come early morning we'll have our troops and by the afternoon begin our journey," he said.

I recoiled from Silvertail. "We have to go now! She could be dead by morning."

I felt Master Tali's gentle hand upon my shoulder. "It's high night and there's a lot to fear that lurks in the darkness that could easily be avoided in daylight. We will go high morning. We all need our rest. It has been a long day and we'll need our strength."

I snatched away from her hand and stormed out of the study, leaving them standing there. Outside the study, a few nurses had gathered with bandages and rags around a babbling figure. I noticed the fine robe and snobbish spectacles and knew immediately that it was Alag's attendant. A huge knot had formed on his head. I knew this was Silvertail's doing—even the calmest of spirits can be overturned by a sharp tongue and the attendant had not only the sharpest but also the most condescending. I had to admit it amused me.

The rest of the palace was quiet. I passed by the Crystal Parlor on my way to my chambers and could see a few still lingering about. Madja sat at the table, facing my direction, looking through a large book. She held up an ornament, a flower from the Remni's garden that had been pressed and preserved in a book. I stood there, unnoticed, watching her pick up and examine each flower, probably every one representing some memorable day she had spent with Mira. It amazed me how Mira made every object, every moment, every person feel significant, and I regretted how long it took me to warm to my shadowing little sibling.

Behind my bedroom doors it seemed a lot colder. Chills ran down my spine as I climbed into my grand bed, pulling the sheets over my head. I tried to go to sleep, knowing that rest was vital at the moment, but I couldn't. My mind summoned every dreadful memory from the past few months. I saw the charred faces of dead elves, the bloody steel of a knife coming from Yann's head, and the ghostly corpse of Sir Calo. I grew ever colder, even as sweat started to form on my figure. For a moment I thought I was sick, my body twisting and turning under the bed sheets, digging my hands under my fine lace and cool linen covered pillows. A round stain of perspiration formed on the cool cloth, dampening my cheek. As my hands dug even deeper into the heap of pillows, my hand grazed something small and grainy. As I ran my finger along its tightly stitched seams, I recognized the seed pouch Mira gave me. I pulled it from under my frequently used safehold. I poured from the pouch four or five seeds, swishing them around in my hands as the light from the moon turned these dark growths into dazzlingly sapphire spectacles more beautiful than the most stunning of diamonds. This small memory of my sister broke down the guard I had built around myself. Tears flowed from my eyes and small high-pitched wails came from my mouth. I cried because Mira didn't deserve this. She didn't deserve any of this. I continued to weep, and just as my tear ducts gave their final release of watery agony, I slipped into a slumber and a calming cool overtook me, ceasing my discomfort.

***

I tried to remember what I dreamed about during the night as I packed my sack for the journey. The nightmares I anticipated never came, and instead my mind was ushered into peace by a beautiful dream. I suppose the heavens granted it since my day would be filled with so much dread.

I received a knock at my door to find Silvertail packed and ready to go. He came in and settled on one of my chests, tossing his sack on the floor. I looked around, eyeing my belongings as I stroked my necklace, running my fingers over the emerald jeweled eyes as I did so often. I was careful to only bring things that I really needed. I packed two pairs of britches, five summer shirts, a few undergarments, and *The Three Burdens,* which I felt would prove most useful if our journey took us beyond the edgewoods into the wilds, for I would return with Mira if I had to go to the ends of the earth. I patted my pockets ensuring that I had grabbed the pouch of seeds she had given me, one of the things that would calm my ever-moving mind.

"This might prove to be quite useful."

I paused from checking my packing to notice Silvertail perusing my tall wooden wardrobe. He pulled from the back of it my bow and sheath of arrows. I hadn't forgotten it. The same bow and arrow I had used to defend the city I planned on using to bring death to those who captured my sister. I took it from him, throwing the sheath and the bow over my shoulder, aligning them with the knapsack that was strapped tightly around my shoulders and waist.

"We have not a moment to waste. Where's Master Tali?" I asked.

"She said she would meet us at the gate at the hour when the sun is high. I've passed along the proposition to my company as well and have beckoned that if any of them are bold enough to take on this task to meet us at the gate at the same time." He nodded, not looking for any extreme token of thanks.

"Very well, let us be on our way."

The sky was eerie this morning. Mist had risen from the rain, making the air hot and humid. I added the heat to the list of the many things that would burden me during this trip. I heard the gates creak open and standing just outside of the golden blockades of the purple ring were two herding animals grazing on the fresh greens that had grown in with the coming of spring.

"I had my charge prepare them. These are rutor, closely related in appearance to the moose and deer, with the exception of their dagger horn of course."

They were beautifully built, their muscles rippling under their shorthaired coats. Their antlers were magnificent, both nearly the size of my entire body. I had never seen such beasts—all the nobles I had known rode atop bucks or great horned goats that had herded into Keldrock after straying too far from the mountains. In the center of their heads was a sharpened horn, like a metal stake. I watched as one dug it into the ground and pulled up a small plot of earth, sending dirt and ripped roots into the air.

"For hence they were named," Silvertail said with a laugh, "for their love of roots."

They donned saddles with bulging sacks of food hanging from their sides. The captain helped me up onto the smaller one, his fur prickling against my hands. He trotted back a little; upset we had disturbed his meal. I grabbed the reins, rubbing the back of his neck to calm him and soon he settled, lowering his head to finish off his remaining shoots of root and grass.

It wasn't long before we were in the heart of the yellow ring. The yellow dome had been torn down with the arrival of spring. I noticed the few trees that stood, shading the newly planted saplings that stretched up from the soil. It only brought sad memories as I clutched the seeds in my pocket. I could see where Mira's plot had been, where a few weeds and a mixture of dead flowers sat, having not been removed yet for the new planting. We pressed forward down the hill and to my surprise, nothing remained of the Remni. The rubble had been cleared and fresh grass and wildflowers grew in its place and nearly all the burnt pasture had grown back again. Humming bees floated towards us, hovering next to the wet noses of the rutor. The other estates of the yellow ring continued on as they had before, most having been only minutely damaged or not at all during the siege of the city. Their huge oakwood doors were painted bright reds and oranges, bringing cheer to the atmosphere of the yellow ring where much was needed.

The blue ring was an entirely different spectacle. The signs of misery were hard to miss. Most of the shops and cottages had been damaged by the invasion and now bricks lay on top of buildings, or near broken glass, or in heaps after colliding with fountain statues. We passed the remains of the School of Talents. There was nothing left of its high tower. The courtyard wall was nothing more than crumpled debris and the pond was murky with charred remnants. I thought of the small fish and knew without a doubt that they were probably lost as well.

"The fort is this way, Alya." I turned, following Silvertail, letting slip another memory that would be lost forever.

It took longer than expected to reach the fort of the Guerr. The sound of rushing water alerted us of our close proximity. Upon our arrival, two heralds, older elves, met us, standing before a moat that was dug around a large iron fortress. Their faces were wrinkled, heavy bags hanging from their necks and under their eyes like sacks of sand. Random scars were placed around their ears and mouths. Finally, one whose nose was bent and knotted in such a fashion that it had to have been broken many times addressed us.

"State your business."

Silvertail hopped off of his rutor, walked up to the sirs, and said with authority, "Hear me now, elder sages. We come requesting the audience of the czar. Our business is with him alone."

"Ya think yurself high nuff tuh enter the ranks a heroes an gods?" the herald said with a chuckle, which sounded more like a congested mixture of a cough and a wheeze. "Now begone wit ya. Ya marked wit the seal of the guard so I'm sure ya could use some rest fore you stand watch hind these city walls." The awful chuckle sounded again.

"I come with more than the seal of the captain of the Guards of Candor." He turned to his side, holding one hand outstretched toward me. "I come with the Protector of the Light. You'd do well to honor my request and signal your gatekeep."

The ancients looked at each other, muttering amongst themselves, eyeing us with disdain, and I knew their bigoted minds were against me now if they weren't before. The snarkiest of the two who seemed to be the hard head, finally spoke, with a greasy, nearly toothless smile.

"My regrets, Protector. We meant no offense, an we still mean none but only lords of the Guerr are loud beyond this point an there will be had no exceptions." He sneered.

"…but if you'd like…" the quieter one finally spewed, "you may stand a few paces, cup your mouth, and squeal like a damsel. Haps one of the younger lads will hear ya cries an come to save ya."

The mouthier one began to put on his best imitation of a damsel squealing for help with mock moaning and bent flopping wrists. I thought to get off of my rutor and knock them into their death a fortnight earlier than it would come, but just as I was about to retort, a shrill, sweet sound, like a combination of a chirping bird and the roar of mighty beast, bore from the skies like a call to arms. I could feel a great shadow pass over my head like a rain cloud, blocking the sun's rays. It floated down closer and landed with one more call, causing all of us, the elders included, to plug our ears.

"Settle down, Athena," called its rider, a fit he-elf of mid-elven age relative to the kooks that stood between the moat and us. He patted his great beast of a bird.

It was the same that I had just seen the day before, against the curses of pouring rain and vengeful lightning. It unruffled its feathers as its rider slid to the ground. The rutor grew a little uneasy, backing away and rearing up as the great black fowl sharpened its talons against the hard earth while pulling at its loosened feathers. Silvertail rushed to grab their reins, holding them steady as the rider approached me.

"I've caught word from the prince that you would be visiting my soldiers today." The he-elf took in a deep breath as he looked me over. "He warned me of your quest, and whether noble or folly, he has assured me that no form of authority is to be used when requesting their involvement."

"We are sorry, Czar Icar," the gaffers sputtered. "We just wanted to be sure. More than a few have sought the refuge of our fort due to the times."

"Very well then," the czar said as he returned to his pet. "Lower the bridge. Let's see what our visitor has to say." With that he ascended on the back of the black bird until he cleared the high barred gates.

Chapter Twelve

Silvertail seemed all too enthusiastic to enter the Guerr's sector. I remembered him telling me how it was an aspiration of his to join this band of elite warriors and if he had not had the chance unfairly taken from him, he might have succeeded. I could only hope that his mind remained on the task at hand.

The bridge was quite wide and made from sturdy metal. It landed with a thud against the ground, causing the rutor to trample a little. Silvertail started to pull them towards the bridge but the sounds of rushing water steered them in the opposite direction.

"Leave them, Captain. They are in the company of moral soldiers," I said with enough sarcasm for Silvertail to pick up on what I was doing but with enough flattery to entice the guards. "They are so strong and noble." The mouthy one's face, although tanned to caramel, scarred, and burned could still turn a deep blood red from blushing.

"You're quite right, meh lady," he bragged as he puffed up his chest and licked his chops. "I have mastered more than a few steeds in meh day. To what are these… whatever these are… to me?"

I thanked the two coots and handed them the reins. With that settled, Silvertail and I made our way across the moat, the treacherous water beating around us, slapping up on the metal bridge, begging it to move from its path. The gates to the fortress slowly opened as painted faces of warriors stared down at us. The ground was softer behind the walls like some mix of clay and sand. It settled under my feet, providing support and comfort with every step. Around the fortress, different training sessions were being held. I watched as archers took shots at small targets and swordsman did lunges and lugged stones. Even the smaller recruits from my rotation were sparring, rolling around in the dirt, trying to pin one another. None of them seemed in the least bit happy to be here. Some of them even had scarred backs and large bruises on their shoulders and foreheads.

"Bring him here," I heard a boyish voice order.

The sparring session had ended, and a winner had been declared. He got up off of his opponent and lifted him by the hair and tossed him to the owner of the voice. He couldn't have been any older than Alag but his build and his authority weren't of self-proclamation or right but had been earned. The opponent fumbled to the ground, burying his face in the sand. Silvertail continued walking as I stopped to watch the outcome of this loss. Surely a sparring match was nothing more than a game of brute strength where the largest and quickest succeed, and this lad was nowhere near the size of his opponent.

"My scourge." One of the other lads who had been standing to the side slowly handed over what was asked of him with trembling hands. The ringleader snatched it away and sent it flying against the lad's face, his victim spoiling to the ground.

"Animal," he said under his breath as he twisted the pieces of heavy leather in his hand, turning back to the lad who lay with his face buried. "This is your fourth battle lost to the same opponent. You were given four days after each defeat to better yourself and you have still failed. You know what that does to me?"

He looked around at the onlookers with a satisfied grin as he raised his whip. They seemed to have no choice but to stay and observe all that was about to unfold. I saw a few trying to shield their eyes and cover their ears but they dared not do it while the elder juvenile's eyes wandered. The lash ripped through air, howling like the north wind that whistled during the darkest days of winter. It slapped against the skin of the losing party like a wasp's stinger, pinching at his skin and then pulling out and coming back down to sting him once more. I watched the young observers flinch, some seemingly holding back tears. I boiled in rage as blood began to trickle down the receiver's back and blisters swelled on his skin. I had had enough.

It only took a few moments for me to have the scourge in my hand and just as quickly sending the bully to the ground in a pathetic heap. My clenched fist was in agonizing pain but not enough to quell my anger or stand down. The lads shuffled back in surprise. I could see in their eyes they feared for me.

"You miserable wretch of a harlot!" the bully said, stumbling to his feet as blood streamed from his mouth. He rocked his jaw a little, making little popping noises and wincing in pain. "You've broken it."

He unsheathed from his side a hidden blade and prepared to lunge at me. I balled my fists, knowing that he wouldn't win. Today he would be taught humility.

Unfortunately, that lesson was to be taught by another. Silvertail gripped his wrist, forcing the knife from his possession and wrapped the bully's arm around his back into a hold. The lads weren't quite sure what to make of this situation. Some moved to try and stop Silvertail, but with a twist of their leader's arm, a painful cry of agony kept them at bay.

"Mercy please! Mercy!"

After a few more moments of begging and squealing, Silvertail shoved him into the dirt. As soon as the young sir had regained control of his limbs, he darted away. Silvertail then snatched me by the arm, and we hurried to a collection of buildings, him nearly dragging me the entire way. After dodging through bunkers and what looked to be large training facilities with weights and sparring dummies, we settled down on a bench to cool off from our encounter with the idiot of a sprite.

"Quite a brilliant idea there, Alya. Assaulting a ranked lieutenant in front of his charge. Quite brilliant indeed. It's almost like you don't need anyone to join you on this quest."

I looked at him with disbelief. "What would you have me do? Allow that lad to be beaten to death?"

Silvertail let out a harsh breath of air, obviously disturbed by my excuses. He pulled from under his coat a sleeve, sloshing with the sounds of drink. He popped the stopper, releasing the smell of ale, and sipped from his load, guzzling it down like a drunkard. He obviously needed something to ease his nerves. Being in a camp full of our nation's most skillful warriors would make even the bravest heart nervous.

"So how should we go about this?" he asked of me as he wiped his upper lip and returned the stopper to its place.

I leaned back on the bench and wiped the sweat from my brow. I didn't have the faintest idea of how we were going to recruit anyone to come with us into the edgewoods. I knew what we were up against and the largest numbers among their ranks were the new recruits. Most of the older sprites would likely align with the prince and probably wanted nothing more than to return to their homes and reunite with their families. Our best bet was with the sprites and there were two who I knew would go.

"We should find my friends Segun and Rayloh."

Silvertail stood up, a little less fearful and a lot more jovial after his few swigs. "Very well. The younger lads are plentiful in this camp. It shouldn't be too difficult to find them."

We made our way around the bunkers and the training facilities and back out to the center plot. At the far end, there were a band of sprites taking a break while their overseer slumped under the shade of a metal awning, obviously more interested in sleeping than keeping watch over his youngsters. They whispered amongst each other, laughing ever so quietly. Silvertail approached them, trying to be as stately as he could summon.

"Greetings, my young sirs. I have a request of you on behalf of your Protector." The lads burst into laughter. I stood just a few feet behind Silvertail, trying to figure out what they could be so giggly about.

"We know why you have come sir, and you will find none willing among us who would join you on this quest back into the hell from whence we've come. Take my word," one of the answered. "We have no interest in revisiting that dreadfully awful forest." They all nodded in agreement.

Another one chimed in, "In fact we have no interest in being here at all. We want to go home." I didn't bother with their idle banter. My sister was my only goal at this point. I needed to find my friends.

"I'm looking for a few near your age. Their names are Rayloh and Segun," I said. They all eyed each other and I knew they knew of whom I spoke of.

"What's going on?" a voice questioned from afar.

We all glanced around to see the overseer coming to. He leaned up on his palms, squinting, letting his eyes adjust to the sun and his mind recall what he was supposed to be doing before he had fallen asleep. I turned to the lads to squeeze an answer from them.

"Please. Where are they? Do tell me."

They looked around at each other again until the first who spoke gave us an answer. "I do not know of this Segun but with Rayloh, I am familiar. He was one of the most skilled premieres I've seen in my four years at Shiloh. A natural talent he is. He was punished for being insubordinate on behalf of a tick. They aren't given names or allowed to be with the rest of the troop. Rayloh, because he came to a tick's defense, was sent to their quarters."

"Laps! All of you, laps!" the overseer shouted, his voice hard and deliberate.

"Where is this place?" I asked, urging them to answer faster.

"They call it the brig," he said quickly. I could see in the switch of his eyes that the overseer was marching our way. "It's behind the czar's hold. He oversees them personally but no one dares venture there who isn't a tick. Bad enough things have happened to the ticks. Much worse is said to come to those who stick their noses into matters that don't concern them."

We retreated just as the overseer was about to lecture his troop. I could still hear his hoarse voice, trumpeting as we rounded back into the huddle of metal buildings. I could see through their windows that they were all empty right now, and well enough. The metal, even from where I stood, radiated the heat of the sun, making my skin twitch. We found our way somehow back to the bench and Silvertail pulled out his ale. He took a small drink, not as much as before.

"Damn this heat." He wiped his forehead. "Well, what now? The czar has made the Guerr very much aware of our arrival today and anyone we question will not dare to join us, even if they wanted to. Seems to me that they are scared for some reason."

"Or just as bigoted as the prince!" I retorted. "I've seen the edgewoods, spent more days marking trails and following streams than they could possibly imagine. My comrades are all I need. We get them and we get out."

Silvertail chuckled. He was a little merry and I knew I had the sleeve of spirits to thank for that. "Very well." He rocked up to his feet and looked around. "You heard the lads. We have to find the czar's hold."

A shadow lurched overhead high in the sky. The large raptor that belonged to the czar circled above, stretching its wings out wide as it glided down. I had seen the way birds perched and this great beast made it easy to observe the facts of their nature that I knew to be true.

"The bird. See it?" I pointed to the heavens. Silvertail shielded his eyes as he followed my finger up.

"Yes I see it. What of it? It's just the czar's carriage."

"You see the way it's circling lower and lower? It'll soon be landing. That's where the czar will be."

I darted off into the metal huts, keeping my eyes on the skies. The bird was coming down faster than I could go and soon I could barely see it over the roofs of the alloyed compartments. I rounded a high partition and ran along it until it came to an abrupt end. I stepped into a large clearing just as the bird landed, uplifting with its great beating wings, a large gust of wind and dirt. Silvertail had rounded the metal partition just in time to see the sand settle and the bird shake the debris from its feathers. In the center was a large hold made entirely of a charcoal-colored metal that even in the bright of the sun seemed dark and archaic. It had great pillars and beams coexisting together in this elaborate construction of steel, iron and other ores. It reminded me of what an estate belonging to some horrible tyrant would look like.

I had made it halfway across the yard when I spotted the czar coming from this citadel of metal. In his hand was the carcass of what looked to be a domestic dog, its neck broken, hanging over its back as he lugged it across the sand. The czar heaved it up above his head, his body a lot more able than what his age would show. I watched as the fowl cocked its head back and with its great beak and neck in unison snatched its lunch from the air. The czar looked at us coming and then with the beckoning of his hand retreated back inside the metal fortress.

I looked at Silvertail who seemed to be waiting on my lead. I took a few steps, approaching with caution as I watched the large bird still guzzling down its meal. I wasn't sure of its reaction to unfamiliar guests. It soon finished, and its eyes focused in on us. I slowed my pace, trying not to frighten it into feeling that it had to defend itself. The sound of blades in the ground startled me as it dragged one of its talons across the earth, ever so slowly, never taking its eyes off of me.

"She won't hurt you," the czar called from inside. "She hunts on command. Not that you would make much of a meal anyhow." Silvertail chuckled at the czar's banter. The bird, tired of intimidating the strangers, returned to tending to her feathers.

The inside of the citadel was even more frightening than the outside. No sunlight lit this windowless fortress. A few torches lined the walls, barely cutting the lingering darkness. Silvertail grabbed one and led the way, looking around in amazement. Not only was he inside the Guerr's camp, but he also had the opportunity to visit the czar's hold. The air was unbelievably cool in the citadel especially for the black metal that surely should be emitting a large amount of heat.

"Beautiful, isn't it?" I could barely make out a figure sitting in the center of a dais with his legs crossed and his hands on his knees. "Oh, you can't see without light, can you? I must say I quite enjoy the darkness."

He took the torch from Silvertail and walked back up the dais to where he was waiting to receive us. I heard a key switch in a lock and soon there were two more torchlights flickering. Trickles of light began to surge about the metal innards of the hold, spreading like tiny winding streams through the black earth all the way to the zenith of the hold, heating the unnaturally cool air. Soon the entire hold was filled with light. All around, frozen in near animation, was a bounty of stuffed fowl and other beasts. Some had their wings outstretched as if they were just about to take flight while others were simply perched like ornaments along the walls. Some were big like great dogs and monstrous cats. Hawks hung from the ceiling with chains around their necks and talons poised as if they were soaring above prey alongside pink-necked vultures seemingly be circling above looking for a carcass to indulge. It was an unusual display to find amongst my people who found all life so sacred. Any animal hide we used was taken from the dead and even that was rare. These creatures were killed for sport, that much I could tell, and it made me wonder about Czar Icar.

"What of this collection?" I said as I approached a stuffed bird similar to an owl. Its neck was burrowed in its shoulders, a behavior I noticed in the small ducks and white billowy swans when they were about to engage in a quarrel with one another. I knelt to observe the details of its face. It was flat, like the barn owls I would sometimes see retreating back into the edgewoods. Its beak was open, and a long slithering tongue sat poised in the air, like a garden snake. It was a light tan color, the ends of its feathers glowing white with the exception of a small, black hole where its heart would beat had not an arrow took its life.

"I am a collector of rare things. In my travels over the years into the edgewoods, I have discovered many treasures. None however can top the beauty of a bird. The art of flight, of being untouchable, is quite fascinating to me."

I rose from my kneeling and turned to the czar who had returned to the fiery prism that I had seen in the darkness. The glow was fiery but was redder than the orange of the torchlight.

By now Silvertail had found his way up on the low platform. "What is such a light that can bore through stone, my lord?" he inquired, leaning over the shoulder of the czar just as he was about to shield the crimson-colored luminance behind its barrier of stone.

"Aha!" the czar exclaimed with gusto. "These are the questions that should be sought. Most of those who are fortunate enough to enter my hold are immediately captured within the talons of my collection." I sauntered over, feeling the direct impact of his comment that I knew was meant for me. He fully extended the stone wedge that he had just begun to close. Its heat warmed my face, and I wanted to move back where the air was cooler. "This is a type of elemel. Although its other four brothers are not common in these parts, a great amount of infernmel remains here." I settled on the dais while they conversed, trying my hardest to seem uninterested even though the topic was quite intriguing. "These gems are like life, their element their breath."

"I've never heard of earth with such properties. Fire and metal working together is uncommon." The czar nearly leapt in the air with excitement. I could only roll my eyes.

"The earth is special because it is living! It is the remnants of living stone, or at least that is what legend holds. Each mass has its own heart or crystalized gem that acts as the control center for the specimen and any other elemel it touches. When I add fire to the gem, it seeps through the entire body of stone and metal."

It sounded like nothing more than a fairytale, so I began observing the stuffed fowl once again. One of them looked like something out of a horrible dream and was much larger than any bird I had seen out in the edgewood wilds.

"What made you decided to collect dead things?" I asked as I ran my hand down the feathers of the owl-like bird. "It seems quite odd for an elf."

I heard the abrupt close of the stone wedge hatch, and the sizzling response of the torch being put out in a container of water. Only the light of the small rivers of bright orange that lit the czar's hold remained. He marched toward me, flapping at my hand so I would stop touching the bird. "If you must know, I found that from my training in the edgewoods; live targets were more effective than dummies."

"You don't think that is dishonorable? I figured that—"

"There are a great host of dangerous beasts, the likes of which you will never know," he snapped. "Some of which have taken the lives of brethren of this city who stood to defend against them, protecting you who so gingerly stands here now and tells me what is *dishonorable*."

Silvertail deferred as he always did when the subject was going in the wrong direction. "We're looking for two lads. We spoke to a few of your cadets and they informed us that they would rather stake their claims here, stating that their allegiance lies here with you."

The czar smiled, reveling at his company's flattery. "They say our best chance is with a lot they called the ticks," Silvertail continue. The czar's smile disappeared. "We were wondering if we might request their hand on this journey."

Czar Icar eyed Silvertail and then me. I knew he was wary of me but when he turned back to look at Silvertail, an expression of trust was somewhat evident. We had him just where we wanted him.

"What if I denied knowing of such a group? My soldiers could have been leading you astray for their own amusement."

"If that be so, then simply say so." Silvertail leaned in close to the czar, speaking so softly that I barely could make out what was uttered. "You yourself said this mission is doomed and from the looks of things, I am most inclined to agree. If you allow us to inquire from them whether they would want to accompany us on this quest, it could show that you are being cooperative while she in turn was most difficult to entertain. Not to mention a thorn would be plucked from your side should a few of these so-called ticks perish in the wilds."

"That's not my intent," the czar warned.

"And I very well understand you wish death to none of our descent, but soldiers are made through experience. Those who fail to rise to the occasion are not worthy of such titles."

The czar thought about it for a moment, scratching his chin and staring intently at Silvertail. "If you round my hold, a hatch marked by a metal staff leads to an underground cellar. You won't be needing a key being that the latch can only be opened from the outside."

I nearly burst into tears of happiness. The czar was allowing me to seek my friends. "A thousand thanks, my lord. You are most kind."

"Don't thank me yet. You have yet to receive the answers from these lads, but if you are to thank anyone, you are to thank your captain."

I nodded with a gracious smile as I turned for the exit with Silvertail by my side. Just as we were about to step out, the czar called, "And if you ever want to submit yourself for evaluation, Silvertail, I feel there could possibly be a place for you within our faction." Silvertail nodded at the czar and we broke back out into the heat of the day.

***

It took a brief moment for my eyes to adjust to the blinding sunlight after being in near darkness for so long. The great winged brute was tucked on the far end of the sandy arena, squatting with her head under her wing in the partial shade of the metal citadel. The air was dry and of all the times that I had hoped it wouldn't rain, I wished today that it would. The heat was unbearable against the grassless and treeless field of this artificial desert.

"This way. The czar said it was around the hold," Silvertail said as he began leading the way.

I followed him as we shielded our eyes, standing a few feet away from the giant mass of metal as to not burn ourselves from its hot exterior.

Silvertail pointed out into the sands behind the citadel to a small slender marker that seemed to be a mirage the way the sun frazzled its image. "The czar said it would be marked by a metal pole, stemming from the earth."

Our pace strengthened as we closed in on our goal and soon we were upon the latch which I thanked Olörun was forged from wood instead of metal. Silvertail kicked the barred latch from its hold and lifted the door.

"After you, my lady," he said with a kind smirk.

I jumped down into the cool underbelly of the hold. The air was thick with the smell of urine, feces, vomit and other bodily excrements. Chains hung from the low ceiling of the tight bunker like waving vines in a willow tree. No sounds came from the darkness.

I decided to speak up. "Show yourself. We mean you no harm."

I heard the dragging of something against the metal underbelly of the bunker and rushed to where it came from. A round face sat in a corner, eyes wide with anger and distrust. He held up a slender iron rusted cell bar, separating me from the other blank faces that stared at me with terror. His face was covered in grime and he was deathly thin, his shoulders and cheekbones like razors.

"State your name!" he called out. With all the muck on his face and the darkness, I couldn't quite make out the being that remained so distrustful even after my assurance that we didn't wish them harm. I thought to go with another name in order to gain the wary defender's hand in helping me find my friends. I didn't want my role as Protector, which disrupted my missions on other occasions, to falter me now or for fear to be stricken within them for even being associated with me. That much, no kind words or promised favors could overcome. I decided the best route was to get right to the point and avoid the question all together.

"I'm looking for two. Two friends." I stepped a little closer and the figure jabbed the pole just inches from my throat.

"Don't come any closer. Name."

"Their names are…."

"Your name!" the figure barked with the demanding power of a leader and a familiar voice from my childhood that I would recognize no matter how much time passed.

"Rayloh…" I called out in a soft, inquiring voice, but there was no question who stood in front of me. My mind began to shape him, even with the frailty of his figure and the smudges on his face. The bar hit the ground with a clang, rolling into the shadowy recesses of the bunker.

"Alya?" he said incredulously.

I watched a series of bony digits comb through my white mane. I remembered that I didn't look the same either. Just as his fingers came upon the ends of my hair, he lunged forward into my arms, causing me to fall right with him. He grabbed me, wrapping his arms around my shoulders and I around his back. We just sat there and cried, and it didn't bother me that Silvertail or the wide eyes in the bunker's shadows were present. I had found my best friend. So many months had passed since we'd seen each other and so many things had changed and even in the midst of all the pain I felt, in this moment, I felt a void had been somewhat refilled, making the hope I'd lost fuller than it was before. He sobbed and sobbed and soon I was holding him against my bosom, comforting him as soft tears fell from my cheeks onto the crown of his curly head. We stayed just like that, trying to collect ourselves every so often but as soon as our eyes met and the memories resurfaced, it all would begin again.

"And where's the other? We don't want to keep Master Tali waiting." Silvertail was not the emotional type. That much I knew, but then again, neither was Rayloh. Yet here we were, pouring out our deepest emotions to one another. The vulnerability that I saw once as weakness I now knew as strength.

Rayloh stood and gathered himself, remembering those he sought to protect. Silvertail began to approach but the wide watching eyes recoiled. Rayloh started to turn away but then returned his eyes back to me. They weren't joyous and grateful like they had just been but conveyed a sense of despair and regret. I almost didn't want to ask for fear of the answer.

"Where's Segun?"

Rayloh turned back to the watchful eyes just as some bobbed up and down while others disappeared. They soon produced silhouettes of scrawny bodies, approaching clumsily together. It was an odd way to walk, timid and close as they did. They, however, were not walking oddly. They carried something and before I knew it, a clear face the color of dark oak was produced from their arms and placed at my feet. I collapsed on the ground trying to understand. It was so strange the way my life was turning out. How as soon as I gained enough ground to where I could sleep at night or feel happiness again, I would be knocked back even further than I was before. I began to wail and nothing could comfort me. Silvertail tried to pull me up from the gently placed figure but no one could remove me. Nothing could heal this sorrow. I held his cheek in my palm, the warmth just barely holding to his beautiful form, my dear sweet Segun.

Chapter Thirteen

"Are you sure the others won't come?" Silvertail asked Rayloh as the drawbridge was lowered over the moat.

"None will. They'd much rather stay in the brig than face the edgewoods. They are gentle spirits. Not warriors," Rayloh confirmed. "Mind his head."

Silvertail adjusted Segun's small body in his arms. He was barely breathing, and his eyes would open ever so slightly before closing again. He was still so small and even in his distress somehow seemed to be happy with his lot in this world. His back was scarred and torn. There were bruises on his chest and sores on his neck and around his ears.

I looked at him in silence, wishing with all my might to end Czar Icar. For the moment, I had to find my sister and bring her home but as soon as she was safe, his head would be mine. I had never thought of using my power to hurt anyone, but that's another part of coming of age. The problems and feelings you experience are more than selfishness and jealousy, but you entertain the idea of revenge, hate and heart-nabbing greed. The spray from the water misted the air as the bridge collided with the ground, allowing us passage. The ancients had kept their word: our rutor held within their frail grasp, ready to go.

None of us bothered riding on the rutor as we made our way up the long path away from the Guerr's fort. It seemed like I couldn't get far enough from that wretched hold, the smell of hot metal still in my nose. We soon came upon the junction in the blue ring where the main roads met leading to either deeper into the blue ring or away into the black ring. Master Tali sat under the shade a small tree near the gate, smiling as we approached. Her smile quickly faded as she saw our gloomy expressions.

"What happened?" she inquired.

"He's hurt… badly," Rayloh responded. "He needs help. His father is a physician. He will be able to treat his wounds."

Master Tali looked to the bundle of pain and agony in Silvertail's arms. "At mid sun, we will meet at the city's gates and begin our journey, being as high sun is upon us and we still don't have our bearings," said Silvertail. "It would be risky for the young sprite to wait any longer before seeking healing so in the meantime, you two find the rutor something to eat. If our journey is long then it will serve them well to take in all they can whilst food is easily attainable. They will also need some rest."

With that they were off, leaving Rayloh and I standing alone. I didn't want to waste time when I could be searching for Mira but mid sun wasn't far away so I accepted Silvertail's plan.

"There's a place I know where we can get them food. It's in the black ring and I'm sure they can spare a few pitches of hay," Rayloh suggested.

We saddled on the rutor, Rayloh leading the way. The streets weren't busy whatsoever. In fact, they seemed to be unusually empty. The few faces I caught in the open windows appeared surprised—whether it was because of the stately grazers we rode or because elves were in the black ring, I wasn't sure. When I used to visit before there seemed to be a sense of curiosity and awe but now it seemed that the presence of an elf in the black ring could only mean something terrible was going to happen.

I spotted the black ring's market and Rayloh with hesitation led the rutor through the awful archway, ducking so the jagged wood wouldn't catch him in the head. The market was abandoned, splotches of light shining onto the floor from holes in the ceiling.

I knew once we started up the path to the black ring that we were going to the children's barn where Nazda and I had taken refuge. I didn't bother mentioning it to Rayloh for a number of reasons—the most prominent one being that Cadon, the new leader of their orphan band, forbade me from returning. Rayloh also didn't know about what happened with Nazda, Sir Calo, or any of the other secrets that I wanted to remain safe for the moment. We soon crested the hill and the pungent, familiar scent of farm animals made it evidently clear that we were almost upon the barn. Rayloh hopped down from the rutor and slowly opened the barn door, being careful not to let even the creaking of the hinges sound.

"I want to surprise them. Nazda is the hardest to catch unaware."

Rayloh darted in, already in the horse stall that led to the barn's loft by the time I had hopped off of my rutor, leaving me to guide both of the beasts in to graze. Before I could even get them across the threshold of the barn door, he had disappeared in the attic. A cow had been added to the small tribe of animals in the barn. The new heifer was obviously fed well, her stomach bulging. It took me a moment to realize she was pregnant. I gathered some hay and stray grains for the rutor to eat. I took in a large breath, the presence of the sour air bringing a nagging taste to my mouth.

"Alya!" I heard Rayloh call down from the loft. I couldn't tell if his tone was upset, fearful or disappointed. My heart beat fast as I made my way up to the hatch. I peeked up through the opening to find that no one was there. Rose, Cadon, and Meca were all gone. "They're not here."

I was somewhat satisfied that they were absent and thought perhaps we would finish feeding the rutor and be able to leave without seeing them at all. Rayloh pulled a sack from the center of the wall and lay on it, ready for a nap. We weren't leaving any time soon.

"I'll go get the rutor some water," I announced but no response came. He had already dozed off.

He was exhausted and I wondered how long it would before he divulged what happened in the brig and how he ended up serving a sentence with those they called the ticks. I remembered the young recruit's words. *Bad enough things have happened to the ticks. Much worse is said to come to those who stick their noses into matters that don't concern them.* I knew, with a little time, he would tell me everything. Strange how I made it sound easy to do, divulging secrets, when I had kept mine to myself for so long.

I slipped back into the barn and found a pot in the corner across from the stables. I went outside, trying to figure out where I could get water. I thought to go to Kala's home, but considering the distance and that I would have to carry the water back, I thought another plan might be better suited. I picked up the pot and headed toward Mister Harmon's front stoop. I thought to knock on his door, requesting assistance, but I remembered how he was interrogated concerning my whereabouts—and although nothing became of the interrogation, I knew that he wouldn't be too excited to see the one that could have possibly cost him his freedom.

My mouth began to water as the scent of fresh pastries filled my nostrils. My stomach roared in response. With all that happened, I had forgotten to eat. Thinking about Segun and my sister made me lose my appetite. I decided now I should get something since I could feel the pangs of hunger. I made my way down the hill to the homey bakery of rugged wood and worn shingles. The scent of freshly kneaded dough and crisp pear tarts emanated from the building. I opened the door to find that it was entirely empty which was surprising since only a great amount of desserts could create a scent that would escape the shack and meet me at the crest of the hill. With no business, it seemed that baking such a large quantity would prove wasteful. I could hear someone, assumedly the baker, bumping about in the back room as I stood at the counter and peered at the large piece of parchment listing the menu, perusing the different delicacies that changed with the seasons. Most of the pumpkin and cinnamon influences were less prominent, replaced with the sweet berries and soft fruits of spring. I finally decided on a jam-filled pastry and continued to wait for the baker to emerge.

A loud bang from the back of the bakery nearly caused me to jump out of my skin. Through the swinging door came a face I had not intended on seeing. Our eyes met and for a moment we stood there, both just as disturbed to see the other. A heavy sack hit the ground and from it oil stains began to seep out. I assumed it was the host of mouth-watering pastries I had caught wind of.

"What are you doing here?" Meca demanded. His face tensed from either embarrassment or fear. I could tell from his reaction that no one was supposed to be here during this time and now that he was discovered, he wasn't quite sure what would become of this situation.

"I knew of this bakery and sought to get a bite." I looked at him and then to the bag. "Where's the baker?"

He sniffled and his eyes fell to his feet as he wrung his hands, mumbling under his breath. I couldn't make out anything that he said but I didn't want to frighten him anymore than I already had. He seemed to have reverted back to that shy boy that I met not too long ago.

"Here, let me help you." I reached for his sack of baked goods which he let me take without objection. I grabbed his hand

and threw the bundle over my shoulder, leaving the pot in the bakery for me to return for later.

We walked to the barn in quiet, Meca's face still pointed at the ground as we climbed up to the crest of the hill. Upon our arrival, I noticed the rutor had slipped out from the stables and into the empty plot between Mister Harmon's house and the barn. They were lapping loudly at the large puddles that had formed from the season's rainstorms. They looked up only to see us pass before lowering their heads once more. I thought with the sun being so high now that the puddles would have dried but since it wasn't the case, I figured they would serve the rutor fine for the moment until I could find more water. Meca and I entered the barn and made our way quickly to the loft before the large animals and the pecking chickens made the connection between the smell of sweet grains and the large oil-stained sack I carried.

"By my light. You found food!" Rayloh exclaimed. He hopped up and was digging in the bundle before I had time to sit it down.

"Actually, Meca discovered these delights." I decided not to tell Rayloh that I had actually caught him pilfering from the baker's stores. Meca wandered to the wall and slid to the floor, letting his feet kick out as his bum kissed the worn wood planks. I watched Rayloh devour entire loaves in only a few bites, taking such large mouthfuls that would put fully mature he-elves to shame. I wondered more about the Guerr's camp and thought this was as good a time as any to discuss it since he acted as if he were starved. "You eat as if you have not been fed, friend. Were they not feeding you behind those heavy iron gates?"

He didn't pause to answer as he began to force another loaf of what looked to be honey oat into his mouth. I had begun to pick at a loaf myself when he finally spoke. "Food was scarce. Not much to go around."

"Well, you know there's plenty here. Keldrock is not going to run out of wheat, Rayloh." I giggled a little, but his eyes remained on his prize as he scoffed down the last bit of the loaf. After finishing nearly half of the bundle on his own, he settled back on his sack and let his eyes close. I would ask him more at another time. Rayloh rarely reacted strongly with his words, but his body language was a dead giveaway. I knew that right now he didn't want to talk about it. I turned to Meca. "Since you discovered the source, I think it right that you have the remaining pickings. That is if Rayloh hasn't inhaled them all already." From the corner of my eye I could see Rayloh's giant grin. This made him smile and for that I felt comfort.

"I won't have any, I think." His head still hung as he muttered, "Not until Cadon and…"

"Cadon! Rose!" We all shook from surprise at Rayloh's outburst. It was so surprising in fact that even the horse and cows cooed in response. "Where are they?"

Meca's eyes didn't leave the floorboards and not a word was uttered. Rayloh looked at me for an explanation but all he received was a confused shrug. Even though Cadon had deemed me unwelcome, I didn't think Meca shared his feelings. The mooing of the cows ceased, and it was as if nothing moved below. The very stench seemed to leave the place, the air becoming clearer and crisper to my nose. Particles of dust shifted and rose, moving as if little feathers could ignore gravity and climb back to the skies just as they did when they fell, spinning in small circles.

"Are you alright, boy?" Rayloh asked. "You don't seem the same."

Meca looked up but only a little. "If I tell what came to pass, what happened to Rose will happen to me," he whispered.

Rayloh curled his lip as he gritted his teeth. I could tell he was becoming angered but trying to remain patient. "Where is Rose?"

Meca simply shook his head so quickly as if ensuring his tongue was so befuddled that it wouldn't let slip his secrets. As calm as Rayloh was trying to sound, I could tell a rage was boiling in him that couldn't be contained. The smell of burning straw began to drift in through the barn window, as smoke clouded the air. Someone trying to keep warm from the cool.

"You can tell me. Was it Mister Harmon?" Meca returned his stare down to the floorboards. "Mister Harmon, boy. Was it Mister Harmon?" Rayloh urged.

It's spring and hot as hades, I finally realized, snapping out of my random spell of stupor. I was so surprised I had let my mind slip that fact as sweat began to run down my face. Who could be burning anything at this time of day? I walked to the barn window that overlooked the little lot between Mister Harmon's house and the barn. There was no one. Not even a cinder was lit down in the lot. It was clear outside, the bright blue sky as luxurious as the many likenesses of vast oceans I'd seen in books and paintings. But where could the smoke be coming from?

"No…." It was still and the room was quiet. I turned my back to the light from the window to see the room had grown darker. The smoke had sifted in like a thief in the night, quietly overtaking us.

"Rayloh…"

"A moment, Alya," he said without losing eye contact with the hung head of Meca. "Was it a guard or one of the boys from Nazda's band? Tell me!" By now he had his large hands around Meca's shoulders, shaking him.

"Rayloh! Smoke! There's smoke everywhere." He looked around just as puzzled as I was before.

"From where does it come?" he asked of me as if I could provide some answer to this strange phenomenon by simply having discovered it first.

There were no flames that accompanied this dark cloud. It was coming in faster now through the cracks in the floorboards but stopping just short of the loft's roof, lingering in the air. I could feel it filling my lungs. I remembered the charred faces and burning drapes and even thought I caught the scent of burning flesh. I could feel myself beginning to panic, slowly losing control, the fear that the scenario that had nearly caused my death outside the judgment chamber was happening again.

I rushed to the loft's window again where smoke rose, making its escape to clear blue sky. My eyes began to water, causing my vision to blur. I nearly toppled out of the window as I gulped for fresh air. The smoke lifted to the skies and I could breathe again somewhat. I could see the rutor wandering about aimlessly with the few other animals, far enough away from the flames to be safe and still close enough to observe their home burn to the ground, because it was the barn that was burning. I saw the flickering of orange hot fingers beginning to climb up the side of the old cowshed.

I searched the surrounding area trying to find someone, anyone, who had noticed what was happening. But no one was outside. The streets were bare and if people were nearby, they were safely tucked in their homes. I looked to the bakery down the hill and recalled the water pot I'd left sitting there, empty. Although it would have proved worthless against the flames that produced this curtain of smog, I couldn't help but wish that I had retrieved that pot of water. I could feel the heat beneath my feet now, through my fine boots.

Voices. I could hear voices.

I looked out the window hopeful and was rewarded to find a team of boys running by. I thought it very strange that they'd jog right past a raging fire but all I needed was for one to look my way and our lives would be saved.

"Help!" I screamed as loud as I could. The entire band of boys turned around, staring with stunned faces. I could see some glancing towards others in fear, panicked expressions on their faces. One remained poised, calm and collected as he continued walking away from the burning barn, not bothering to turn over his shoulder as he urged his troop onward.

"Help, please!" I begged. They all stared up at me and I could tell they wanted to help, but they remained stilled.

"Come now!" Their leader had reached the crest of the hill, preparing to descend when I recognized him. An anger that caused my lips to tremble surged through my body as I watched Cadon grab one of his thugs by the arm and lead him away.

"Up to the roof!" Rayloh urged. I couldn't believe my eyes. They had to have been deceived. After all, Meca was in the barn. Cadon had to have known that. He wouldn't burn his most loyal of siblings. I turned to Meca, who was coughing and wincing as the smog became unbearable. "Quickly!" Rayloh shouted. "Up to the roof, you fool!"

He shoved me up through the loft's window, nearly causing me to tumble down to the unyielding earth. I caught myself, stiffening my legs as I reached up to the barn's overhanging frame. I pulled myself up onto the roof. It was quiet up there, so peaceful and still it would seem that the danger beneath couldn't harm us. I knew it wasn't so and I immediately began searching for a way down. Mister Harmon's house was out of reach. A jump from the barn's roof to his small abode would surely end unfavorably.

"Alya!" A child's voice called to me and for a moment I had forgotten the two victims that were in just as much danger as I. I could see Meca's red tiny fingers straining to reach the rugged rooftop and I rushed to receive him, lugging his boyish-sized body up. Rayloh didn't need much assistance as he shot up to the roof, his eyes darting about just as mine had, trying to find a way down.

"Someone help us!" Rayloh called out. No one answered. There was something unfamiliar about his tone and it made me uneasy. No matter the trouble, Rayloh's confidence and his ability to face any situation brought comfort. But today, fear had overcome his strength and I sensed that much good couldn't come from this.

Rayloh ran to other end of the roof, the shingles rattling under his feet. Meca trailed behind him, trying to stay as close as he could, hoping that this headstrong elven warrior could rescue him. Suddenly, Meca's foot sunk, crumpling a patch of the roof beneath him.

"Meca!" Rayloh called out as he started towards him. The old wood beam under Rayloh began to crumble, creating a tide between him and Meca who was slipping down into the furnace below, his hands dragging cross the roof's rough surface. Smoke encircled his body and plummeted up to the sky.

"Help!" I could see his body slowly slipping into the darkness below. The smoke. The smell of burnt flesh was summoned once again and I couldn't move. I wouldn't move.

I could hear my name being called over and over. *Help him, Alya. Help me! Pull me up! He'll burn!* But my mind remained unchained as I watched his body begin to slip down into the pit. Meca continued trying to pull himself up, gripping his elbows against the roof, refusing to fall under. I had to do something, but what if I fell too? I took a step and the slight tremble of the shingles on the roof caused me to recoil. I looked over at Rayloh, who peered at me imploringly. I knew the importance of self-sacrifice. I had fought on the Day of Unveiling and had given up my life to serve as Protector. I deserved some peace. I deserved to be fearful and to have limits. I watched Meca continue to cry out as his face began to disappear in the smog below. He was lost, and I had done nothing. As I watched the last of the fumes take his silhouette, a large bulking figure rolled over onto the roof. His face was wrapped in a scarf and on his hands he wore leather gloves with tiny holes beaded along the tips of the fingers and palms. He brushed through the fumes like a mast against the winds, causing it to dissipate around his large frame. He tossed Meca's body over his shoulder. His skin was blackened and red with blood and I dared not assume the worst. The rescuer slipped over the side of the barn and disappeared as quickly as he had come.

Rayloh didn't need any kind of invitation to follow. I followed just as he had done, hopping to the edge, not taking any more steps than necessary on the unsettling roof. I peered down over the edge and found a ladder, missing most of its wooden slats, leaning against the burning building. I lowered my body, my toes just inches from the first rung of the ladder. I dropped down on it, causing the ladder to shake. I leaned back to catch myself and in turn removed the ladder's bearing from the wall. Blessedly, Rayloh had touched the ground by now and before I could even begin my terminal fall to the earth, he slammed the ladder back against the side of the building. I raced to the ground, as fast my legs could carry me.

Once safely on the ground, I looked around, waiting to be embraced by Rayloh but he was fixated on Meca whose body lay still, covered in ash. My heart stopped as I saw the hurt in Rayloh's eyes. I didn't even want to ask.

Our rescuer had in his hand damp rags and began cooling Meca's forehead, wiping away the soot to reveal burned skin. The barn continued to crackle, and the sound of toppling debris could be heard from the side lot. I knew that the roof had finally given in. Soon the whole building would collapse, and I didn't want to be remotely near it when it happened.

"Into the house. Grab the boy." Our savior's voice sounded like he had spent the previous night guzzling spirits and mead until he was in a stupor.

I ran to assist Rayloh, each of us clearing a side of Meca's body, and followed the burly man into Mister Harmon's house. By now I knew who our savior was and I wasn't sure what to expect next. Mister Harmon removed the scarf from around his nose and mouth. His face was sweaty and full as if he had been holding his breath. His cheeks looked flabbier with the layers of sweat and soot attached to them. He tossed the leather gloves aside and grumbled over to his dining room table, sweeping empty bottles and old pipe fillings to the floor.

"Place em on the table. I've told those brats to be more careful. I knew somethin would come if Nazda weren't here to keep an eye. Now they've gone an set my damn barn on fire. You're lucky I didn't let ya burn," he lectured. "That wouldn't do me no good. You and those buffoons are gonna have to work this off." He probably didn't care about saving Meca's life as much for the simple honor in it but for the fact that he wouldn't be repaid for his barn if he hadn't.

Rayloh lifted the young boy up on to the table. Meca's breathing was staggered and his eyes were distant and glassy. I remembered how just yesterday the smoke made me lose consciousness, how I awoke in my chambers alongside a medic. If a medic were here now, much worry would be set aside. But Meca's only hope lay with Mister Harmon and two elflings. It seemed that his every inhalation and exhale were strained as he gasped like a fish out of water. Rayloh held his hand tightly, staring into Meca's great big questioning eyes. I figured he was just as confused as we were about what to do. He opened his mouth but nothing came out.

"Oh no," I heard Rayloh softly utter. "It's just like before, when the inferno took his father."

As soon as the words were spoken, Meca's eyes widened and he began to cough hysterically. His body remained still, his arms and legs still fixed on the table, but his chest bucked wildly. This episode lasted for a few minutes. I got the damp towel and wiped his head, but it was no use. Suddenly, a spray of blood shot from Meca's mouth. The tears stopped flowing from his eyes and he was still again. I couldn't tell if his breathing had returned to normal or if it were abnormally slow, considering the only apparatus I had to measure it against was his stifled gasps.

"You could have prevented this," Rayloh muttered. He didn't bother meeting my eyes or even facing my direction.

"Rayloh! I was…." I began.

"You were scared! I know. I'm just upset." We were quiet for a moment, the sounds of Meca's breathing breaking the quiet. "I'll just wait outside."

"We're leaving." Rayloh said before I could make my exit. "We have to depart for the edgewoods if we are going to have any chance at saving your sister." He arose, apparently having gathered himself well enough to resume his commandership. "I must have a word with Mister Harmon before we go."

We found Mister Harmon outside gathering his animals with some old rope. They all seemed to be a little startled but none were injured. From the stoop I could see the top of Mister Harmon's head. His balding scalp was reddened and peeling, burned from the sun's rays. Every so often he would pause from his task and scratch his crown, sending dry flakes of crusted skin into the air. My stomach cringed at the sight and my face turned sour. Mister Harmon turned just before I had time to restore decorum.

"You'll see much worse things in your life than me balding head, missie," he said as he stretched out revealing his gut. He settled back down to the old cow, tightening the leash around her neck. "What of the boy? Will he be fine nuff to work?"

"I'm afraid not, sir," Rayloh said. "Being almost burned to death requires more healing than a few moments can hold."

"You being quick with me, sprite?" the farmer said with a spraying hiss that caused beads of spit to form on his chapped bottom lip. His beady eyes were now bold and crazed, staring hard at Rayloh.

"He meant no offense," I interjected. Rayloh, as usual, would let his outspokenness get the best of him, but we had no time to amuse this ass of a man. "It's just that he has suffered much today."

"As have I." Mister Harmon gestured in the direction of the now broken heap of shambled wood. "A loss that will take the lot of his company to reinstate."

"They have worked for you tirelessly for this pity of a place. Not to mention you offer them no food or revenue from the livestock or even their own animals to tend," Rayloh retorted.

"I have done more for those runts than you will ever know, thank you very much!" Mister Harmon had now risen, and it seemed he and Rayloh were going to stand off against each other.

"Whatever price, I will help them pay, but for his keeping, I need assistance. He is after all your kind and under your watch," Rayloh finally submitted. "You must know of a nurse within the ring, perhaps one who aids in birthing or nurtures the sick."

Mister Harmon scratched his chin, mulling this over. "There is a nurse who has recovered my livestock an checked on the chillen when available. Relations with me are her only payment, for she is barren and isn't married because no one will have her."

I cringed, my face taking on its own expression once more. Just like before, Mister Harmon caught wind of it. "I'll have you know, dearie, that there are many a woman folk who would have me as a suitor. Believe you me." He seemed to want to illustrate this illusion because in this moment he chose to finally stuff his stretched shirt into his trousers.

"So you'll take care of the boy?" Rayloh pressed.

"I'll let the nurse look at em and he can rest for a few days but after that, if he won't be quickly recoverin, then there's no place for him. I've got a barn to raise and I won't have a sick mouth on my hands."

Somewhat satisfied, Rayloh treaded to the rutor. "Here." I offered Mister Harmon two markels. "This should be well enough to feed you, the boy, and your livestock for more than a fortnight. That alleviates that problem."

He sniffed, sucking in air. I knew he was about to spit up mucus, just as he had done the first time I met him. "For that problem, yes. But for me time, there's no currency worthy." With that he shuffled into the house, letting out tiny grunts as he climbed the few steps up to his porch.

Rayloh had by now saddled up on his rutor and was ready to go. I ran to the other, quickly saddling myself.

"The sun is nearing its middle course. We must hurry if we are to meet Master Tali and the captain."

We trotted along, not saying anything as we made our way to the front gates. I could tell Rayloh was thinking as he stared off into the distance. His gaze didn't shift as we passed ruined cottages and the few quiet faces that stared from their windows. Most of the houses seemed abandoned as if all life were draining from the black ring. I thought to comfort him but there wasn't much I could say or explain. My head kept trying to make excuses or make what I saw an illusion but I knew that was Cadon darting over the hill with Nazda's former band of adolescents.

"Ahh! There you are!" I heard a boisterous voice call from up the path. It had been so long since I'd wandered the path leading to Keldrock's marvelous gates which had been replaced with nothing more than a cheap imitation. Wooden flats hinged and barred with logs was a pitiful attempt to keep even the smallest and frailest of barbarians at bay. I remember how the metal of the old gates lay twisted and wood trembled in splinters as I rode to the chamber of light atop that brave mongrowl. I thought of the boy Niegi and the love he had for the beast. I remembered wondering how strange it must be to connect with something so monstrous and unpredictable. It seemed that I would always be in this state of longing for what I had lost.

"What came to pass since we last parted?" Silvertail inquired as we approached. He had exchanged his captain's garb for a simple shirt and an old pair of trousers. I guess the heat got to him and he thought it better to leave his uniform behind. He kept on his patrol boots which would serve him well in the forest.

"We were caught in a fire, but all is well," I grumbled, looking down at my clothes and realizing the smoke and embers had left dark smudges and singed fabric.

"I hope that you are well enough to face whatever dangers lay beyond these walls. This is a rescue mission and we will need to have all our bearings. Especially since Master Tali has chosen to stay behind with the lad."

I nodded, accepting Master Tali's absence as sensible. I knew what I was facing and was all the more willing to enter the edgewoods, no matter the danger.

"Whether my sister is alive is the only thought that nags my spirit. For death will come to whomever stands in my way." Silvertail gathered himself on my rutor, saddling in front of me. The gates were opened, and the sound of pounding hooves ushered us into the once-familiar unknown.

Chapter Fourteen

The edgewoods seemed different in the most wondrous of ways. While our city dwelled in constant hammering and destruction, life seemed to flourish within the forest. The storms that brought with them tumultuous deluges made the vibrant green leaves ever more flamboyant. The trail that had once been marked by me and the lads was now overgrown. We came upon a stream and decided that this would be an appropriate place for us to stop and figure our way. The rutor were very apprecreative, not even waiting for their riders to climb from their backs before herding over to the smooth-running current.

Rayloh was the best with directions. He remembered the streams we passed and the fallen trunks that played host to all sorts of slimy critters. He was a being of the earth and all wild things. It is a wonder his talent was summoning flame as opposed to the sweet petals of flora or the waters of powerful rivers. He knelt and picked at some moss that was stretched across massive, weathered stones along the stream's embankment, using it to wipe at the sores along his arms and legs. His teeth ground against each other as he patted and prodded the tiny cuts and bruises on his body. There would be more than one awaiting justice once we returned to the city.

I looked out into the wide span of woods. I watched as a wild bunch of lorikanaries, the beautiful little birds with voices like angels that fluttered about the city of Keldrock, flew into the air, shimmering like oil paints as they floated up past the canopy of green toward the bright sun, probably appearing ever the more beautiful exposed in its full rays. I remembered the lesson Master Tali had taught using the birds, the song they sang of the exiled sisters and how now these women were stronger than ever. I wondered if those who witnessed their exile thought that this combination of daughters, mothers, and sisters would one day rise up and be the threatening force that could take the whole city. I looked off into the distance, tracing how far we had to go. Wood Haven was a day's journey on foot, and the rutor would make it quicker, but every minute was precious. At any moment my sister's life could be gone. It could have been ended already.

"Let us be on our way," I urged. "We've dallied long enough."

Silvertail took a swig from his sleeve.

"Very well." He faltered a little when he stood which I wasn't sure was due to his drinking or misplaced footing.

Rayloh tossed the moss back onto the riverbank and resettled himself atop the rutor. "Ride with me, Alya. We will travel faster as a pair than you and Silvertail." He reached out his hand and with one strong lift, I was saddled behind him. With a jerk of his heel we were off.

Darting through the forest on these steeds was thrilling. They were fast and seemed to already be calculating their next jolt before completing their current move. Their broad horns wrangled vines and small branches that seemed to reach down to grasp as we passed.

A few hours passed and soon the terrain began to rise into a hill. I knew we would be upon the grove soon. From behind Rayloh, I jerked the reins, halting the rutor in its rhythm. Silvertail did the same, nearly toppling over the beast's head as it slammed to a stop. I hopped off of the rutor's back and looped the reins around a slender but strong trunk of a tusking oak, known for the way it grew from the ground like the tusk of an elephant. Nothing sprouted from these trees, but underneath their smooth bark was a hold of water. With my bow and arrows already over my shoulder, I pulled from my traveling sack a canteen and a few small trinkets, a blade, and a pair of spotters, leaving the rest on the back of the rutor. Silvertail hadn't bothered bringing much—only his double-edged sword, a few knives he tucked in his belt, and his sleeve which he hooked to the back of his trousers. To Rayloh he tossed a smaller sword. With everyone prepared, I began my lead, peering into the quiet brush that held so much life.

I crept quietly, not having to say much to direct my company as we moved soundlessly through the underbrush. Silvertail seemed to have regained his full capacity because he moved effortlessly through the shrubs with stealth equaled to the great mountain cats who every so often picked off one of the grazing goats in the pastures to the west of the city, leaving behind only footprints. I began to recognize a path, a way through the forest that had obviously formed from the constant tread of feet over the grasses.

The clouds overhead moved in front of the sun, bringing near darkness to the wilds of the edgewoods. The air seemed to still as I saw at a distance the intertwining grove of trees, looking like one giant organism in the center of the woods. From this angle, it was hard to determine whether a scout lurked in the branches above or patrolled the circumference of the small camp.

"I'll look ahead. The last time I was here, they knew of our arrival before we could even announce ourselves. For Mira's sake, we must not be given away."

"Then wouldn't it be wiser if the lad and I search ahead?" Silvertail suggested. "At least if we are discovered, our connection to you might not be assumed."

"The point is for us not to be discovered," Rayloh retorted.

"I know that!" Silvertail returned with a hushed roar. It apparently wasn't hushed enough, because a flock of dark feathered birds shot from their nests. Rayloh leaned back on his knees, looking puzzled by the slight combativeness of Silvertail's tone. He seemed to be on edge about this whole trip and even since its conception had kept to his sleeve of spirits. I saw him start to pull it out but caught our glances and decided not to, playing it off as if he was adjusting his trousers.

The captain cleared his throat. "Then it is settled. I will go ahead and chart the area. I should return within the hour but if not, go on without me. If I am caught, this would serve a distraction that may allow you to enter the camp more easily."

He galloped off across the terrain, bringing with him only his horn and sword. I looked to where he disappeared until there was nothing but the sounds of nature and I knew Rayloh and I were alone. We started to look for a safer place to wait but thought it wise to stay in the general area to make it easier for Silvertail to find us once he returned. Sounds of life that I hadn't noticed before were now louder and cacophonous amidst the stillness. Birds called to one another while tree frogs croaked and moaned. Cicadas sung up above in the trees, out of sight, seeking safety and nourishment within the canopy. Rayloh seemed unbothered by the racket as he settled down atop a soft mesh of grass and rested his eyes. I would have thought he were falling asleep had he not intermittently opened his eyes to check his surroundings before returning to that same state again. I decided to follow suit, settling underneath some wild plant with great big leaves that nearly covered my entire body, just in time for the drizzle that was about to ensue. Only tiny drops made it past the dense canopy. It sounded like the marching of tiny feet the way the droplets pattered against the forest. The toads continued to croak while the birds and cicadas retreated, their conversations halted. I watched the mist fill the air around us as I drifted off, slipping into sleep.

***

I was shaken awake by a pair of strong hands. My eyes popped open and I scrambled for my bow but was relieved to find that it was only Rayloh.

"A full round has passed and the captain hasn't returned."

I looked toward the intertwining trees of the Wood Haven camp and then back at him.

"All right then. We search the camp on our own. If he is caught, he will need a cavalry."

I stood up, wiping the grogginess from my eyes. I slung the sheath and bow over my shoulder, allowing it to rest in the crevice that my spine made in my back. Rayoh didn't bother sheathing his sword. He carried it perpendicularly to his upright form, ready to cut down enemies at a moment's notice. We eventually reached the grove and tucked ourselves behind a few bushes, peering out into the small clearing. I pulled out the spotters and brought them to my eyes. I first scanned the edge of the trees. No one was out circling the perimeter but as I turned the spotters to the heights of the grove, I could see two watchwomen on platforms.

"There are two in the treetops." I stared at them through the spotters to make a more precise observation. They were older, their hair beginning to turn grey. They were obviously ill-suited for this task because they were barely paying any notice to the line of trees just a few meters from their posts. "We will need a distraction!" I received no response. "Rayloh?"

I turned to my side to see that Rayloh was nowhere to be found. I shot from the cover of the brush, looking to all sides of me and then out into the small field that lay between our post and the grove. There darting closer and closer to the Wood Haven camp was Rayloh, his fiery head floating like a torch as he treaded through the tall grasses. I looked through the spotter to where the watchwomen had been. They were gone. This being the most opportune time, I darted behind Rayloh just as he had begun to slip into the grove. I picked up my pace, trying to catch up to him.

It didn't take long to cross the small span and I was soon rounding one of the intertwining trees into the camp. I expected a group of warriors to be upon us by now, just like before, but it didn't come to pass. Rayloh walked clear into the center of the grove, no one in sight to overtake him. I looked up into the branches to the platforms and zip lines, so naturally woven in the trees. Colorful flowers had sprung up in the grove's center, bringing a feeling of subtle paradise to the assailants' hideout. I knew we were being watched. The grove was too still. It was too quiet. Just as I was about to call out to Rayloh, beckoning retreat, my fears were confirmed.

"Who should be had first?" A calm, hushed whisper came from behind me. I didn't dare move. My heart cringed as the sounds of stretched bowstring against pressured wood reached my ears as my capturer raised her arrow and bow. I knew she was pointing it straight at Rayloh as he looked about the field, searching for anything that would point him towards Mira. He tore through the fields, slicing his blade through the wild plant stems and calling out her name to the dark huts that sat overhead.

"Please, we're looking for my sister. We didn't come to harm you." She came in closer to where I could see her just from my peripheral. Her eyes were fixed on the red hair in the distance.

"Your sister isn't here." She sounded appalled at even the accusation. "My warriors are waiting for my signal. Death is the punishment for trespassers."

I tried again. "Please, that's all we want. She was taken by a masked night crawler. It looked like..." I started to turn to face her, but a quick shift of her arrow stopped my rotation. "…Well, it's hard to explain."

"It looked like a bird. With a beak surround by feathers, the sockets the size of walnuts." I could see the bow being lowered. She whistled into the air and I watched as her signal passed to hidden archers and spearmen that dropped from the dense foliage of the linked treetops with bows and javelins ready.

"This way, young elf." The archer came around to face me. She didn't wear a mask like the rest of her troop. Instead, she wore a shiny piece of iron pierced through her septum. I swallowed hard, remembering the warrior who chased me into the edgewoods before meeting wits with the mongrowl. "You and the he-elf can join us in the huts."

She seemed to not recognize me. Then I remembered my hair and the way it shimmered white now, so different from the dark tresses I had when we initially met. Somehow she must not know about my ascent to the crown and how the light passed from Shiloh to me during the Unveiling. For her ignorance, I was grateful, but still wary. Yann was tactful but I thought at the very least her warriors would know everything she did prior to her defeat in the yellow garden's dome.

Within the heights of the trees, everything seemed different than before. We had used the ziplines just as we had before to get to the highs of the branched community connected by wooden planks and sturdy platforms. Few people were left within the camp and those that were seemed to be rushing about, carrying sacks and wrapping food and other provisions. I watched as the two older watchwomen, who up close seemed to be in much better shape than I had assumed, returned to their posts.

We settled in the same large hut where Nazda, Niegi and I met before, except this time Amazja, the matriarch of Wood Haven, wasn't there to greet us. I looked about the room as other archers and spear throwers joined us, surrounding us with recessed weapons. Some looked as though they were sizing us up, while others probably just wanted to see an elf up close. The woman with the pierced septum stood in Amazja's former spot, her bow now slung over her pointed shoulders.

"The mornowl has taken your sister. This much can be said."

The mornowl? What fairytales does she speak? The mornowl was no more than a creature of folklore that took pleasure in waking up right before dawn and letting out its boisterous call. I couldn't say that I didn't enjoy the wonderful tales of Keldronian folklore, and part of me wanted to believe that the mornowl was real.

"We've all grown up with the tales passed down through the generations. The same sun that used to rise at the call of the mornowl in the city could be heard sailing over the grove of Wood Haven." Many birds would coo at the sight of dawn, but the mornowl's call would burst just as light broke the night. I wasn't quite sure if I could trust her words or if she was just stringing me along. She began pacing around us as she continued. "There are some legends that say the mornowl can take the form of something similar to that of an elf but most favored is a great bird." I thought of Czar Icar and his savage raptor. I couldn't imagine a bird like that transforming into a thief as common in build as any being seen walking the streets of Keldrock. I listened as she rambled on, her eyes growing wide with excitement. "The mornowl is said to be angry because the veil has fallen and the balance of this world has been thrown askew. The former head of our defense and two of her charge were murdered by the mornowl."

I sucked in my breath, remembering that cold morning in the yellow ring's garden dome. I remembered turning away as I felt the knife slice open her face and the bloodcurdling screeches of pain that followed. I looked at Rayloh, leaning against the support column in the center of the hut with a skeptical expression on his face. Out of anyone I knew, he refused to believe such far-fetched stories without solid proof.

"Then where can we find this heavenly angel bird turned murderer?" Rayloh demanded. A few of the younger girls giggled, amused by the banter of this handsome he-elf.

"Your pompous friend laughs now since a dozen arrows have not crossed through his frame." The girls laughed again. Rayloh sneered at the warrior with the septum piercing and she turned back to me. "My sisters and our children are leaving these lands. The mornowl is angry and since the veil no longer contains us, making the world free to explore, we will migrate elsewhere. The mornowl—"

"Why not have assembled during the Unveiling and migrated then? Why did your warriors kill Shiloh?" Rayloh sneered.

The woman with the pierced septum remained serene. "It matters not since what is done has come to pass, but the death of Shiloh wasn't our doing."

I looked at Rayloh in disbelief. He looked ready to blurt out curses and insults. Just as I held my own rebuke, I knew it to be in vain, for I could always count on Rayloh to encourage his.

"Then who attacked Keldrock? Warriors with masks that shield your battle maidens' faces today were in the tower the Day of Unveiling." I wanted to snatch him by the collar but the woman with the septum piercing seemed too eager to finish her story to address his contempt. She just smiled but I knew she wasn't pleased and that it would only be a matter of time before her patience wore too thin.

"The city was not supposed to be under siege, at least not by the mother of our order. I am ashamed to say that I myself took part, although I was blinded. The head of our guard, Yann, was so consumed with rage at the state of our people within the city's walls that she wanted to bring the veil down for them all to cross, and so that's what came to pass."

She let out a longing sigh as she sat down on a wooden frame at the back of the hut where Amazja would have probably been seated if she were here, ready to govern her haven. The hut began to empty out, the unamused onlookers returning to their business, leaving Rayloh and I to discuss our own matters.

"Our clan leader Amazja was not pleased and warned that if any more death ensued, the culprits would be banished from the haven. Yann was upset. She felt her work was nothing more than the mighty hand of justice, but her mother thought otherwise. She decided to leave, stating her purpose had yet to be fulfilled, and with a few others too young to see reason, they left Wood Haven." She stood up from the chair and turned to face it as if worshipping it as some special ornament that contained magical properties. "That was a horrible day for Amazja and a few months later, she heard that her daughter had died. An injured party who saw Yann's lifeless form fought through the forest to deliver the message to Wood Haven only to die herself soon after. She accounted in her last breath of a bird, large, with fiery colored wings and the utmost *terrifying*. Amazja wasn't the same after that, and a week later, she disappeared."

"I'm sorry…" I uttered. It was weird hearing the story from another's view. Yann's insanity suddenly turned to slight reason. I spoke so disgustedly of her murderous taste which I still believe was well beyond the standards of any noble being, but she wanted more for her people. Even now, it's insulting that I can judge her life so harshly, a life I took with my dagger.

"It is alright, Protector." I looked up at her in shock as she strode toward me, laying her hand on my shoulder, her eyes beaming with regret and revelation. "It is I who should be apologizing to you. For I drove you into the very events you were trying to avoid. Many mistakes have been made on both sides, and my path hasn't always been one I am proud of, but it is mine all the same."

Rayloh looked confused but remained surprisingly quiet to keen an understanding of all that unfolded and what was to come of it.

"The people of Wood Haven and the Dwala are leaving these lands. The few of us who remain are waiting until the Celebration of the Fawn in case any others have mustered enough courage to leave the city walls."

I thought of Rose's words about a migration. I thought of the invitation she gave and the wrath of Cadon who so help me would pay tenfold should any harm have been dealt to that sweet little girl. The woman with the septum piercing withdrew her hand and walked back over to her seat, composing herself as a queen on her throne.

"As for your sister, I would seek the western woods. Before the veil fell, we would hear the glorious calls of morning climb over the trees from the west. I would think that the mornowl, having taken your sister and not dealt with her right then, isn't out to harm her. Perhaps it seeks her council. Maybe it seeks yours."

"We thank you for your kindness, Mistress…"

She smiled, delighted in the fact that she had not introduced herself but went straight into business. "A name, although important to share, is not all that important. For the sake of my title, now that's where true nobility lies. Neont is my name and it is Neont you can thank for your life, little elf master." She and I giggled while Rayloh blushed, attempting to hold back a creeping smile.

Neont had stopped her banter and looked to the hut's entrance where two of her order stood like great giants among women with a humiliated creature in their grip.

"We caught him lurking around the grove and thought it best he be joined with his party," one said with a snicker. Her hair was cut short and her arms, bulking with small thumping veins, were decorated with blue inked tattoos.

"Ah." Neont stood and faced none other than Silvertail breathing heavily as if he had tussled and lost a most defaming defeat. All this time I had almost forgotten that he had gone to scout the area. She turned to the woman who spoke. "Tell me Worsk, was it you who captured this he-elf?"

She smiled, while Silvertail hung his head woefully. "Alas, it was not I but Caman. She just celebrated her twelfth year not even three moons ago. She netted him and hoisted him up all on her own with us supervising." I fought to hold back my amusement at this tale but Rayloh made no such attempt. He whooped and hollered and just as he let go all decorum, the rest of us joined in his mirth.

Silvertail whipped away from the two strongwomen, smoothing the wrinkles out of his shirt, most likely a guise for soothing the bruising from their grip. "We will be off then," he said, lurching for the door.

"Very well," I answered, remnants of laughter still rolling off of my tongue.

***

We set off while the sun was still high in the sky. The days were longer now that we were well into spring, and more wildlife emerged in the wood. We decided to leave the rutor behind, feeling that they would cause less harm to themselves there than if we encountered a crazed fowl, considering what happened when Czar Icar's Athena swooped down upon them. Neont was kind enough along with Worsk and the other guard to usher us in the direction where they believed the mornowl to be and providing us with a bounty of nuts and bread for nourishment. She described the most promising area to search being near a river whose dropout ran down into the same deeps as the river that ran through Keldrock.

Rayloh led the way, practicing with his new sword on low hanging twigs and spiraling vines. We kept our eyes peeled for any sign of Mira or this supposed mornowl. I tried to recall the figure from that night, its face and feathers, but as sure as I was before, I felt distanced from the memory now having only gotten a brief glance. Silvertail remained quiet the entire time, his eyes straining beyond their limits at what seemed to be every single detail of the forest. Every subtle sound of some wild insect or flick of a branch by a tree climber, he would brandish his sword. I reckon he felt he had something to prove after what happened in Wood Haven. We crept for hours and the sounds only grew denser. My nostrils flared and my ears were perked, hoping to catch any sign of rushing water. The sounds of crickets and croaking frogs filled the air as dusk began to set in.

"Damn these gnats," Rayloh sputtered as he swatted in vain at the little black specks with his sword. "They're drawn to the smell of his ales, they are. Finish that sleeve and be done with it!" he said to Silvertail.

The captain didn't respond. He didn't seem to have even heard Rayloh's banter as he trudged forward ahead of our band, taking the lead from Rayloh. He veered off in a different direction, slightly south from the trail we had been on which followed the setting sun. Soon the smell of wet soil filled the air followed by the sound of running water. It grew louder and louder until with the last day's light, we spotted the peacefulness of the river, running like icy blue silver strings over large brown stones. A few fish swam quietly through the water, strong enough to battle the current. Little gnats clung just above the river, causing Rayloh more hassle as he swatted at them.

"Seems Neont was honest in her directions," Silvertail said as he settled down on the hard stones by the riverbed. He washed his hands and the sweat from his face and trickled a little water down his back. The day was beginning to cool but even still, we were hot from traveling and the gnats didn't make this experience any more tolerable.

Rayloh knelt down cupping his hands and took water to his lips for a drink. "Are we to wait for the bird to come to bathe in the river or will we seek it out?" There was no sarcasm in his voice. The water must have calmed his edgy nerves.

"A plan must be devised before that," said Silvertail. "Neont believes the beast can change form. If this is true…"

"Then we should span out. Find its burrow," I said. "After all, that is where Mira would be kept and if this river is the main source of life for these woods then it can't be too far." It made sense.

"And what if our lead was wrong? What if the abductor simply wore a guise in the likeness of a bird? What then to evoke the wrath of something so sacred for nothing?" Rayloh said calmly, trying to seek reason with Silvertail who had already set off to cross the shallows of the river. He stopped short just before the water passed his knees. It seemed that he was actually considering this.

"Very well, Alya!" Silvertail said as he stared up at the sky, ignoring Rayloh. "The heavens tell me we have nearly an hour before total darkness falls. We should spend it wisely. Each of us will look for the mornowl's den and once it is discovered, you are to return to the river. In any case, we should all return before darkness falls." I nodded in agreement and although Rayloh did reluctantly, seemingly thinking this unwise.

Rayloh and I followed Silvertail across the river, each taking our own route. Rayloh spanned north, I walked east, and Silvertail went west. For a while I walked along the river, searching the mud for any footprints, scrapings, or even large animal droppings. I didn't find much aside from the remnants of fish bones, so I decided to go into the woods. The trees were thinner in these parts and grew exceedingly tall. The air smelled different, a stench that was not necessarily unpleasant, but simply unfamiliar. I walked along quietly, happy to be free from the nagging gnats of the river. I kept my eyes peeled, peering through the trees for anything that moved. Long shadows stretched along the ground, shading me from the last heat of the day. I walked a ways before deciding the direction I was heading most like led to nothing. I turned around to find my way back as the shadows began to grow deeper and longer.

Night had fallen by the time I had almost reached the river. Hearing the sound of rushing water, I picked up into a trot.

That was when a crackling voice rang out in the pitch of night that I couldn't make out but sounded like scraping whispers that made me feel cold inside.

"Rayloh!" I called, thinking that I had come back west a few more meters than I had intended and our paths had crossed.

No answer came. Suddenly, the ground began to tremble with so much force that I almost lost my footing. The trees seemed to screech as the cracking echoes of the sound reverberated through the woods. Just as quickly as the tremor had begun it was soon over, the peaceful chirps of crickets resuming. I sprinted through the night, dodging trees. I came down over a small ledge, not noticing it in time to stop, and tumbled forward into a rather large puddle. I landed with a splash, contorted in a weird fashion. I sat up in the murky mess, wiping muddy smudges from my face. I took in gulps of air, trying to regain the breath that the surprise fall knocked out of me. That's when I noticed it.

Like an oasis in the desert it stood. The puddle where I sat stemmed from a larger pool of water settled in an enclosed moat around a mound of shimmering white rock that reminded me of the snowcaps at the top of the mountains that lay behind Keldrock. In fact, if I hadn't known better, I would have thought it was frosted with snow—but I was sure my eyes deceived me.

The perfect place for a hideout, I thought, as I waded deeper into the moat. The beautiful clear water sparkled with a growing shine that can only be compared to the brightening of the stars. This structure was so rare, it had to be the home of something great. I walked steadily forward, sending ripples to the ends of the ever-growing puddle. As I got closer to the magnificent white rock, I realized it was much larger than I anticipated. I spotted a small opening in the rock, arching into a giant triangle, as if to swallow the water and me with it.

Return to the river, my conscience urged. I began to turn around, but this could be the mornowl's den, and what if Mira was inside? I let my bow slip from my shoulder and nocked an arrow just in case. I took one step inside the glowing interior of the cavern and immediately the chill penetrated to my core as little puffs of visible breath fumed in the air. This was very odd, but I didn't heed my senses' warning. The ground started to shudder and the water around me began to sweep away out of the opening of the cave, knocking me to the ground. It was soon followed by the thunderous crunch of rock and I watched in horror as the mouth of the cave began to seal shut. I shot up like a trapped rabbit, realizing that this was too unusual. I shot my arrow in a fury of contempt and watched it soar through the sliver of opening that remained right before it closed. I couldn't see outside, the insides of the rock like mirrors. I nearly toppled over again as I stood on unsteady ground. The cave was *moving*.

Chapter Fifteen

I gave up pounding and clawing at the white crystal mirrors and collapsed on the glistening smooth floor. I didn't know how long I and the cave had been moving or where it was going. By now my panic had subsided and all I could think about was getting out—or more accurately, when I would be let out. I could only hope that peril wouldn't befall me.

I sat next to a jutting crystalline stone, rubbing my hands together, trying to stay warm. The universe seemed to have a weird way of making me appreciate its natural climate because now more than ever I would have welcomed the sweltering heat. Up through the ceiling was the only point of light, a glowing orb that could only be compared to starlight. I turned my eyes away, tired of this beautiful spectacle, and just stared at my shivering reflection across the way. Soon after, I closed my eyes, touching the silvery scales of my necklace. It felt surprisingly warm like a kiss in front of the hearth after spending a time in the freezing snow. I stroked it, allowing it to warm my fingertips as I felt the cave come to a stop. The mouth of the cave parted and the floor slanted, causing me to slide out on my back in a pitiful slump. I stared up at the stars twinkling peacefully above as a large boulder came straight for my head. I let out a loud yelp and covered my face, preparing for it to pulverize me.

"Is it broken?" I heard a crackling voice of what sounded like an old crone question. I peeked out from under my arms to see the boulder scrunched up with small stones on its surface and creases as if it had a face—a very stern face. I sat up, stunned as the part of the heavy geode where the mouth would be split apart, opened wide. A voice spoke. I couldn't move as I watched the stone lips open and close. An icy splash pulled me from my trance.

"Get up, you lot," came a voice from behind. If it had not come from the giant white hunk of crystal rock, I would have thought to come from an elderly drunkard, bringing to mind Mister Harmon. The white mass of rock's face was just as chipped and jagged as his body, random shards sticking out around his chest and along his arms. I watched the water that he had thrown on me climb back up his form and become a frozen hand of ice, like the rest of his arms and legs. I stared in disbelief at these two monstrous rock creatures.

"Get up now!"

I stood up and saw Rayloh a few feet away, struggling to free himself from a wrap of vines that bound him.

"Tricky one this was!" said the stone woman, who I could now see was covered in a thick layer of moss, vines, and had sprouting in different places tiny plants and flowers. "His hair kept turning to flames and burning my vines."

"Quite lucky you are, sister," the shimmering water crystal being bellowed, who in all his eeriness was still somewhat beautiful. "If he burned your..." They both eyed me and Rayloh, who was now standing next to me, staring up at his capturers with furrowed eyebrows and bold, accusing eyes.

"He reminds me of brother. His embers were so lively, they were. That is, before he took that terrible tumble into the river. What a pity." She sounded so sad that I almost felt sympathy for her.

The boulder creature settled down on the ground with a hard thud and began patting her face as tiny streams of flower petals floated down from her eyes. I could see held around her neck with a slew of vines a shiny green orb right below her chipped stone chin. The watery crystal mass settled atop a great stone with a ledge like a stoop and begin picking away at his glimmering toenails flakes of carbon, sprinkling them about like blackened hail.

"What are you and what do you want with us?" Rayloh shouted loud enough to disturb the gorge. It looked as though we were in a very large, mountainous bowl.

"Oh joy," the earthy creature shot back, nearly falling on top of Rayloh with overexcitement. "It talks. Did ya hear em, brother?" she shouted over her shoulder at the water crystal. "We are Gigantourmoutherantines," she explained to Rayloh. "Although some call us unbefitting names like mountain trolls…or…or…" She looked puzzled and wrenched her head towards her brother who answered. It seemed to be somewhat a normal ritual for them.

"Boulder beasts!" he sputtered, spitting as he spoke tiny ice diamonds out of his mouth that tumbled onto the ground and tumbled about like pieces of glass.

"And we'll be killing ya," she said just as cheerfully as before. "We've been given all the finest of things to be done with you two….and…" She looked around where she sat hunched over, scanning the ground in desperation. "Where might it be, brother?"

"Calm yer nerve, sister. I put er some place she couldn't get out. A lot smaller than these two, she is." He stood up from the stone he was sitting on and lifted it high into the air before tossing it halfway across the gorge, it landing with a thunderous display of earth-rattling. "Here it be!" he said after reaching in a hole the rock was covering and pulling out a youngster, wriggling like a mouse in a cat's paw.

I couldn't believe my eyes as the little creature that he sat down turned out to be Mira, looking more disgruntled than scared. I grabbed my sister and hugged her tight, and she seemed just as happy to see me, wrapping her little arms around me. I stooped to see her face, pushing her hair back and wiping the little smudges that had stained her cheeks.

"You came to find me! You really found me!" she squealed through tears with a smile so wide pinned to her face. I pulled her in close again.

"Of course I came to find you!" I looked up at the stars, grateful that we were safe—at least for this moment.

"Where are we, Alya?" Mira looked past me up to the mountain trolls who were putting their heads together, quite literally, debating something or another. I remembered the earth wench's words and knew we had to escape. Perhaps there was a way out of this that would require just a little cleverness which I imagined was all that was needed to outsmart these halfwits.

"Pardon me, my good sir and madam, but what exactly were you offered for our lives? Whatever it was has to be quite wonderful," I said with the most beseeching of tones. It would be good to find out what exactly was promised to them in order for them to be done with us. Perhaps we could double it and buy our freedom.

"Ah, right ya are, sprite," the crystal mountain troll spat, sending trickles of glittering ice over Mira and me. "And we'll not be sharing with the likes of ya. They're only for me!"

The earthy mountain troll gasped, pulling at the tufts of her vines and thorny hair. "*And* for me!" she exclaimed, now standing upright with her moss-covered hands on her boisterous boulders of hips. "And might I tell ya, they er fascinatin, they are."

"I would like to see them. If my eyes are to view their last, I would want that last to be whatever wonderful treasures you were bestowed."

She smiled, her teeth nothing more than corroded stone chips. I could see a few were missing here and there.

"Oh, I'd be delighted." She started to rush off to the lower edges of the gorge when a large stone came flying across and hit her square in the back of the head, sending two of the small trees that sat atop her head, a heap of moss, and a whole lot of flowers tumbling to the ground. She recoiled, her mild temper now replaced with terrible fury. "What'd ya do that fer?" she questioned her brother, who had in his hand another rock ready to hurl. Rayloh, Mira, and I backed out of their line of fire as not be crushed by any projectiles that would falter and miss their mark.

"Don't go blabbing on to these lot, yer stupid big fat ogre. It's none of their business." Another splendor of sparkling gems flew from his mouth. She seemed more embarrassed than anything as she looked to us then back at her brother, realizing she had been belittled in front of company. Although I wanted to figure out some way to deal away with the two and be gone from this place, I hated more than ever the crystal troll, whose words were as harsh and disrespectful as Mister Harmon's and even my father's. Recognizing an opportunity, I decided to force this disagreement further.

"Oh, I am sorry my lord," I said with believable sincerity. "I didn't know you were the head of your sibling." Mira, whether she was playing along or just caught up in the familiar banter she had seen with the ladies of the Remni, gasped and looked at the earthy troll to see her reaction.

She reacted the very way I had anticipated. "Fer yer business's worth, he is lord to no one. Especially not me, ya miserable river stone!" she shot at him. Before he could let the stone slip from his grasp, she was on top of him, hurling her huge rocky fists at the jagged, glistening shards that formed his head. They rolled about hurling each other against the ridges of the gorge.

"Follow me," I whispered, grabbing Mira and Rayloh's hands, leading them away.

We reached the low barrier from whence the earth beast had come. The two mighty boulders rocked against the walls of the gorge, uplifting and loosening rocks and bits of earth.

"Up you go, Mira!" I began lifting her up to barrier's break, pushing her little body up against the wall until the tips of her toes were on my shoulders. "How close are you to the edge, Mira?" She wasn't heavy at all, being thin for her age, but the urgency created by this situation made it a challenge.

"I'm just short of the ledge," she called down to me. She was making small, straining sounds as the tips of her toes dug into the pockets of my shoulder blades, the weight on my neck becoming unbearable. "Almost there!" she assured through what sounded to be gritted teeth. She forced down her right foot too hard into my shoulder blade and pain shot through my entire body as I gave in, sliding down to the ground in a terrible heap of defeat. Mira screamed as she tumbled down the side of the rocky wall, sprawling next to me on the ground. A quiet rushed over the gorge as the mountain trolls came to a still, each one holding some piece of the other.

"Ya see that, sister? They meant teh set us against one nother!" He choked as he stood up, letting go of a boulder with moss and thorns covering it. I was surprised when it turned itself on the ground revealing the stone woman's face, more of her teeth missing than before as she spoke.

"Ya are right, brother. They're tryin teh escape, they are!" Their disembodied portions slowly began to reassemble themselves from the battle, even down to the last of the she-troll's ragged teeth.

"I think they meant to steal my treasure as well," he said as he crept forward, the last of his spitting, diamond-like fragments trailing up to his mouth. I gulped hard, clutching my throbbing shoulder.

"Stand back," Rayloh warned as his hands became engulfed in flame. "I'll burn you to bits! We just want to be on our way." I stared at him in amazement as his talent had advanced since the swirling of a small ember cupped in his hands no bigger than match flicks from our adventures into the edgewoods. I watched his hands burn bright with coarse fire beating like it had a pulse of its own.

The ice troll laughed, its boisterous sound rolling over the mountains, making them tremble. The earth troll who at one point seemed to be so timid and kind smiled eerily at us as the last of her tiny trees rooted itself to her head.

"That kind of magic won't help you, little lad. Now be still." She began cupping her hands and arching her back as if to lunge out at the lot of us and grind us up in her palms. "It'll only hurt fer a second."

As she approached, I saw gleaming just beneath her chin—the sparkling stone that would glow marvelously even without the moon's light. It was a sight to behold on something so wretched. I watched as vines began to lift from around her rugged fingers and coil at our feet, snapping like vipers as she toyed with us. One of her longer vines that had thorns dripping with venom reared its neck. I grabbed Mira's hand and she grabbed mine, almost instinctively. Rayloh did the same, his hands surprisingly cool, even after holding such heat. I shut my eyes and began counting slowly as if to anticipate the strike. *One, two, three, four…*

An agonizing howl shook me to my core. I squeezed Rayloh and Mira's hands and they squeezed mine back. I didn't realize until a few counts later that they were alive and well—so then who was screaming? I squinted into the moonlit darkness to see scrounging on the ground the earth wench, crying out in agony.

"It burns!" she shouted. "It burns!" I watched as the crystal troll melted the ice of his hands and sent it flying towards the eruption of flames on her neck, but it was too late. Large pieces of rock, leaves, moss, vines, and tiny trees and shrubs all tumbled together in a terrible heap on the ground, burning to a crisp. The fire erupted her entire body leaving nothing more than tiny broken fragments of the boulders. From the heap rolled a glittering green stone more beautiful than any emerald I had ever seen, even the ones on my necklace. The gem landed at Mira's feet. Lodged into it was a burning arrow that had hit its intended mark. The she-troll was no more.

"What magic?" the crystal troll thundered, peering up at the cliffs and high ridges of the surrounding mountains. "Show yourself, scum, so that I might wreak justice on your being for this crime." No one appeared but instead a voice was heard.

I listened intently, not even bothering to protest when Rayloh slipped the bow off of my arm and pulled from my quiver two arrows. "*Eremet,*" I heard. I tried to sound out, as the voice continued to repeat itself, unsure if the word I was hearing was in fact what was being said. "It's *eremet.*"

The monstrous crystal ice giant seemed to have heard the same thing as I because he cried out, "What is this *eremet*? Speak, you treacherous fiend!" He picked up a piece of what had been his sister and attempted to hurl it up to a nearby ledge, but it only went a few feet in the air before crashing back down to the ground.

I watched the last of the arrow burn away and the light fade from the green gem that now lay dormant on the ground. It was as if it had died. As if it were life itself. I was struck by lightning, remembering something Czar Icar said, and I deciphered what the hoarse voice from above was saying.

"Elemel!" I said to myself. "It's elemel!" I exclaimed to Rayloh and Mira. Mira was still gripping my hand, staring at me with a shocked expression as the crazed frost giant cursed at the unknown. Rayloh had strung my bow, the points of both arrows flickering with red flame.

"Rayloh! No!" I screamed, just as he released one of the burning arrows.

My warning sounded just in time to warn the crystal troll. He turned, the arrow landing in his leg. Rayloh quickly loaded his bow with the last of his burning arrows since he had missed his target. As soon as the arrow reached the troll, it froze, the flames instantly smothered. I watched the boulder beast smile, showing sharp incisors of sickled ice that could cut through bone, dripping droplets of ice-cold water from their points.

Before he could fully process what was happening, Rayloh had sent another arrow right at his chest, and this one hit its mark. The icy shard that I saw while caged in his center that lay just beneath his chin had been pierced. A spurt of snow shot from his throat and he stumbled back, frantic. Rayloh jumped in the air, reveling in his success. Mira had let go of my hand and was now staring at the frost giant, the glow of victory written across her face, but her joy was premature. There were no cries of agony or wailing on the ground. Something wasn't right. Rayloh froze as we all watched the arrow fall to the ground, free of flame. The frost giant laughed thunderously and called out to the mountains with an evil tone.

"Whatever magic took my sister resides not in flame for me."

Do something, I thought, hoping my necklace could sense my desperation. I half wished that my necklace would do something. Something that I couldn't explain but always suspected. But the silver remained cold and unyielding around my neck. I watched the giant inch forward, seeing that we were all out of options.

"I've only but escaped hell in the form of an iron bunker. If I am to see death, she will have to come herself and deal me so."

Right then, Rayloh's sword became engulfed in a vibrant blue flame, the heat smacking me in the face like a wrathful furnace. Mira and I backed away in both surprise and fear. Rayloh let out a battle cry before lunging toward the crystal boulder beast. His voice was so powerful that it shook the canyon, uplifting stones from their holds just as the large mountain trolls had done. I knew fire could stall the beast, but wouldn't end him, and if I didn't do something, Rayloh surely would meet death. I ran through what I knew in my head.

The elemel belonging to the earth troll only was severed from her with fire, but nothing happened to the ice giant's gem when the flame was sent to his stone of elemel.

I wanted to pound my head against the surrounding rock. Mira was panicking now. Rayloh had sliced through the wrist of the frost troll and was now wiggling in his other hand. The giant lifted a flailing Rayloh high into the air, ready to slam him into the ground. Rayloh, with at most a few seconds before the crystal giant's balled fist came crashing down, sent his fiery sword through the giant's hand and fell to the ground with it, landing in a pile of snow and crushed ice. I let out a breath of relief and returned to my thoughts.

The earth wench mentioned her brother and compared him to Rayloh. He must have been a fire troll. That would make sense since we had come to know a troll of ice and earth already. I seemed to be making some headway as I watched Rayloh dodge a close call from the boulder beast, who had turned his severed hands into sharpened points, using them to dig at Rayloh in an attempt to skewer him. And the river defeated the fire troll. Water defeated him. I could hear Mira screaming again and I needed nothing more than silence since I was already panicking myself. The fire troll was defeated by water. Flames destroyed the earth wench. The crystal giant must be conquered by…

I began looking around for anything growing but the ground was barren. All the plants and trees that had been a part of the earth troll had withered away or were burned to a crisp. I grazed my trouser pockets, feeling a slight bulge. I grabbed at it, thankful to find the pouch that Mira gave me. This would be the very thing that would bring our victory.

I reached inside of the pouch and pulled out a single blue seed. I didn't have any idea how I was going to get it into the frost giant's gem. It would never sit in a bow and I didn't have a sling, nor would I have time to fashion one. *Sift, Alya!* I told myself. *Sift! You know the words*. But I knew I wasn't sure, or perhaps I was simply fearful of what would happen if I got it wrong and something terrible came to pass.

Rayloh tumbled to the ground, gasping, as the frost giant continued jabbing at him with large drill-topped sickles where his hands used to be. The giant leapt in the air and drove his blade into the ground, missing Rayloh and splintered the point all the way up to his shoulder blade, breaking the ice limb into jagged shards. The monster seemed to be crumbling and he didn't find the time to gather the severed pieces of himself during the course of the battle.

"Rayloh!" I called out. I reared back, ready to throw the seed to him. Just as I had let the seed fly, I saw the boulder beast blow a breath of ice, freezing the watery floor of the gorge. Rayloh rocked forward unsteadily, his sword fumbling across the ice, but he didn't move from where he stood. His legs were frozen to the ground. The seed landed just a few feet away from where he stood. The boulder beast was smiling, I could tell even through his smashed face where segments of ice and crystal were missing. With what was left of his severed arm, he began crawling, trying to get closer to Rayloh. Rayloh jerked his right foot as the giant inched forward looking like an injured bear that was still intent on killing. Even in his deformed state, he was terrifying. He wanted blood and if I didn't do something fast, he would have it.

I heard ice cracking and I saw Rayloh's right foot break from its hold. The sword was too far away, even with one of his feet dislodged. Instead, he leaned to his side and began reaching for the seed. The ice giant was nearly upon him as Rayloh strained to reach the seed.

I rummaged in the pouch and quickly pulled out another one. I started grasping for words as the giant rose up on its base, where his legs had been parted from him and let out a large rumbling laugh. I picked up my bow and looked at Mira, who was staring at Rayloh through glistening tears. The sky had cleared and now the moon lit the gorge in its entirety in a beautiful white that made blue the once-black shadows. I could also see the look of defeat in Rayloh's eyes and for the first time I saw him accept what he believed to be the inevitable. He lowered his head as the giant reached the sharpened point where his hand once was into the air.

"Flechyil!" The seed shot across the gorge, shifting in the air from a small container of life into a broken cavity. Sprouting from one end of the seed was a winding branch and at its tip a single thorn. On the other end, another branch sprouted, but at its end were three crisp blue leaves the same wonderful color as the seed's oval sapphire shell, imitating the fletching on arrows, the thorn acting as the arrowhead. The giant's sickle of a hand had nearly speared Rayloh when the arrow formed from a tiny seed like a miracle, sliced through this arm, shattering it into nothing, before driving into the ice giant's crystal glowing orb.

Yet the ice giant soldiered on. Rayloh, Mira, and I stared at the beast in awe. Perhaps he had more will than the others, or maybe he was immune to whatever poison outdid his siblings. The ice giant didn't cry out or spit curses to the air. He didn't smile as he did before either.

Just as I had resolved to our ends, the arrow began to root into the crystal boulder beast, surging through his body like ivy on fencing. It coursed through his eyes and climbed through his head.

I watched the giant scratch and tear at himself, trying to remove the roots that were forming. They went down, out from under his chin, wrapping around his sharpened shoulders and breaking them off into chunks of ice and snow. Then I watched him begin to diminish as the roots sucked him dry, leaving behind only the hard crystal that formed his base, sitting elegantly on the ground. As the last of the water disappeared, so diminished the light of his beautiful gem. The ice giant was no more.

Chapter Sixteen

Rayloh was still frozen to the ground, gawking at the empty shell of glistening white stone that sat on the gorge's cold bottom. The sky was beginning to lighten, and I knew the night had almost passed. I rushed to Rayloh, helping to free his remaining foot.

"You did that?" he said incredulously, looking to where the ice giant had been. I couldn't tell Rayloh about the lessons that I had with Master Tali and how she had taught me how to sift but I wasn't sure how I could deny what had just happened with the seed sprouting into a formidable arrow in midair. "Weaponry conversion is a difficult feat in itself, let alone a skill reserved for the Guerr and the Guards of Candor. How did you come about it? I never knew those born with talents of earth to be so clever."

Making the earth yield was easy for me to some extent, but weaponry conversion, such a skill I knew I hadn't been taught. I envisioned Rayloh's sword engulfed in fire. One thing I could confirm was that I was in fact clever—or a great liar.

"As a part of my royal ascension, I had to become accustomed with all of the measures of my talent, no matter how obscure. A simple arrow is nothing compared to a flaming sword of course, but it evidently served us well in this time of need." I giggled a little but Rayloh's expression remained skeptical. However, for the moment, it seemed that my answer was satisfactory because he moved on to another pressing subject.

"They wouldn't have happened to educate you on where we are currently located during your royal ascension?" He inquired with a lightly comical tone.

I looked to the high ridges of the gorge and thought of the voice calling to us and saving us from a most certain death. It was hard to believe that this elixir of gems was what Czar Icar had deemed elemel. My eyes wandered to the two gems that lay just a few yards from one another. Even though their inner glow had diminished, their shells still shimmered handsomely in the last light of the moon. I strode to the earth wench's gem, poking at it with a shaking finger. It was cool to the touch and seemed to maneuver around my finger, shifting, allowing my finger to pass through it like tilled, moist soil. It did not fall apart, which was a strange nature. I felt a hard grip on my shoulder and peered up at Rayloh who looked with intrigued but hesitant eyes as I was just about to pick up the beautiful stone.

"You don't suppose this elemel is dangerous?" he said.

I responded with a sarcastic tone, being somewhat familiar with the properties of elemel thanks to Czar Icar and having just touched it and finding it more inviting than ever, despite the earth troll's horrid disposition. "I never thought I'd see the day Rayloh Emberstone would cower before a simple rock."

He lurched back, snatching his hand from my shoulder and just like that summoned enough bravery to pick up the crystal stone. He brought it back over to me just after I had placed the earth elemel in my sack. The crystal was transparent, the inside splintered into a multitude of tiny diamond-shaped cutlets that magnified the tiny lines of Rayloh's tanned, battered hands. I tucked the crystal into my sack and gathered my quiver and bow while Rayloh cleared the slosh of melted snow from his sword. We then rejoined Mira at the low ledge where she had been waiting patiently, seemingly deep in thought. This must have been quite a lot for her to take in. It would have been a lot for me as well if I hadn't seen so much in such a short time.

"I'm tall enough to get Mira up to the ledge," Rayloh offered. "Then up you'll go next."

With little effort, he placed Mira close enough to the edge of the break that she could climb up and onto the solid level of the ledge of what seemed to lead to the trolls' keep. Rayloh began the awkward procedure of pressing me up against the wall so that I could climb up after her and soon I saw Mira's wide smiling face at the edge. She helped pull me up and I commended her for her effort, although much wasn't contributed considering her frail and timid nature. I bet if Madja were here, she would have been grateful for the skills I'd gained during my wanderings into the edgewoods, climbing trees and rolling down hills. With some strain, Mira and I pulled Rayloh up to the ledge where we all collapsed, exhausted, breathing deeply. I could smell a scent on the air that I recognized only to come right before a storm.

"Alya! Look!" I flipped over onto my stomach and looked in Mira's direction. She was lurching away from us, peering at something in a distant corner.

"Wait, Mira! Let me have a look." I shot up without a moment to spare, racing to my sister before she could disappear again. I snatched her by the hand before turning to look where she was pointing.

It was a small hollow in the mountain against the mountain's base, adjacent to the nook was a slab, rounded around the edges like a wheel. It seemed that the two imbecilic mountain trolls had forgotten to seal up their plunder. Before I had time enough to worry about the darkness that concealed the treasure inside, Rayloh had lit a lying branch. He led the way, filling the chamber with flickering orange light that cast long shadows of our small figures. Tiny jars of powder sat along the walls as well as multitudes of what smelled like fertilizer. There were also wooden barrels with red tags on them. They smelled awful, the pungency of their scent burning the insides of my nostrils. No doubt that whoever paid these buffoons had given them spoiled mead and aged beer, and they very well hadn't noticed. We moved deeper into the hollow, looking around to find broken, useless trinkets that the trolls had collected. A sound like walnut shells cracking echoed off of the walls quickly followed by a horror-filled screech. I scrambled to Mira who nearly collapsed in my arms. I lifted her a little ways away before sitting her down, and after realizing she was safe, she let herself be calmed. I stood, breathing heavily next to the petrified little sprite, her eyes watery and her breath heavy. I inched into the shadows from whence we came, attempting to spy what caused Mira such a fright.

"Rayloh! Do you mind?" I beckoned for him to come closer with the torch he carried. I watched as the darkness began to slowly creep away like a living plague being vanquished by the flickering swords of heat.

I spotted what caused Mira to violently convulse and I nearly keeled over in disgust at the sight. A few ends of fingers, not more than an inch's worth, stuck up from the dirt, bent awkwardly and peeled in a most unnatural way. The fingernails were blackened where blood most likely had congealed.

Rayloh passed his torch to Mira and began removing the dirt in the area around the hand. A part of me wanted to stop him and leave covered whatever was buried in this catacomb. I didn't want to see. I didn't want to believe that *she* was dead. Rayloh dug, scooping up dirt filled with earth insects that raced away. A nasty stench began to fill the air and he had to stop for a moment. He continued soon after, cupping the palms of his hands and scooping out the dirt quickly. I began to sweat. I felt like I couldn't breathe. He brushed away soil from what seemed to be the body's head, and suddenly a patch of black curls came into view.

"Stop!" I screamed. Rayloh let the dirt he had just cupped fall back into the hole and stood up, shaking soil off his breeches. "Everything here is lost. No treasure exists in this hold. Burn this rubbish along with everything else that lies in these stores."

I walked out of the cave into the cool pre-dawn air. I breathed in deeply and sighed, pushing out of my mind what I knew to be true. Anger boiled within me, but I knew Cadon wasn't capable of this. Not to kill her. I conjured an image of beautiful Rose, just a few years beyond toddlerhood, being buried while she still pulled breath, with her large, beautiful, questioning eyes. *If I tell what came to pass, what happened to Rose will happen to me.* I recalled Meca, his head lowered, avoiding my eyes, as he said these words. They continued to echo in my head as I lingered outside of the cavern, waiting for Mira and Rayloh to join me.

It wasn't long before Mira appeared, staring at me with wondering eyes, the same eyes that Rose and all youth, whether elf or human, possess at this age. Then she opened up her little arms and wrapped them around my torso, squeezing me tight. She was so much like Madja, her hair, her beauty, and how she knew just what to do in order to comfort me. I embraced her, burying my face into Mira's crown of long black. Rayloh emerged with his torch. Mira and I released each other and I instinctively received the torch from him. I stared at the dark mountain vault that held all the pungent powders, the scented barrels and the tiny body with black curls and tiny broken fingers. I took in a large breath as if it were my last, pulling back my arm as I did, and then I released the torch. I watched it whip through the air like one of the beautiful Jalla dancers that performed at special occasions in Keldrock. I thought of how they would look at the Celebration of the Fawn, with their shimmering skirts and elaborate headpieces as the flame disappeared into the darkness and flickered, growing steadily with everything it touched.

"May Olörun deal heavily to whatever evil is in this place," Rayloh said with anger in his voice as he turned, heading up the gorge's sloping walls.

With Mira now safe within our company, we made for the mountain to begin the journey back to Keldrock where hopefully Silvertail had returned. It seemed all of us were in deep thought as we trailed along like a funeral possession. When we were a little more than a quarter mile from the troll's keep, a sharp hiss stopped us in our tracks, breaking the silence. It reminded me of the gentle pops and hisses that came from burning firewood except a lot louder. It came from the hollow in the mountain, the flames now flickering wildly from the opening like trapped demons struggling to be freed.

It wasn't but a breath later that an explosion happened much like the ones I had experienced in the judgment chambers and during the Day of Unveiling. It surged through the gorge like an earthquake, causing us to lose our footing. Rayloh, knelt, shaking, as he clung to the panicking earth. Mira held to me as we tumbled down to the ground and watched the boulder giants' hold flourish with bright sparks of light orange and deep reds against the once-still walls. The harsh scent that I recalled coming from the barrels filled the air. Rocks began to fall outside the nook and I was more than relieved that we got well away after setting the place ablaze. I held Mira's head in my arms as a louder explosion surpassing all that had come before it caused the ceiling of the cave to fall and a pile of crumbled rock and large boulders to spill out of the opening, blocking the entry. Soon everything returned to quiet. Mira lifted her head from my shoulder and we looked at each other with both fear then relief in our eyes, which quickly emanated into grateful laughter. Rayloh hadn't moved.

"Quiet," he commanded.

I stared at him intently, trying to figure exactly what was going on. He got up and began climbing up towards us, agony wrenched across his face.

"Up! To the ridge! Now!" he screamed, not leaving any time to explain the cause of all his dramatics. What could be running from?

A shift in the earth disrupted my passiveness. It felt like a crunch followed by another that seemed to echo within the ground. A single patch of snow landed just along the round door that had sealed the boulder beasts' den. Then another fell and I looked up to see the snow-capped mountains like sketched marble against the sky. More rafts of snow began to slide down the mountain's face, landing a few yards from where we stood.

"Run, you fools! Run!" Rayloh called from behind us. I grabbed Mira's hand and yanked her to her feet, and together we ran for the ridge across the rumbling gorge, heaps of sloshing ice crashing down all around us. One nearly fell atop Mira and me as we raced for the mountain's edge.

I lifted Mira quickly by her waist up to a hold, and she looked down at me even more frightened than before—but there was no time for fear. If we didn't get out of this gorge soon, we would certainly die.

"Climb!" I screeched, and she did as I said, placing her hands on small holds and footings in the wall of the ridge. Rayloh was almost to the top of the break of the ridge and would soon begin his way against the next rocky face, up to the main ground.

I pushed Mira up to the zenith just in time to hear the rough cracks echo off of the walls of the gorge. Clouds of displaced snow and ice from the disturbed mountaintop puffed in the sky like smoke as I watched a great portion of the frozen ice caps begin to slowly break from their holds. I pushed Mira up and shoved her toward Rayloh, who had waited for us before scaling up to higher ground. The avalanche was moving faster and faster, sheets of ice, snow, and rock, sliding down together.

"Come on!" Rayloh shouted as he lifted Mira up to a low ledge.

"Get her to safety." I ordered.

"Alya! Wait!"

But it was too late. I had already begun climbing back down the ridge, nearly losing my balance, but quickly regaining it as I bounded from ledge to hold like the beautiful brown goats with large curling horns, until I was back on the floor of the gorge. The avalanche had made it halfway down the mountain. I could see it hurtling, cascading down, bearing all its weight against the hard earth. I looked back and saw that Rayloh and Mira hadn't moved, and even if they had, there was no escaping this unless I did something. *It's important that you construct these phrases as to not suffocate and eradicate yourself from existence.* I remembered these words from Master Tali. Still, what choice did I have?

The avalanche had just touched the floor of the gorge, crashing down, destroying the boulder beasts' treasure chasm indefinitely if the fire and explosion hadn't. The words came like a whisper but spoke louder and louder to me as the avalanche tore across the gorge, heading straight for me and my friends like a stampede of white horses. I closed my eyes, tasting the chilled air as I breathed deeply in and out, focusing my energies. The ground was shaking more, but I remained unmoved. I clenched my fist and locked my knees, regretting that I hadn't been able to come up with a cleverer plan. I took in one last breath as I let the words slip from my lips.

"Detenon Avalanchayil!"

They sounded beautiful, like the whistle of a gentle breeze, but just as they had built in my mind, they began to slip like a memory one tries too hard to grasp. The stilled avalanche began to fade into black, blending with the dawn.

Chapter Seventeen

There was voice rising over the sound of flutes and strings. It was melodic and enticing, more beautiful than the song of the lorikanaries. I looked around for Prince Alag, or a white fox, or the serpent, or some other strange figure. I felt around my neck and found that the ornament that normally rested against my collarbone was missing. The fields of sweet grass were missing as well and in their place were the charred remains of burned earth. The beautiful sounds of flutes and strings that I remembered from my previous dreams suddenly filled me with sorrow as I watched the gentle breeze lift tiny puffs of soot and ash into the air. It appeared to be the same tree with the distinctive reddish brown bark from the journal. Except it was split open now, pieces of the tree twisting in different directions, wound in knots and spread open like a blooming flower, its branches perched at awkward angles. I began to walk toward the tree. It was so destructively artistic in its death. The tree had to be dead, but something was drawing me nearer. The sound of drums beat louder and louder with my every step, vibrating through the ground and up to my outstretched fingertips. The branches seemed to come alive as I approached, untangling themselves, then stringing together to a unified point, trying with all their might to reach me. I stuck out my hand, just a few feet away, when—

***

A terrible hiss and the head of a serpent was the last thing I saw before I awoke in a cold confusion, looking around to see a world of white. I was in a tiny pocket, somehow having avoided being crushed and buried by the snow and ice that surrounded me. I remembered the avalanche rushing toward me. I studied more closely at the tightly packed walls of snow that formed the ceiling and walls that sealed me in this chilling cocoon. I didn't know how deep I was beneath the surface or how to get out. A worried voice called out from above and the ice began to shift slightly, loosening. I felt around for my necklace as I often did only to find it missing. Remembering my vision, I thought it may have actually been lost. I had not the time now to worry about such trifles no matter how dear it was to me. The voice continued, growing nearer and nearer. Tiny streams no bigger than the threads that went into the colorful tapestries that hung around the palace ran into my tiny cell. Water began to fill my cocoon, the streams growing larger, dampening my clothes and making me ever more cold. Chunks of sloshing snow dripped down from above me. The cocoon began to enlarge as the puddle grew and light began to make its way down into this deep-frozen den. I looked up, puzzled. It didn't seem possible that the sun could melt the snow this rapidly. Then, as if answering my questions, sunlight broke through the last of the ice above, creating an opening through which I could see the sky.

"Alya!" A voice called down to me.

"I'm down here, Rayloh!" I screamed up to his silhouette, which was the only thing I could make out against the morning sun.

"Thank the heavens! She's alive!" I heard him report. "We'll have you out in a moment."

Rayloh was right. I was alive. Had I stopped the avalanche, or was it all a dream? Had I dreamed the avalanche stopping in mid-fall in the air? Had I never spoken those ancient words and I had only but fainted?

A rope dropped down into the freezing pool, splashing cold droplets all over me. I was already soaked so it wasn't as unnerving as before. I grabbed the rope and began pulling myself up, scaling the wall as my feet pressed uncertainly against the packed snow. I could feel the sun's rays beginning to warm my face and it wasn't long before Rayloh and Mira were pulling me up. Mira collapsed into my arms as I observed the aftermath of the avalanche, dumbfounded. The gorge was filled with snow.

"What happened?" I asked, confused. The avalanche had covered everything and yet we were still alive.

Mira looked deeply into my eyes with a grin on her face. I couldn't look at my sister and not see the youthful spirit that was stolen from Rose. Now wasn't the time for grieving. I focused on Mira who was now trying her hardest to explain to me how they survived the avalanche.

"It was the oddest thing, Alya!" she went on. "Rayloh and I were standing there, not wanting to leave you behind, when the avalanche swept over you and was hurling towards us. I love snow, but this was way more than what I'd deem enjoyable." I smiled at her comment, but she was altogether serious. "Then it was as if a wall was built in front of us. The snow right in front of the lower ledge where Rayloh and I stood stopped and packed against itself like a mound of mortar. It was like magic!"

Or sifting. Still, this occurrence was odd indeed. I remembered focusing my energies and forming what I wanted to happen in my mind. I pictured the walls of ice and snow packing together, stopping in its rampage. I hadn't stopped it—or had I? Had I just stopped it for Mira and Rayloh, leaving myself to freeze to death in an icy cocoon? I didn't picture a hollow in the snow and definitely didn't picture that I would be in it.

"How did you find me? How did you know where to look?" I asked Rayloh, who had used his talent to rescue me from my frozen prison by melting through the ice and snow.

"Well, after scaling up to the mainland, we crossed piled snow from the avalanche looking for signs of where you could be. We searched and searched but it seemed that we had lost you. I have Mira to thank for not giving up. She's the one that found it on top of this large bank and figured you lay beneath it."

The smile wiped clean from my face. "What is it you found? Tell me!"

Rayloh looked at me with a mixture of bewilderment and amusement, as he pulled from his pocket my necklace, the gleaming silver head of the serpent still poised as if were investigating the matters of its territory. Without thinking I snatched it from him and fastened it around my neck. Soothing warmth streamed through my body and I closed my eyes to revel in it, glad to be reunited with my most prized possession.

"I thought I'd lost you," I unintentionally said aloud. I opened my eyes upon realizing my odd behavior, hoping that the other two hadn't noticed. Rayloh stared at me with curled lips and searching eyes that I tried to shake off with a smile. Mira simply giggled.

"So which way is home?" I questioned, looking around at the endless expanse of white.

"I'm not sure," Rayloh responded, "but a great start would be solid ground."

He turned and began making his way to the mainland with Mira and I close behind him. She ran ahead, kicking up snow, stopping every so often to scoop some in her hands and toss it into the air. I still felt odd about my reaction to finding the necklace. I had never before found myself highly infatuated with anything material until now. I pondered these thoughts as I walked, hearing Mira's childish banter, as she ran about the snowbanks shrieking with giddiness. Perhaps it pained me to be separated from it. It also in an odd way protected me even if I couldn't quite explain that theory. I rubbed my fingers over the scales as I looked up at the sun and then in the distance to the green forest. I closed my eyes, feeling grateful to be alive. To my surprise, a cold projectile smacked me in my face, causing my teeth to chill and my eyes to water.

Upon recovering my vision and composure, I saw Rayloh standing there smiling, with his hand behind his back and Mira to his side, laughing so hard that she nearly fell over. I brushed the remnants of snow from my shirt and trousers, and then quickly scooped up a hunk of snow before Rayloh had time to launch his snowball at me. Instead, he mushed it in the face of an amicable Mira who only laughed more before gathering up her own snowball and launching it at Rayloh, who teased her by running backwards, dodging her aims. We did this all the way to the woods, even stopping for a moment to draw snow angels by lying in the snow and swishing our arms and legs back and forth. We stood up, the three of us together, admiring our angels. Rayloh, feeling somewhat threatened by the beauty in his, ran his foot against its wings, giving them the semblance of bat wings and drew horns with his fingers, claiming he was a demon before darting off into the woods shouting as if he had gone mad. Mira and I chased him, darting behind trees and bushes until we grew tired and settled atop a fallen log.

"These aren't the edgewoods, I can say that much," I noticed, looking around at the multitude of pines and oaks that stood spaced out from one another, feeding the forest floor green and brown pine needles.

"Of course it's not the edgewoods. These trees are more similar to the groves of the city, not to mention we just escaped a gorge cradled by a mountain," Rayloh said with so much sarcasm that I had to accept that fact that the answer was that obvious. "I'd wager a few markels that we are in the high mountains or perhaps to the rugged slopes in the west. Can't be so sure right now. Probably the slopes to the west eh?" He stood up and looked around. "I don't think the czar would allow such beasts as these Gigantour…" He paused, trying to recall the proper name of the mountain trolls. "Those kidnappers to rampage anywhere near the city. I think we should head through these woods until we reach something familiar."

Mira yawned widely. It occurred to me that we hadn't slept all night and upon this realization, I felt exhaustion catch up to me. I knew it wasn't in Mira's nature to complain. While I could probably carry on in this dreary state, I knew she couldn't. Before Rayloh could start off into the forest, I suggested, "Why don't we rest for the day and continue our journey tonight?" Mira perked up and I knew this was exactly what she wanted, especially since this was her first time outside the city's walls.

Rayloh shrugged. "Very well." I figured a full day and night without rest would make even the strongest weary. "It might be for the better. We've made a little progress and the sun will be high soon. At night, we'll have the cool and the stars to guide us. I'll take first watch."

"Are you sure you won't rest? I'm sure we're safe way up here."

He shook his head wildly as if the idea of not acting as watchman was preposterous. "I had some rest at the barn. I'll be fine. I could use the quiet time to sort through my thoughts." He sat down on the fallen log with his sheathed sword across his lap.

Mira had already found herself a spot on a small bed of pine needles. I settled down next to her, wanting her to above all be comfortable and feel safe. She had been through so much. We all had. As my mind began to clear, the sounds of nature filled the space. I could hear the gentle calls of birds and the crunch of leaves. I began to drift into a deep sleep, the quiet hums of nature ushering me into slumber.

***

"Wake up!" I heard Rayloh call. Mira was already up, staring out into the forest alongside Rayloh who was standing still, his neck stretched as if he were a deer listening for a stalking cougar in the bush.

I stood up and stretched. I rolled my shoulders and neck, little pops of ecstasy crying out from my bones creating a wonderful sensation of relief. I picked up my bow and sheath of arrows along with the sack of food we received from the women at Wood Haven. It was late into the evening now, the sun slipping over the mountaintops leaving a trail of red across the sky. Rayloh hadn't moved and Mira seeing I was awake ran over to me, looking up at me with questioning eyes.

"Is something wrong, Rayloh?" I asked, trying to be quiet as to not interrupt his listening.

He lingered for a moment, staring out into the lengthening shadows before turning around and replying with a smile. "It's nothing. We better get a move on."

"You haven't had a chance to rest. You need your—"

"I'm fine," he retorted, a twinge of annoyance in his voice. "I'll rest when the morning comes." With that he set out, not bothering to wait for my response, and reluctantly I followed, Mira tailing alongside me.

These woods were still, unlike the wilds of the edgewoods. The trees grew farther apart and had great trunks with shielding branches. I would have deemed them uninhabited if I hadn't heard that voice when I was down in the gorge nearly being killed by a mountain troll. A part of me wanted to stumble upon my savior, but whoever it was didn't want to be seen or known or else they would have revealed themselves. I couldn't shake the feeling that we were being watched. Every so often the wisp of the leaves in the conifers or the crack of a fallen branch would startle me into dashing forward to Rayloh. He wasn't deterred at all by our being lost. He would stop by the trees and rub the trunks or dig into the dirt, rolling it around between the tips of his fingers. I suspect he learned such practices from his time with the Guerr.

Night crept over the trees and with it came the sharp sounds of insects emerging from their underground nests with the heat of the day gone. Rayloh moved as quickly as his feet would carry him, jogging through the trees, down small slopes and through brush. Mira kept up the best she could but I could tell she was tiring out, and the distance between Rayloh and us grew. We had been going for hours, and by now Rayloh was just a little silhouette up ahead. He stopped, not turning back as we trotted to his side, Mira panting heavily. Once at Rayloh's side, she collapsed on to her hands and knees. Rayloh looked at her with no sympathy.

"We'll never make it back to Keldrock at this rate. We must keep going."

"Mira isn't used to the terrain or the distance. If she can just have a moment to gain her bearings—"

"We don't have time," he insisted, with a serious, authoritative tone. "You've had time to rest and at the very least by the stars and the endless trees, we could be days away from the city."

"She's exhausted Rayloh. What would you have me do?"

He reared back, anger firing in his eyes. "You're the Protector, maybe you should act like it."

"What does that mean?"

Rayloh didn't back down. "It means that you should take some responsibility. Maybe you need to grow up!"

I couldn't take his insolence anymore. Friend or not, I couldn't let him treat Mira and me with such disrespect. My sister needed my help and for that I returned that which he was giving me.

"Well, maybe you need to accept some things about yourself. You don't know the responsibilities of Protector or all I've been through. Half of which you probably couldn't endure."

"I'm sure I've seen worse than you, Alya. You sit in a castle in luxury while your brothers are dying under a tyrant and starving in the edgewoods. You've done nothing but worry about yourself."

"I came back for you! If it were not for me, you'd still be a tick. If I weren't Protector, Segun would be dead right now. You have no idea the responsibility I've taken. I didn't ask for this."

"What about ticks? What about the Dwala? What about the warriors in the woods? You only have risen to the occasion because your sister went missing. You only came to the Guerr's barracks because you needed help on this quest. Otherwise, you wouldn't have even thought to retrieve Segun and I. You are not a victim, Alya!"

"This isn't about me. My sister was abducted. What would you have me do? Leave her?"

"You know I don't mean that, but you are no leader. At least not now, so stand down." He turned to walk further down the mountain. I couldn't bring my legs to move. By now, Mira was squatting on the ground staring at me, intent on following whatever decision I made.

"We're waiting for Mira to catch her second wind. Then we will continue." I heard the rustle of Rayloh's feet on the forest floor come to a stop.

"What did you say?" It was as if my defiance struck a nerve and I realized that this was probably the first time I had went against Rayloh.

"I said we're resting for a moment and I think it wise that you do the same. Your restlessness seems to have made your anger ever the more poignant."

"I don't need rest!" he shouted, his booming voice resounding across the woods making even the loudest of crickets cease in their movements. "I need you to gain your bearings so we can get home. You're spoiling her just like your mother. Weakness it is. Weakness is the lot of you."

The words that made me cringe with rage were last to come out of his mouth and before I could stop them, the worst thing I could say to Rayloh slipped from my grasp and into the quiets of the forest.

"Well at least I have a mother! If you had one, maybe you would see this as compassion and not weakness, you horrid bastard."

He stared at me stunned, flushing away the anger that once bore into me. I felt sick. I wanted to disappear. He didn't say anything. I turned away, leaving him there without an apology, without another word. I began to help Mira up to her feet, her eyes shifting as the crunch of leaves started up again and trailed off into the distance. I didn't dare turn back to Rayloh as Mira began calling out to him, starting at a small step before stopping, still too exhausted to keep up. Soon the patters of his feet against the earth were just distant echoes and we were overtaken by the returning sounds of purring crickets.

We trudged on quietly. I knew Rayloh was gone and he wasn't going to return. And I wouldn't blame him. I had called him something I would never do to someone I loved, someone I would consider a brother, and yet I had. It seemed that was always my constant battle. I was always in situations that I found unusual or dangerous, but I could always seem to find a way around to blaming them on something or someone else. This time, it was all from me. Rayloh was angry, as was I, and probably regretted what he said, just as I did, but I can't say that he wanted to hurt me. He didn't want to make me feel pain by his words but I had. For a moment, I hate to admit, when I saw the hurt in his eyes, I was pleased. I was happy that I had caused one who was so hell-bent on proving constantly that he was the strongest and bravest of us all crumble.

***

Mira and I still did as we had originally decided, sleeping during the day and traveling during the night. I had rationed the bag of provisions that Neont gave me, but they were for a day's journey at best, and we were now five days into our journey. I wasn't even sure if we had made any more progress getting closer to Keldrock. I took it as a good sign when I noticed the grasses beginning to become long and the trees growing shorter and closer together like the ones at the beginning of the edgewoods. I dug my fingers into the ground just as Rayloh had done and I had now done every day since he had been gone. The soil was moist, sticking together, instead of crumbling like sand as it had done before. I knew we were nearing water and with that being the case, I knew I could figure out where we were from there.

We continued on as we had the days before in near silence. Mira had mostly given up on reuniting with Rayloh. She would try her hardest to keep up, not complaining at all about the small rations of food and water. At night, I would hear her crying, shuddering in the spread of leaves and pine needles, until exhaustion took her. We decided to begin today before nightfall, trudging through the forest groggy and half asleep. We came to a ledge that jetted high above the lower grounds of the continuing forest. Suddenly, a gleam from the last of the sun's rays caught my eyes. The gleam came from something familiar and even though it was farther than I would have liked, there was no mistaking what it was.

It was like a horror in the creeping night, a castle of black. Across the treetops, over a gate of stern iron was the czar's citadel. It was both disappointing to see as well as blessed to see the dark metal hold in the distance ahead. I couldn't believe that we had found our way just to realize that even from this distance, the city wasn't the same. The two watchtowers that were so tall they seemed to touch the heavens had fallen. Still, excitement overpowered whatever grief was summoned from this surreal view.

"Look, Mira!" I shouted, pointing towards the faraway palace. "There's home! Do you see it?"

Mira stood on the tips of her toes trying to spy in the distance, the gold-plated monuments that housed the royals and elites of our city. She looked amazed, staring at the great buildings and humble homes that from this distance seemed no more than the size of dollhouses. Her face grew long as she settled back on the flats of her feet.

"Do you think we will make it back in time for the Celebration of the Fawn? I don't want to miss the Jalla dancers' tribute to the doe."

I hadn't thought much about the Celebration of the Fawn let alone Mira's love for the beautiful dancers. I faintly remembered it being discussed at the council meeting. It's hard to focus on such trifles when dealing with such pressing issues as the city was facing. In truth, to make it this great a distance on foot would be cutting it extremely close with the festival a few days away. The boulder beasts covered such a wide expanse of land to have gotten us from the beginning of the western woods to the gorge, but they were much bigger than Mira and I and the terrain easily passible for their giant limbs.

We began the tricky task of scaling down the wall of the ledge, down to the next span of forest. I decided to go first, just in case Mira slipped and tumbled. She hadn't had as much experience with the complexities of climbing as I had. It hadn't rained for some days now, so the slope was dry, which served as a small favor as I began placing the insides of my feet against the hardened clay. I gripped onto patches of grass and roots that stuck out like islands in a sea of red earth. Soon I was at the foot of the slope and realized just how high it was for an elf that hadn't even seen a decade. Mira's tiny feet began to peek over the edge of the slope as her hands held on to the break in the ledge until she found enough security with her prodding toes to begin her descent. To my surprise, she scaled it with ease, reaching the ground faster than I had managed. She looked at me beaming with pride.

The rest of the journey seemed to be no more than distance. We hadn't made but a league before night overtook the forest. It was darker than normal tonight. The stars and the sliver of moon hung behind heavy clouds, no doubt full of rain. I tried to remember on days when it rained the heaviest if it was like this before the veil fell. I felt a drop on my forehead and was immediately annoyed. It slowly picked up as we continued on and had but covered a league before the weather was too much to bear.

"Come on!" I said darting deeper into the forest. None of the trees nearly were as full as the ones I was familiar with in the edgewoods. The trunks and branches of these trees were thin and went high into the sky, letting the drops of water easily slip through their gapped canopy.

I saw a hollow in the distance much like the one Nazda and I hid in during a fall deluge.

"There!" I said to Mira pointing at the hollow's mouth. We darted together, our feet making loud, distinct splashes. I grabbed Mira's hand to ensure she didn't fall down into the wet muck that was beginning to form. We were nearly upon the cave. It was so small with just enough room for the two of us to wait for the rain to pass.

Then suddenly something snagged my foot and I tumbled into the damp, my body colliding with a painful smack as my quiver slipped off of my arm. Before I had time to recover the quiver, let alone myself, Mira and I were tangled in the net of a snare trap suspended from one of the trees, the rain pattering even heavier as we dangled feet off of the ground.

It was another hour before the rain let up. I gave up on trying to cut through the rope with the notch of my bow, not only because I wasn't making much progress, but also because I wasn't completely sure if at this height we would survive the fall, even if the ground was a soft, murky mess. I would have a better idea come morning, the light revealing more about the matter. Mira and I were pinned together, the lines of rope cutting into our backs and legs, forcing us to adjust every few seconds to ensure our circulation wasn't cut off. The small patter of drops from high branches could be heard dripping down to the puddles that collected on the forest floor. It was pitch black, the clouds overhead floating ever so slowly against the light of the moon and the stars. Every so often Mira's head would graze my shoulder, and I knew that she was resisting sleep. I adjusted so that the majority of her body was cradled on top of mine, allowing her head to fall on my chest. The net swayed as I felt Mira's breathing slow to an even pace. Soon I drifted away as well against the soft patter of water drops and the swaying of the net.

Chapter Eighteen

I awoke with a start, not having gotten much rest since we were suspended from the ground. Mira was still fast asleep, little sighs escaping her lips as she breathed in and out. The woods were beginning to lighten. I could make out bits of my surroundings now. I could see the ropes that made the net, one of its inner crossings completely severed enough to fit a hand through, the metal that formed the notches having served some use in cutting the net the night before. This allowed some relief because at least I knew that freedom could be attained without waiting for someone to find us. My hands were still somewhat cold but most of my body had dried, leaving mud crusted against my clothes and skin.

Mira rolled away from me, one of her arms falling out of an opening in the net. I was surprised she was so calm. Even I was calmer than I would anticipate. It seemed that this trap was just another obstacle we would have to overcome, which proved unsettling to me. I was used to the constant danger and close calls with death, but Mira didn't deserve this. I reached over and pulled her hair out of her face. Even in the fleeting black surroundings, I could see a sleepy smile appear on her face, and it seemed all would be all right.

A rustle in the bushes disturbed my admiration of my sweet sister. Then another rustle, and soon I heard footsteps splashing through puddles and charging through the brush. Before I knew it, someone stumbled into view, swearing quietly. From their barely visible shape I could make out a shallow frame, frail and deprived, inching across the way, one leg seemingly dragging in a limp. I held Mira tighter, stroking her head, hoping that she wouldn't wake up startled and give us away to our unknown visitor. A tight grip squeezed my stroking hand, startling me from my observation of the odd person below, but I quickly realized it could only be Mira. She pulled my hand down, interlacing her fingers with mine.

What could they possibly be looking for? I looked at the figure searching the forest floor. I watched them take to their knees, feeling the ground, when it occurred to me that they were possibly the one who had set this snare trap. I took in a deep breath as their head suddenly twitched up and to the right of where they crawled, strands of scraggly hair hanging alongside their face—the only reason I was able to see it was because it reached way past their shoulders. Mira gripped my hand tighter. I remembered losing my quiver of arrows. They could have discovered them. I pictured them sliding out of my possession as I tripped in the snare and was hauled up to the treetops with my sister. But they didn't need my quiver to know that we were up here because the line of their trap was what they were looking for. If there was any doubt of this conclusion, it was all washed away as the sharp pull of a steel blade from its hold pierced the silent darkness of the woods. Mira clutched my hand tighter.

Their silhouette disappeared into the shadows of the trees and for a moment, I could only hear the sloshing steps of damp leaves and mud. They stopped and I held my breath. Everything was still. Mira's grip eased a little as if she were uncertain that if she let go, everything would fall apart. It started off like a rustling until the strands began to break and I recognized the sound of thick rope bring cut. Mira let go of my hand only to wrap her tiny arms around me, burying her face into my chest.

It felt like the world was suddenly pulled from under my feet. We collided with the ground in a tangled mess as the figure remerged again, their uneven footsteps making noises in the muck. The ground beat alongside my heart timing each passing second as the steps became steadily closer. Then the earth-pounding grew, and I knew it more than my racing pulse. More beats were added, and I knew it as galloping. The figure stopped. Could they feel the ground trembling as well?

They stood there for a moment, still, the shape of their knife stemming from their silhouette, bringing to mind the terror evoked by the speared arm of the frost giant. They staggered forward again, their wet hair shifting in the darkness. The galloping increased and I could tell they were frightened, perhaps by the movement of another party moving through the brush.

"Alya!" A voice called out a few meters away. I dared not answer, simultaneously hoping that my cavalry would somehow find me and at the same time hoping this person wasn't provoked.

I just stared at the shape which had frozen once again from advancing.

The galloping slowed enough to where it barely caused any disturbance in the ground but I could hear the rustle of brush being torn aside. "Alya! Is that you?" I heard the voice call out again, this time much closer. So close that it was recognizable as the voice of Silvertail.

"Yes! Over here!" Mira responded, clambering and tugging at the net to free herself and go in the direction of the voice, toppling over me trying to find the ends of the net that were once tethered to the single rope the awkward figure severed.

Mira finally freed us, pulling the net over my head and letting it fall around my sprawled legs. She urgently helped me to my feet, pulling on my hand, and we sauntered in the direction of Silvertail's voice, our legs having been asleep for so long that it took a few minutes for our limbs to move naturally. I tried to move quickly and at the same time keep watch over what lay behind us, still unnerved by the unknown being who had cut us down.

"Alya!" I heard Silvertail call out once more, now only a few yards in front of us. We continued on, pushing through a cluster of vines until we collided into the side of something large and hot, their hair feeling like bristles against my skin as I slid to the ground.

I heard the braying of an angered herding animal and I knew I had run into one of the rutor, who I remembered were easily startled.

"Oh, settle down!" Silvertail called to the rutor, which was tightly tethered to the other one that he rode astride. Silvertail slipped to the ground, rustling around in his saddlebag, and finally finding what he was looking for, with a distinct popping noise, produced a small flame, dispelling the endless darkness. His face was scraggly and tanned, his eyes burrowed above large bags. In just a week's time he had become nearly unrecognizable. I hugged him tightly, not minding the smell of spirits that clung to his garments. I could feel the tension in his body slowly release and I knew that he had accomplished what he wanted and that he needn't stress anymore.

Silvertail walked with us to the area where we had dropped in the net and crouched to the ground with his torch in hand to examine the scene. He picked up the severed end and curled his fingers in its breaks as if he was testing it somehow. After a moment, I thought to offer what I had come to know about the edgewoods and who it could be.

"I'd assume that the snare was set by Wood Haven, probably meant to serve some use as a trap for an animal." He tossed the rope to ground, and I couldn't tell by his disgruntled expression and uneasy grunt whether he took it as a likely possibility. "There was also someone in the woods who freed us from the snare."

At this, Silvertail's eyes grew large. "What more can you tell me of this being? What did they look like?" he insisted, grabbing my shoulders.

"They looked skinny with scraggly hair. Upon hearing your approach, the figure disappeared into the shadows."

It was as if a merry spirit had possessed Silvertail for only a moment and had now gone, leaving him to his former temperament of stress and all-around discomfort. "Very well," he said as he straightened himself, brushing the moist dirt from his pants. "We must get back to Keldrock. I'm sure the prince is worried about you." He smirked at me, confirming his sarcasm, and I at him as he led the way back to the rutor.

***

After a few hours, we were upon the river, and the woods had just begun to lighten with the near rising sun. The rutor galloped to a stop, hoping they would be pardoned time to gather a drink. Silvertail decided that it was best for them to rest for the moment and slipped to the ground before helping Mira, who had ridden behind him, down as well. The birds tweeted as they slowly emerged from their night's rests and the sounds of chirping crickets died. I washed my hands in the cool water, having gripped the reins of the rutor for so long that deep indentations were imprinted in the skin.

"So, what made your mouthy friend set off on his own without you two?" Silvertail asked as he settled by the riverbank and rinsed out his sleeve, having finally consumed all of his liquid comfort. "I passed him on the way. I even made an effort to offer one of the rutor so he wouldn't have to make the rest of the journey on foot but he declined, stating that he'd rather see you two safely to the city than hinder by taking one of these gentle grazers. He is quite noble for one so irksome, isn't he?" Silvertail bellowed with a jolly laugh.

Rayloh was quite noble. I never had to question his loyalty and bravery. He had risked his life so that Mira and I would be safe. I stared at my hollow expression in the water as tiny fish swam around it, probably hoping to be tossed a free meal.

"I'm sure he'll find his way back, Alya," Silvertail said with a comforting tone as he set his hand on my back, standing behind me now with a sleeve full of water. "He knows these woods. He even knew exactly where to find you two. He didn't disclose what happened to make you all go your own ways but I'm sure it's nothing that can't be mended."

***

The sun was in mid-descent by the time we trotted out of the edgewoods upon the great stone bridge, our only pass into the city a pleasant sight to behold. The city's gates were still a pitiful display of lined logs against wooden flats, but a metal lining had been added for a little reinforcement. I heard at a distance the guard calling for the gates to be opened as we approached.

As we crossed the threshold into the city, the guards bowed their heads, glancing up at us, looking impressed that we had returned unscathed. We continued on through the black ring that was all but deserted except for the flutter of scavengers and the barking of dogs as we passed. I guess these occurrences pointed more to the fact the city had been emptying steadily for a while now. I wondered if they had a hole they dug under the wall that only they knew of, like the one the lads and I discovered. The blue ring was still without its former glory as I saw residents rushing about repairing their damaged homes.

The yellow ring had lost its flair of elegance as we traveled up the long path to the purple ring. I could see elves out in the front yards of their estates pulling weeds and chipping away at stone, tasks that I was accustomed to seeing being done by the Dwala. They looked up to Silvertail and me as we passed with dour faces that communicated blame and insult. Still, at the very least, the glory of the yellow ring's garden seemed to be slowly returning, large yellow ribbons the size of banners bearing horrid faces, probably meant to keep the fowl from nesting and picking off the food, hanging from wooden poles at the corners of the plot. Mira tapped me, pointing at her former flower plot, beaming at the beautiful arrangement that had been set where hers once was. They were quite beautiful; a series of rose bushes, a few finding strength to bloom where their siblings had had barely time to bud, showed beautifully in the sunlight, like little red and pink clouds.

When we reached the gates of the purple ring, the guards didn't greet us as the ones at the city gates had. Their widened eyes, stretching as if they had seen a ghost, and their quick whisper assured me that I was not expected to return from my journey into the edgewoods. They parted the gates, staring straight ahead as to not connect glances with Silvertail or me as we entered the purple ring. The trot of the rutor kept pace with my beating heart as we neared the palace. Silvertail gathered his pack and mine off of the backs of the rutor and with all of our belongings, we ascended the steps to the palace, leaving the rutor with a guard to return them to the stables.

The palace was cool and bustling, servants hanging sets of aged antlers that were used every year around spring during the Celebration of the Fawn—which, if not for Mira's clapping at the sight, I would have forgotten was tomorrow. Mira twirled around in the hall, the decorations so vibrant that they easily distracted her of the troubles she endured in the edgewoods. Just as she was about to fiddle her fingers into a wreath of pinecones, twigs, and berries, Madja's voice came hailing down from the grand staircase.

"They've returned! Oh, thank Olörun, they've returned." The news had obviously reached her, probably from one of the servants who spotted us from one of the windows.

I dashed up the stairs behind Mira who dove into Madja's open arms, wrapping her tiny body around our mother with all her might. Madja made no attempt to remain composed. She let out an agonizing cry, a mixture between sobbing, laughing, and screaming. Servants stopped in their tracks to stare, most after realizing what was happening, smiling with great congratulations while others sneered with their noses upturned.

I stood there smiling, happy that I could do this for Madja, happy that I hadn't let slip away one of the very lights in her life. She looked up at me, giant tears dripping down her robes as she mouthed the words "thank you" before beckoning me over with a wave to join in on the embrace. She wrapped one arm around me while holding Mira with the other as she kissed my forehead. And there we stood like some three-headed sobbing creature but I didn't care. I was home and all the pain that had been caused and all the changes that had passed didn't seem to matter anymore.

A large frame soon shadowed us, wrapping his arms around Madja and me. Dressed in the fine purple robes of the council, the ends of his hair trimmed and his face freshly shaved, was my father. For a moment, I wanted him to remove himself, to take whatever aims he had and to be gone with them, but there was no one to impress. The hall had emptied and a pang in my chest grew that wasn't the normal anger and resentment I felt towards him, but longing. He stared down at me and although he didn't say it, his eyes apologized for him. He wanted forgiveness and who was I to deny him? Almost simultaneously we bore into each other and quiet tears draped our family that was once broken but was now mended.

"Protector!" I heard a surprised voice call out from up the corridor. I released my family, who parted to allow me to face my beckoner.

"Prince Alag," I said in return, my voice containing no enthusiasm in seeing him. He was with his attendant, who still had a healing knot on his head, a few members of the council, and Silvertail, who had wasted no time in forging back to his former post, along with two of his charge. Alag nodded in return, then addressed my father.

"Are you coming, Meoltan?" My father lingered for a moment, staring at Alag with disdain but didn't utter a word before walking towards him. Madja, Mira, and I stood, watching him belittle my father like a pawn on a chessboard. Halfway, my father stopped and turned abruptly with certainty on his face. I didn't have to look at Madja to know her face was full of anguish and warning, but my father didn't heed.

"We're settling matters for the Celebration of the Fawn tonight. There are a few issues to address before the morrow." Alag's smile lingered but had transformed from amusement to forced composure at my father's unconformity. For whatever amusement he lost, I gained as I trotted up to meet my father.

"I would love to," I said. My father and I joined the procession following the arrogant brat.

Chapter Nineteen

We met in the Crystal Parlor since the judgment chambers along with the hidden arena had been destroyed. Guards were already inside lining the walls and although their training had taught them to be stoic, I could see the jolt of surprise as I came in. The edgewoods to them was a horrid place, one they had assumed would end a young she-elf easily. Alag's attendant passed out the agenda to the entire table, about a dozen of us present for the meeting at the time.

"Will we not wait for the rest to arrive?" A few of the council members gasped angrily at my questioning, and for a moment I couldn't fathom why until I recalled my lessons with Mournadam concerning royal etiquette. Alag answered nonetheless, although he did it in a way as if he weren't actually responding to me but making a general statement.

"While it is unfortunate that so many of our brothers were either lost in the tragedy that befell the city, are still healing, or—due to fear—had to resign," this being the part that was valuable to me, "I feel that we are more than capable to proceed with our 776th Celebration of the Fawn." The he-elves nodded in agreement, a few clapping at this affirmation from Alag. "As far as security measures, I'm sure that with Captain Silvertail here we will have no problem taking the proper precautions with his lower shelf that guard the city gates. I want this to be a time of celebration; a time to celebrate the commencement of a long period of peace. I feel the majority of your order can enjoy this celebration along with their families. As long as the gate is guarded, there is no need for any other provisions."

As Protector, I felt that the safety of the city was more my designation—or at the very least should involve my input—but then again, designations weren't required before considering the ruler of the city and the Protector were the same person. Still, I didn't disagree with Alag. The people of Wood Haven and the Dwala had left Keldrock and its surroundings, and although Cadon and his troop had done a great wrong to his siblings, Rayloh and me, they didn't pose any threat to the whole of Keldrock. The meeting finally ended after excited discussions of the pallet of meads and fruity wines that would be had. I didn't bother lingering with Alag and his cronies who were already commending him on his creative ideas. I thought now was a good as time as any to turn in with the sun beginning to set and our journey finally at an end.

"Alya!" I heard Silvertail call out as I was about to go. He jostled through the departing council members who huffed about being nudged out of the way. "I didn't want you to leave without your things." I reached for my bag, tossing its strap over my shoulder.

"My thanks to you, Captain. You didn't have to venture into the edgewoods with me and… you did." I blushed a little, turning away from his wrinkling smirk.

"Make no mention of it, Protector." He nudged me on the shoulder and made to leave but turned around quickly. "Do you think you'd be up for some training by the moonlight to get your mind off things? I could really use the company."

I could feel my head swaying and my body still ached from the pangs of the journey, but I couldn't deny him this one little thing when he had done so much for me. "Very well. Midnight." I tossed my bag to him with my bow and sheath sticking from its side. He caught it with a laugh and strode off.

My room was unchanged even down to my bed having remained unmade, the coverings distorted in the exact way I had left them before I departed for the Guerr's camp. With a sudden realization, I grabbed my housecoat and darted down the stairs and out into the streets to the purple ring's infirmary. I felt ashamed that I had let slip the wellbeing of Segun and hadn't checked on him as soon as I returned. I darted through the dimming streets, choosing to slip out through the west foyer, since it was common for it to be unattended. Gorgeous lamps flickered atop tall poles for tomorrow's celebration, keeping the darkness from enveloping the path.

The lights in the infirmary were out so I ran behind it to the housing quarters, high-quality living accommodations for those who were recovering from ailments and couldn't afford to be too far away from the medic. Most appeared to have never been inhabited by anyone, the royal and elites probably preferring the medic to come and stay in the palace than stoop to such unappealing levels as these wonderful homes. Only one house shined bright with light coming from the inside. I darted to the door, raising my fist to knock, when I heard hushed, disgruntled voices coming from inside.

"It doesn't make sense. What do you think it means? He won't let it go." It was a he-elf's voice.

"I think we should bide our time. Alya has returned. Perhaps if he spoke to—" replied a she-elf whose voice I recognized as belonging to Lady Kalowan, Segun's mother. The he-elf assumedly was his father.

"I won't be made a mockery of," he interrupted. "With the death of Sir Calo, our stores in the department of medicine are empty until another talent masters their gift well enough to better assist in this matter. It could all be some terrible dream for all we know. Who's to say that he's aware of all that came to pass while in the edgewoods or in the Guerr's camp? One thing I'm certain of is that Czar Icar will be dismissed from his post if my life depends on it."

"But what if what Segun says does prove true, Krunal?" Lady Kalawan inquired of her husband. "Tomorrow is the Celebration of the Fawn. It would be the perfect time for—"

"Alya!" I spun around only to receive a chest full of Segun diving into my arms for a hug. I squeezed him back, happy to see that he was so well that he was up and about. He winced a little before pulling away. "My back is still a little sore. Father has done a great job at mending it."

The door of the house shot open and Segun's parents stepped out, their faces stunned with worry. I knew they wondered if I had been listening, but they must have thought better of me because they graciously invited me in.

"It's great to see you've returned, Protector!" Lady Kalowan gushed. I hadn't seen her smile like this since Segun had left to train for the Unveiling.

"Just Alya is fine! No need for such formalities. Especially since the house of Evesong has been so kind to me and my family."

As Segun's mother went to the kitchen to fetch tea, his father led us into the elaborate common room. Lord Krunal was a tall elf although very lean—that much he and Segun had in common even though his son hadn't gained his full potential in height just yet.

"I'm quite pleased, Alya," said Lord Krunal. "Your venturing into the edgewoods and recovering your sister. Those closest to us worried that you had perhaps been lost."

"I wonder if those closest to you hoped that that would in fact turn out to be true," I said with a quiet laugh that was simply returned by the Evesongs with nervous smiles.

"We wanted to thank you for coming to the aid of our Segun, of course." There was a tone of gloom and surprising anger as he said this. "I'm sure you were just as enraged as we were to discover all that occurred while he was in the Guerr's company. If it—"

"Would you mind if Segun and I have a word?" The room was still for a moment as the Evesongs examined one another, slightly put off by this request.

"Very well," said Lord Krunal as he gathered his cooling tea and headed into the kitchen with his wife, closing the door behind them.

Segun still had a bright smile on his face, his lips curling around his scalding tea.

"It's great to see you well, friend. Your father is a great medic."

Segun nodded. "I hope to be as skillful as him one day. That is, if I'm ever released from the service of the Guerr." His face lost its jovialness. "Father received a letter only two days ago saying that as soon as I am full recovered—or in five days from the morrow, whichever comes sooner—I am to return to the fortress."

"I wouldn't worry so much about that. If anything as Protector, my footing in your affairs concerning the Guerr has some influence. You and Rayloh will not be going back to that awful place and if I can, I want to recover all of these so-called ticks from the brig." Segun smiled wide at this, and although I wasn't completely certain that I held any influence or power to make this possible, I vowed I would make it so. I took a deep breath. "Can you tell me what happened? While you were in the brig?" Unlike Rayloh, Segun seemed quite interested in divulging his experiences under the large black citadel.

"I ended up there after refusing to fight one of the older lads. I felt my best fit would be in the infirmary, which my lieutenant found quite hysterical. So he put me against Rayloh. And—"

"Rayloh refused to fight you," I interrupted, proud that my two comrades refused to engage with affairs so barbaric, but Segun's expression returned to me angry.

"No. I'm sad to say that isn't so." He slumped down in his chair as if he were somehow still in the brig at this very moment. "I told him I didn't want to fight but he didn't care. He called me weak, and then that's all I can remember. I woke up in the brig. My head was bandaged with an old piece of a blanket from one of the dirty spares they had down in that cellar."

I lost my breath for a moment. Segun's words were hard to believe. Rayloh wouldn't attack his friends. We were family, regardless of blood. Perhaps Rayloh's encounter in the edgewoods had changed him. Perhaps something different enveloped him after the veil fell.

"Is that what your father feels you shouldn't share with me?" I whispered, assuming that Lord Krunal was probably at the kitchen door listening as intently as I had been outside the front door.

"No." He hushed his voice and leaned in. "I asked for an audience with Czar Icar. By now Rayloh had joined our cohort but kept to himself, which I can't say I had a problem with after what he did to me." Segun clenched his teeth, rage boiling in his quivering lips. His eyes were beginning to water and I suspected that what he was about to tell me would make me do the same. "The heat in that cellar was unbearable. I presented myself to what he thought to be my willingness to adhere to the culture of the Guerr, but when he found out it wasn't…" Segun closed his eyes, pausing before he continued, "he punished me."

Segun took a sip of his now-cooled tea, drinking half of its contents before setting it to the side on one of the exquisitely detailed side tables.

"He wrestled me until he had my hands bound. Then strung me to one of the beams. He didn't care about my cries or the agony or the blood." He gulped hard. "He beat me until I was quiet. I faded in and out and there he left me to hang. I don't know if mere minutes passed or hours, but I had begun to come to when I heard voices. 'They have all left the city. Most of their lot have abandoned our cause,' one of the voices said. 'If we are going to act, we have to do it soon.' The other voice answered, 'I'm with you. I have always been with you, but we've run out of time and the Protector still exists. You don't think she'll pose a problem?' They sounded worried. 'She doesn't know her full power,' the first voice responded. 'You're right. I'll think of something. In the meantime, ensure that the beasts are prepared. Then I will ensure the plan is carried through.'"

Segun picked up his cup of tea and finished it off. "I slipped out again after that, everything fading back to black. I awoke here, Master Tali over my bed. She told me everything," he said, perking up again. "How you rescued me and how you went into the edgewoods with Silvertail and Rayloh but wanted to ensure I was taken care of." I smiled slightly, feeling that I didn't deserve the praise.

"Sorry to interrupt," Segun's father cracked the door, slipping through awkwardly. "Segun has to have a healing session before he turns in for the night. If you'll let me get on with it, you can—"

"Oh, that's quite alright." I stood up, leaving my cup of tea untouched. "I just wanted to make sure he was doing well. He has some strength in him." I let myself out, stepping into the misty night.

Segun had given me a significant case to mull. It didn't make sense. What beasts could these voices be alluding to and what plan did they speak of? I knew a lot of people wanted me gone, wanted my position eliminated, but it sounded somewhat threatening and at the same time a little far-fetched. Perhaps he just overheard the Czar discussing something privately with Alag; something that he didn't want me to know. I recalled Silvertail's inkling. He believed Alag to be false and after this, I couldn't say I didn't either, even though Segun's story was hard to believe. If a conversation did happen between Icar and Alag, then I needed to be involved. I couldn't be ignored any longer.

I burst into the north wing of the palace, guards rustling in their armor as I brushed past them. I quickly ascended the red-carpeted steps and marched until I reached the foyer of Alag's suite. I examined the elaborate stained doors, trying to guess at which one Alag was behind. A mixture of heavy breathing and panting caught my ear coming from behind a door the end of a corridor. I knocked softly but the heavy breathing continued. I knocked a little harder and the panting on the other side immediately stopped. I then heard the sounds of quick movement across the flooring and decided now was as good a time as any to enter and to see what exactly was happening.

I opened the door wide, a blast of warm air surrounding me as a young maiden wrapped in a thin sheet who I had seen assisting in the kitchens and washroom swept by me, attempting to shield her face. I shook in disgust as I turned to face an arrogant Alag slouching under his bed coverings shirtless.

"You ought to wait until you're received before entering someone's private chambers." He began to lift his elegant coverings and just as he was beginning to bare all, I turned my head, clenching my eyes shut until I heard the whiff of his robes being put on his body.

"You've spoken to the czar, have you?" I said accusingly, my eyes now glaring at him, my expression still contorted in disgust.

"Perhaps," he responded, raking his long hair to the back of his head, letting it fall behind his bulging shoulders. "What's it to you?"

"It's no matter," I said, suddenly confounded as to why I had ventured up to his quarters in the first place. "Whatever you have planned tomorrow, I'll be ready."

"What in Olörun's name are you going on about?" he asked, approaching me with inquiring eyes. "Did he tell you—" He stopped abruptly, realizing he had said too much.

"So you admit it! You want me dead. You wished I had never been deemed Protector," I said, spitting my words like daggers.

"What? That's absurd," he retorted.

"Oh, don't stifle me. You've been pigheaded and black-hearted since I set foot in the purple ring and now you've got some scheme in the works with one of the last powers that you haven't managed to put an end to."

"Watch your tongue, Alya!" he snapped, but I continued on, fury filling my insides. He turned away, leaning against a dresser, with a mirror propped on top of it, alongside an assortment of glass vials of what I would assume to be perfumes, scented oils, and body pastes.

"Protector. You will address me as Protector, you rat. How dare you deem yourself worthy to cast judgment on me..."

"That's enough, Alya." He didn't look at me but continued staring down at the dresser, rage evident in his clenching fists.

"I'm not finished!" I screeched. "Tomorrow, if anything goes awry, you won't have the Dwala, or the warriors from the woods, or even the city's leaders you control, but you will have me, the very one who wields your grandfather's blessing, to worry about. Is that what you have against me? That the Light rather have me, a she-elf, instead of the likes of you?"

With one swift movement, the mirror was shattered, pieces of glass springing in the air and across the stone floor. I jumped, never seeing Alag this upset. His eyes were watering and swelled with emotion as his breath became straggled and harsh. I stared at him with a mixture of fury, surprise, and even fear. For a moment, he stared at the pieces on the ground, his chest rising and falling quickly, then looked up at me with an unforgivable rage in his eyes.

"Leave," he muttered, his voice deep and rumbling. I wanted nothing more than to stay and make him feel all at once the pain he brought upon me during these long months of being pushed aside as if I didn't matter. But as much pain and anger as I felt, a stronger feeling of remorse overshadowed all in this moment.

I turned and left without another word. When I reached my chambers, I slammed the door behind me and dove into my bed, drowning my face in my pillows. I let out a powerful scream, releasing all of my bitterness, fury, and sadness into the luxurious bedding. I was angry and hurt and I had let it boil within me, constantly dodging it, but now it had broken free. Then suddenly, like a wisp of sudden chill, I thought of Rayloh, who I wasn't sure had made it back to the city. He who had set out with me into the edgewoods to retrieve my sister had required nothing to do so. I continued to cry until I couldn't anymore, the tears dampening my pillow, until I faded into a peaceful, restful sleep, and with it the promise to meet Silvertail at midnight.

Chapter Twenty

"Alya! Come on! Wake up!" I heard Mira skirting around my room. I was exhausted in more than one way from the previous night's events.

The scene with Alag had been horrible and I didn't want to take the chance at crossing paths with him during the Celebration of the Fawn today. I had overreacted and let my resentment get the best of me. I still shuddered to think of his furrowed face glaring at me over the broken shards of the mirror.

As if to reveal some marvelous exhibition, Mira ripped back the curtains of my large bay window, allowing the morning sunshine to cover my entire room. I didn't want to get up, but I knew I had to. I had no official part in the celebration as Alag had made sure to mention during the council meeting but felt that it would still be most appropriate that I showed that I supported the people, as if my defending the city during the Unveiling wasn't convincing enough.

"Alya! Get up, why don't you. We'll miss the spring prance, and Miliki's father bought her sister their very own fawn," Mira whined. Miliki was her best friend and since my family had joined me in the purple ring, she had only seen her a few times. Still, this wasn't reason enough to get me out of bed.

"Why can't Madja take you?" I returned with a half yawn.

"She said she doesn't feel well. She said you would take me. You have to, Mira. Madja said." I sat up, staring at Mira, remembering the day before when Madja was a picture of health. I remember her bronze skin shimmering in the day, so radiant and neatly put together by her attendants.

"What exactly is wrong with her?" I asked, trying not to sound overly worried.

"She didn't say," Mira replied. "She just said she wasn't feeling well."

My stomach lurched suddenly, and I felt as if the worry had transferred from my head down into my stomach, making me queasy. This had happened before. I tried to convince my mind that it wasn't like the courts who had died after claims of suddenly becoming sick. I forced myself out of bed, trying to remain calm.

Mira perked up. "So you'll go with me?"

I looked at her begging eyes beaming up at me. "Of course. It'd be my pleasure," I said, gripping my side, trying to balance myself as I fumbled to the door. "Why don't you help me by picking out a dress from the wardrobe." Mira clapped her hands together excitedly and before I could get clear of my chamber, she was flipping through the garments.

I started up the hall still clenching my stomach. I nearly fell into my parents' chambers without announcing my arrival to find Madja standing in the middle of the floor, her elegant robe swaying as if she was starting to go about doing something or simply pacing about her room. She looked astonished as if she weren't expecting to see anyone today. Clothes were spread about along with an assortment of shoes and undergarments.

"Good morn, my dear," she said continuing to float. Madja, who normally haunted us with the importance of keeping a clean house, was in the midst of what seemed to be a small whirlwind. "Don't mind the mess. I just got a little upset."

"Was it Father?" I asked.

She sat down, not confirming or denying this assumption, but I didn't inquire any further. The lurching in my stomach dissipated upon finding that she wasn't in fact sick. I settled down next to her, wrapping my arms around her, and for the first time I didn't feel like a child. Her head fell on my shoulder and time seemed to stand still as we sat, not speaking, just warm in each other's embrace.

"I'll take Mira into the square for the celebration." Madja looked up at me, gratitude in her eyes. "You take today for yourself."

"There's no doubt indeed. If anyone denies it, their name is liar because you are indeed the Protector. *My* beautiful protector." She stroked my cheek gently before rising, picking up a long yellow shawl from the floor as she did.

I smiled at this and began making my way to the door. Just as I was about to exit, she stopped me. "And Alya. Don't worry about yesterday. What happened between you and Alag doesn't matter. I'm sure he'll reap his own downfall," she said with a wink, which I returned with a hesitant nod. I wasn't surprised at how fast news traveled through the halls of the palace, as grand as it was. For Madja to know about the altercation so early meant it had to be the top of the news for the maidservants, attendants, and officials. It's not as if it were a quiet disagreement either.

As I returned down the hall, I noticed the patterns and ornaments as the decorations that met me in the corridor. Antlers were mounted to the walls, and pyrocones from the red pines that could hold fire without burning up or passing it along to something to burn other things sat hooked under the antlers, shimmering like little stars, filling the hall with the smell of the woods. Colorful streamers of purple, gold, and cream wove in and out of each other on the high ceiling; tiny flower petals, and smooth, oval shaped leaves, that had been cast up in the air, no doubt by some incredible talent related to my own, fluttered on their own, twirling down up and back down again.

I returned to my room to find Mira sitting on my bed beaming with delight next to her chosen dress, as a maidservant picked up the discarded garments off of the floor. The dress Mira had chosen wasn't at all what I expected. Instead of something with an immense amount of ribbons and bows or rainbow assorted gems, she had picked out a simple gown of white fitted to my arms and chest but flowed out at the ends as if I were some heavenly host. I slipped off my night garments and put it on, letting the material caress and flow down my body like a shower of silk. Mira clapped with approval and I myself had to say that she made a very mature choice.

"I found it tucked between a fluffer dress and a blooming gown. Thought you probably hadn't thought to wear it or seen it for that matter, having been smothered between those two tents," she said with a giggle. I rubbed my necklace, its silver detailing and green emerald accents adding to the beauty of whatever I wore as it always did. I twirled in the mirror, stopping just as I was about to twirl again after seeing the eyes of the snake around my neck twinkle as if coming to life, but I thought better of it. Today was a going to be a good day. I knew it.

We moved along the hall, stopping at the kitchen for a plum cake, Mira urging me along as if we were extraordinarily late for some formal affair. Her dress was a summertime yellow, the color nearly as bright as the sun made her a little jolly spectacle. She had her hair curled, falling in little spirals down her back. I ate the plum cake as we went, careful not to drop any of the purple jam-topper onto my gown. It satisfied my appetite for the moment and although I might have enjoyed a more filling breakfast after all that had happened, I couldn't deny that I was beginning to feel the same eagerness that Mira was experiencing.

We began making our way to the gates and already ahead of us were a few maidservants, attendants, political figures, and other residents of the purple ring with excited elflings. Nearly all of those we passed acknowledged me; many bowed toward me and smiled at Mira. No doubt word had spread—just as much as other news—about my brave journey into the edgewoods to retrieve my sister. As much as I didn't care what these hollow-hearted traditionalists thought of me, it was a welcome pleasure to have them beam at me with admiring eyes instead of shunning me with disapproving glares. I remembered Rayloh and it seemed that he should be here; dressed in fine robes, walking the fine streets of the purple ring to have a well-earned retreat with friends and family. The sadness brought on by his absence became even more vivid as Mira and I came upon the Evesongs approaching the purple ring's gates, with them a tiny toddling companion.

Segun waved and Mira darted to him, wrapping her arms around him before turning to stroke a shy, staggering fawn no more than a few weeks old with a tan coat with freckles of white. Segun, in order to be able to identify his fawn from the many others he'd encounter today, had tied a turquoise scrap of cloth around its neck. The Evesongs waited for us to join them before we clustered at the purple ring's gates, waiting for the next round to open. At the gate, record was being taken by a guard of who all were leaving the purple ring, as families and friends conversed happily about the day's events. A few other sprites had fawns as well, some of them a little older than Segun's, which had already begun their juvenile delinquency, nipping at their owner's robes and prancing about, yipping as they sauntered unnaturally on their hind legs at one another.

Segun passed off his pet's leading rope to Mira who happily obliged. "Father got him for me for cooperating during our healing sessions," he explained. "He said I was quite the lad and expected me to be more than unwilling." I couldn't imagine being well mannered was hard for Segun, being the best mannered out of Rayloh, him and me.

"Well, he is beautiful. I wish I would have gotten one so that Mira would have one to play with." The Celebration of the Fawn celebrated the season of spring and the coming of summer as well as all the triumphs of being youthful and the growth that comes with the oncoming seasons, a perfect holiday for young elves.

"Names please?" I turned to receive a younger guard, somewhat thin and freshly new to the post, looking down at a book, scribbling aggressively, obviously on call today because the higher ranked line that normally held the gate was relocated for more crucial tasks by order of Alag. He seemed annoyed that he had to stand watch at the gate alone, his voice drenched in forced amicableness.

"Alya and Mira from the house of Lightstar," I recited politely. He looked up with widened eyes, his scribbling brought to a halt as his eyes ran down my body and back up again, stopping on the top of my head.

"Oh, Protector," he said with a cracked whimper. "It is my pleasure. Very well. Uh…" His brown face had turned a subtle red and for a moment, I thought I saw him about to bow but thought better of it.

"No, the pleasure is mine," I said with a smile, pleased to see that some held reverence to my name. "And you are?"

"Kurtsley, my lady."

"Well, nice to meet you, sir." He lingered for an uncomfortable moment as if he wanted to say something but before he could, Segun decided it best that the guard move along with his duties, eager to get to the celebration.

"Segun Evesong," he said loud and clear, drawing out each syllable, so that Kurtsley the guard could remember he was supposed to be recording the names of those leaving the purple ring. "And Lord Krunal and Lady Kalowan Evesong." Kurtsley wrote fast, his official demeanor returning. "Oh, and this is Cortis," Segun said gleefully, pointing to the fawn, which Mira ushered forward slightly as if the guard needed to make an inspection of the little critter. With a small smirk and a pat on the fawn's head, Kurtsley moved on to take a few more names of those behind us before heading back up to the gate.

"He was excited to meet the Protector, huh?" Segun said, nudging me softly in the ribs. I nodded unenthusiastically as if it were nothing but it meant a lot that there were some citizens who saw me worthy of my position.

"Make way for the gates!" Kurtsley called from a miniature turret.

The screech of metal pinned the air, celebrative cheers erupting as our passage was finally granted. The golden gates gleamed under the morning sun as a beautiful song and the sounds of instruments far up the path rode the calm winds. Maidens danced with beads and clappers, tiny cymbal-like instruments, as young lads pranced around on flutes and tooters. The path from the purple ring to the yellow ring was lined with streamers that hung from the trees. Tiny paper lanterns holding bright star beetles, their beaming lights still blinking in the bright of day, swayed ever so lightly. The streets were lined with families and vendors, some sitting in their yards or atop ruins from the Unveiling, seeming unperturbed by the past to let this day go gloomily. Revelers shot little sparklers into the air that cracked open with sparkles shaped like beautiful fluttering butterflies, buzzing bees, or some other symbol of spring. Little lads I recognized from the Remni and the surrounding estates waved as we passed with their new litters of puppies falling closely behind them. The smells of pastries and cakes, sweet syrups on fruit, and honey filled the air along with the roasting of vegetables and the simmer of rice-based stews. Flags fluttered from poles being carried by elven children heading to the blue ring's square.

Even Alag who I wasn't so keen on seeing was out among the crowds of the citizens of Keldrock with only his wormy assistant at his side. Before I could avert my eyes from him, he caught sight of me and I accidentally smiled, but before I could recover this embarrassment, he turned and continued on with his mingling and I thought it best to get as far away as possible from him. Games of all sorts were being played in the blue ring and the once-closed shops seemed to be up and thriving again. I saw

Mistress Colar, the seamstress who had made the dress for my birthday celebration, who beckoned me over immediately. She seemed to be in great spirits. She insisted on giving me, Mira, and Lady Kalowan a few scarves, which we took delightfully, and made us promise to tell those who complimented them where we got them.

After a game of dung bags where we tossed bags of gravel into variously sized holes in a board unpleasantly called the crappers, Mira and I parted from the Evesongs to find her friend Miliki. Mira grabbed my hand, guiding us through the crowd as I nodded to a lot of familiar faces, some I had seen with such discord so many months ago during my hearing. I saw Destili in the distance, an attention-seeking sponge from my school rotation, who I knew had seen me but wanted nothing more than to make me feel insignificant so dared not turn and greet me. I smiled at the thought as Mira screamed with glee, having found her friend Miliki. She let go of my hand and darted to her, dodging through the crowd with me close behind. Miliki was with her sister, Cornishel, a slightly portly miss from my rotation, who received subpar evaluations in our class. She was nice nonetheless and made a point to welcome me in conversation as our younger sisters admired their black-coated fawn with a small white patch around one of its amber eyes, a breed I had not yet come to know.

As we lined up at a venue, purchasing cakes with honey and powdered sugar, a clash of a cymbal pierced the multitude of conversations and laughter, causing all to fall quiet. It was followed by another clash as a series of colorful ribbons streamed overhead. The crowd parted as the Jalla, a group of beautiful entertainers, made their way to the sunken platform in the center of the blue ring's square. The smallest of sprites including Mira and Miliki made their way quickly down the stairs to get a decent view of the performance. Petals danced through the air and to my amazement I realized that I could conjure the same talent, remembering one of my favorite lessons with Master Tali. The petals floated together to form does and bucks prancing about each other, courting, and then, joining them, little fawns. Then the petals departed from one another and sprinkled about the floor of the sunken platform. With one last resounding break from the cymbal, the Jalla began.

Their performance, accompanied by flutes and harps, filled my senses, as images of blooming flowers, chirping chicks, and clear streams ran through my mind. The ground trembled and my vision blurred a moment before coming back. Now I saw fluttering butterflies and dashing rabbits. The ground trembled again and I could hear the disgruntled sounds from a few around me, but the visions came humming back. Now I saw large green fields with flickering star beetles against a purple-hued sky. The ground shook again and the visions dispersed. The Jalla had stopped dancing and were looking around as the flutist stopped their playing and the harpist stood up, holding her instrument to keep it from toppling over, as the ground trembled again. Then it began to shake. Unsure faces peered around at one another, some looking questioningly at me as if my being Protector could somehow explain this phenomenon. Suddenly, a shower of cement and dirt shot into the air from the platform, spraying the spectators. Blood-curdling screams stunned my ears as panicking citizens rushed to get as far away from the platform as possible. I watched a leotard-clad Jalla dancer fly through the air and collide with a flagpole. That was enough to send everyone into frenzy as more dirt continued to spray the air and dancers scrambled past, having escaped whatever was in the platform. Over the horrid screams, I could hear my name. It was Mira calling for me.

I began shoving my way through, pushing over crazed citizens. I was almost upon the steps when it shot into the air, black as night, the same piercing eyes from my dreams long ago that I hadn't seen since the Unveiling. The same that I had seen turn friendly and at once, so cold and frightening. It landed on a vendor's cart, crushing it to bits, as food and wood exploded through the air. Its eyes were glassy as if a dingy shield were over them but they were unmistakably the same black slits over vibrant yellow.

It stared at me, its large eyes not darting or moving away. My surroundings seemed to spread away from me, the once-crowded area clearing to avoid the beast's and my standoff. It bore into me with vengeful eyes as if I myself had done something to wrong it. Its slits were wider, more spanned than the ones I became familiar with during the Unveiling. They were altogether different.

"Alya!"

Segun dashed between me and the mongrowl as it steadily inched forward, baring its sharp teeth. Segun, with a stake in hand, jabbed it in the direction of his face in an attempt to drive it away, but it seemed only to irritate it all the more. With one swipe from its apish paws, it grabbed the stake and slung it halfway across the square. Segun remained in chivalry, using his body to shield mine, but I could feel him shaking with fear. Screams continued to blow through the air like booms of growing thunder. With only paces to go before he was upon us, his lips curled, drool dripping from its snout, the beast stood on its hind legs and let out a howl while beating on its hairy chest. He turned away from us, its great black bearlike nose pointing with determination towards the edgewoods. Then like eruptions throughout the city came more howls responding to the mongrowl.

I grabbed Segun's hand and darted down a side path away from the beast. As we dodged through alleys, I could hear the snarls of beasts and the return of screams. All I kept saying to myself was that I was the Protector. I shouldn't have been running, but what was I to do with no weapons? Why had Alag relieved the guard? Perhaps he wanted this to happen. I couldn't believe I felt sorry for him. Deep in thought, without noticing where I was leading Segun, we ended up at a closed end. By the time we realized it and turned around, the humped, bulging shadow of the snarling mongrowl was edging the corner and soon came into full view.

I looked around, panicking, not wanting to die this way. Of all the times death had almost taken me, this was the most unnerving. For I remembered the vivid dreams of lamp-like eyes in the pitch of night and remember seeing Niegi's body tossed in the air and its lightning speed as it raced through the woods. Segun grabbed me, wrenching his arms around me as if to protect me but before the mongrowl could take any more steps, from a nearby roof came someone I would never have expected. Draped in scarlet and blue robes was Alag with a spear in hand, landing right between Segun and me and the beast intent on bringing about our end. With one jolt of his spear, he ended the beast, driving the point into its shoulder and wrenching it around in its neck. He yanked it from the lifeless mongrowl and urged Segun and I forward and up a side street.

He ushered us along without speaking, not even to give direction, Segun and I sprinting breathlessly as we edged further into the blue ring. I was utterly confused. Surely Alag couldn't have been behind this attack on the city if he had saved me. He had killed the very beast that would ensure his return to power. I wasn't sure how the Light passes from person to person but if it was by proximity, he was closest. No one would have known either except for Segun who with a second thrust from Alag would have come to an end, but the prince didn't do any of this. He stopped and turned to us with wide eyes of the utmost seriousness and spoke.

"Continue on east. You're just upon the fort of the Guards of Candor. Tell them what has happened and to come armed and ready." Another howl from a few streets over caused all three of us to jump in fright. "Hurry now! Don't delay!" I turned with Segun ready to dash away. "And Alya!" I looked back, hoping that of all times, Alag wasn't choosing now to make a snide remark or tear me apart with an insult about having to save me. "We'll be needing you to come back armed, Protector." And with no more than a very subtle smirk, he darted away, using his spear to row him back on top of the roofs, and disappeared from sight.

Segun and I continued on, the sounds of screams blurred with the cries of retaliation, the crumbling of brick and stone, and the snarls and barks from the mongrowls. I looked back once as we made our way out into the path that led directly to the Guards of Candor's fort. Many of them had heard the disturbance, having chosen to take this day and rest instead being around a crowd of celebrating citizens. A few darted past me on horses, but most were still scrambling around to prepare, this event catching them off guard. The officers that had families and were likely the most highly trained chose not to live in the fort, so it was important that I retrieved weaponry for anyone else who wanted to take part in the efforts of defending the city. I gathered some spears, tucking them under my arm.

"Here's a wagon and hitch," Segun shouted, nodding, his hands filled with metal rods, spears, and a few arrows he had gathered around their training arena.

I tossed the spears into the wagon before sprinting over to the stables where a few guards were beginning to trot off astride a few does that were smaller than most that stemmed from the breed. Which could mean most likely one thing. My fears were realized once I peered into the stables and saw that not a single animal lay in wait. Still, time couldn't be wasted, and I gathered a few more minor weapons in a shattered barrel, some pitchforks, hoes, and spokes. I cut across the fort's inner yard to the cart where Segun awaited. After I quickly explained the situation, he grabbed the hitches and began pulling the cart in the buck's stead. I quickly placed the weapons and items I got from the stables onto the wagon and assisted Segun at the rear.

It was an intermediate feat for the most part; the carriage and its high wheels allowed our efforts to not be fully resolved. We attempted once to go through side streets, allowing us quicker and more covert passage than the main road, but the constantly jostling spears and rods and the tight fit of the cart made it a real hassle. So with great reluctance, we decided to keep to the main road. The incline recessed in our favor and soon we were simply ushering the cart. We could hear fighting and the barks of the mongrowl and every so often the cry of a citizen meeting their end. *Get to the square. They need you in the square.*

With every step, I pushed harder until I could see the overhanging arch above the road and a high raised flag that marked the blue ring's square. I rushed to the front of the cart with Segun, who was using all his strength to get the cart to our destination, and helped him pull. The cart clattered along against the sounds of louder war cries and snarled growls. I could now see the runes etched into the wood of the overhang as warriors darted from its mouth with panicked but determined expressions on their faces. A bigger, more brutish mongrowl than the one I had seen before emerged through the archway behind the fleeing guards, ripping it from the ground like some garden marker before slinging it with such excessive force that it toppled a nearby cottage. Realizing the significant difference in size between the two beasts, I knew at once that the one sent before was no more than a disposable scout.

"Weapons!" shouted a guard who had blood splattered on his uniform caused by a nasty bite mark on the side of his stomach. He toppled over as he said this, breathing heavily.

His comrades grabbed the spears that lay in our wagon and immediately began casting them at the beast. Those who managed to even get their spears close to hitting the mongrowl had them merely swatted away by the raging beast. The beast pounded its chest, roaring loudly, sending shivers and uncertainty through the discomforted guards.

"Fall behind the line, Protector," shouted the guard who was grimacing in pain from the mongrowl bite. "There's nothing any of us can do now. We must retreat to the fort."

The mongrowl's eyes shifted behind their glassy allure, and it was as if it were listening to something we couldn't hear. Even its ears perked in response. Suddenly, its gaze shifted to me, digging into my skin. I turned immediately, deeming the injured guard's words as a better course, but by the time I had placed my footing in the opposite direction, the mongrowl had me within its grasp, feet above the ground as it reared on its hind legs, glaring up at me. Its ears perked again, eyes returning to fuller slits of pitch black, but just as quickly as it had halted in this odd stance, it was interrupted by a loud shout from a distance. Suddenly, an arrow spliced through its throbbing wrist, causing the mongrowl to wrench in pain, swinging its arm violently while letting out high-pitched whimpers. The beast fell to the ground and so did I.

Another thud hit the ground alongside me, and I was surprised to see a person robed from head to toe in black except for the space of their eyes. I was utterly confused as they scrambled to their feet, but before they could dart off, another arrow came soaring through the air into the chest of the figure in black, causing them to once again tumble to the ground. Galloping with all speed was Silvertail and his rutor, bow and a sheath on his person and on the buck's back was my bag, the end of my bow sticking out of its slightly parted opening. Silvertail flipped back its flap to grab the bow and with its sheath, tossed it to me so that it landed at my feet like a gift from the heavens. I picked it up, feeling all my fear tuck behind the certainty that had demanded my conscience's attention. I looked up to Silvertail with the impulse to hug him and thank him but before I could, he assured me that none of that would be necessary.

"Keep your gratitude. Next time you'll remember to keep our meetings, won't you? I might be too enraged after being stood up to save your life." He cracked a small smile. "Now let's see about saving the city, Protector."

Chapter Twenty-One

On the rutor, Silvertail and I entered into the blue ring's square where chaos reigned. Bodies ranging from the beautiful Jalla dancers and overtaken spectators to newborn fawns and noble steeds having died alongside their riders lay in every direction. Blood formed in runny puddles on the floor of the sunken platform, gathering in rivets where the dirt had been overturned. I noticed among the lost a few others wrapped in all black—most likely, just as the former had been on the blue ring's path, the riders of mongrowls.

Along with Alag, who had managed to lessen the numbers by taking out two more large mongrowls, heading the charge, we soon were making some headway. One mongrowl we gathered in a corner. It was cowering, its floppy ears falling back along its back. A half dozen guards and some he-elves who had gathered what they could from their nearby homes jolted spears and makeshift weapons at the beast, which it timidly swatted at. I looked at its darting, bulbous eyes, round and begging, as a guard raised his spear to finish the deed. I remembered the mongrowl who helped me in the Chamber of Light. I recalled in the edgewoods how I let the young mongrowl feel my intentions, how its eyes turned from narrow slits to wide and welcoming. The guard lunged forward, the point of the spearhead just a few inches from the mongrowl's shuddering neck. I couldn't let this happen.

It wasn't throbbing at the mouth or snarling, or even gritting its teeth but cowering like an overgrown puppy. *It must die,* I heard a flickering, hissing voice say in my head, just as clear as if standing right behind me. *It's just a mongrowl.* The guard crept nearer to the terrified creature and I turned my eyes. Somehow this death was different than the others that came before it.

"Stop!" I opened my eyes to find my body had somehow found itself at the side of the guard and my hand was wrapped around the spear. The guard, with utter shock, backed away, a confused expression on his face, leaving me to face the cowering mongrowl. I turned to face it, its searching eyes watching me, unsure why the guard who was about to skewer its neck had now retreated behind this odd young she-elf.

I looked back around at Silvertail who had his bow and arrow ready as he sat astride the rutor who seemed to be just as intrigued and confused by my sudden outburst as my kin. Silvertail simply stared at me, his brows furrowed, surely debating whether he should send his arrow straight between the eyes of the once-volatile beast. I felt altogether ashamed that— although the voice was in my head—I had agreed with it. I had, just as Destili had described the women who were banished to the edgewoods as "only Dwala." The same bitter taste that brought me against her, I now felt about myself.

"It's alright." I said clearly, as spectators watched my standoff against the mongrowl. I wasn't sure if I was saying it to Silvertail, the beast, or trying to convince myself that everything would turn out just fine, but in truth I wasn't sure what I was doing. I stretched out my hand, my fingers quivering.

I slowly stepped forward, my eyes averted. I could hear hushed grunts and startled gasps coming from the witnesses behind me. It took more tries than one, but finally I brought my eyes to its own just as my fingers, then palm, pressed against its cold, wet nose. *You have to be open. Let them see you. Let them know you.* I remembered telling myself this when I was faced with the mongrowl in the edgewoods, and it was only a sudden movement away from tearing me to shreds. Instead, it gave its life to save the city. The least I could do was spare any of its kin that I could, because they deserved life just as much as we Keldrons did and they, just like us, were capable of great harm but also great love. I curved my arm around its furry jaw, scratching, digging my fingers under its thick, black mane. Slowly, as if it were unsure whether or not my kindness was a trick, a long, sloppy tongue emerged from its lips and licked my face, leaving it covered with saliva. I laughed, patting it again as its eyes engulfed me in their golden yellow.

It shot into my ears, a sound so piercing that it enraged me beyond any annoyance that Mira, Destili, or even Alag could summon. I stared at the beast before me, wanting nothing more than for it to take me far from here. The same thing seemed to be happening to the beast. Could it hear the same thing that I could? Did it want to take me away as well? Its eyes became slits of black again, his hair raised, its lips curled into a snarl, its teeth gnashed against a hoarse but powerful roar, but for some odd reason, as the guards behind me backed away in fear, it sounded like the sweetest sound, overpowering the annoying pinging sound that dwindled with each snarled bark the mongrowl made. I opened my arms wide, taking in deep breaths as the mongrowl continued to growl, its eyes now keen on me. The world around me became nothing more than a distant light moving in a blur. I seemed to be bobbing in air, light as a feather. Buildings flew past my eyes, then cottages, then trees. Then everything stopped as I was laid down on the ground. Everything was now coming into focus. The piercing sound had stopped and the mongrowl was whimpering, looking about as if it were just as confused as I was, before darting off into the edgewoods.

I sat up and held my palm to my forehead, my brain feeling like runny cream waiting to become solid. I turned to look over my shoulder and found myself at the foot of a hollowed-out potbellied tree. Rayloh, Segun, and I called this the base, the place we used for our hideout during our ventures into the edgewoods. I heard footsteps approaching, crunching on the forest floor. Soft drops of water tapped at my face, pecking my eyelashes and the edge of my nose. The sky had turned a murky mix of gray and blue, which I hadn't anticipated given how the day had been so kind before. I could hear the footsteps drawing nearer, now running, and appearing in the small clearing in front of the base like a ghost was Meca, his eyes watering and wide with fear.

"Meca!" I shouted in joy before piloting over to him and grabbing him in my arms. I felt his tiny frame quivering. I heard the crunch of more footsteps off in the distance.

"It's too late. They are coming." His eyes were darting around the woods. Like a deathly assassin, I took my bow from across my back, and an arrow from my quiver and placed it on the string, ready for release.

"Who's coming?" My eyes continued darting around, the head of my arrow following. "Meca?"

I turned to find him backing away slowly, tears now streaming down his face. "I'm sorry, Alya," he sputtered. I opened my mouth to respond but before I could, he turned toward the base and screamed, "She's over here!"

He backed away from me, his eyes darting around as the sounds of movement in the forest drew nearer and nearer. From all sides of the base emerged figures like the ones in the city draped in black uniforms with nothing more than their eyes revealed. The last to come forth, a burning torch in hand which they slammed into the soft ground in front of the base, pulled his mask down from his mouth and from over his head to reveal a sweaty-haired boy, slightly smaller than the others. He smiled, thin lips prickled with beads of sweat peeling back.

"You won't get away with this, Cadon." I pointed my arrow so that it would pierce him square in the chest but as I turned, his company, who were much larger and brutish, drew out swords, daggers, and crossbows. Even Meca pulled out a dagger, although his daring was absent, unlike the others that stood around waiting for me to make a sudden movement so that they could attack.

"It seems I already have," Cadon said with a smirk. "Drop your weapons."

I dropped the bow and arrow at my feet with an angry grunt.

I tried to figure out his angle. "But you've been defeated. The last of the mongrowls has abandoned your cause."

"The mongrowls served as no more than a means to an end. We first began capturing them and imprisoning them with the help of a few of your kind, which is why they are defensive to the likes of you. Once we had them, it wasn't hard to get them to do what we wanted, thanks to the moon and the power it possesses."

"But that's only legend!" I protested. "No more than a myth."

"However!" he shouted over me. "It didn't help as much as one would expect from animals. Mongrowls are after all more intelligent than most beasts that roam the wilds, which Yann should have predicted. Still, it did help in their temperament, their minds now more open and trusting. We were able to ride them and command them within their own course of reason. Still, we needed more, so we recruited the help of another. One who could make the animals listen and do as they were told." My eyes gleamed with eagerness and—obviously having noticed this—he didn't want to give me the satisfaction. "But I've already told you too much. After we ensure the end of elven reign, we will…" He paused. Galloping in the distance caught his attention as he halted from reaching inside his garments as if to remove something. "Aw, I expect this is your cavalry."

The galloping drew nearer and nearer, and it seemed that all of the boys around us were ready to end whatever came bursting into the clearing. The two with crossbows aimed pointedly in the direction of the sounds, and those with daggers reared them back, ready to hurl them into the chest of the intruder. I hoped and prayed that it wasn't Silvertail. Then again, what other animal had I known to whip through terrain such as this so easily? From out of the thicket of surrounding brush came the rutor, which dodged two or three simultaneously thrown daggers easily before darting off into the edgewoods, my satchel tossing around its thick neck as it disappeared.

"Arrrrrrggghh!" A harsh, startling battle cry filled the air as Silvertail, Segun, and Alag emerged from different sides of the clearing with swords raised and bows arched. They began with those who had lost their daggers, beheading one and leaving the other with a severed arm to bleed to death, while Silvertail with his bow and arrow took out the third. I quickly gathered my bow and arrow with just enough time to recover it before Cadon released the hold on his crossbow and sent an arrow flying, missing me by less than an inch. I rolled over onto the ground, recovering myself as quick as I could. I threw the quiver over my shoulder and with my loaded bow sent an arrow flying at Cadon as he fumbled to reload his crossbow. The arrowhead disappeared into Cadon's shoulder, sending him plummeting to the ground, moaning in pain.

I ran up upon the wretch, pulling another arrow from my quiver and thought to drive it through his throat without even bothering to place it in the bow. *He wouldn't spare you.* The whisper of a voice returned. I couldn't tell where it was coming from, and didn't feel the need to find out why. It would be near maddening if it not for the fact that everything except my mind wanted to do exactly what the voice was saying, egging me on as if after doing this one deed, all my problems would go away. *It's his fault the city is under siege. He deserves death,* it continued. Cadon was breathing hard and clutching his shoulder, small, hushed spurts of pain coming out of his mouth as I stared down at him, the arrow in my hand. I imagined his neck, skewered, the sensation it would bring me to feel the skin break from the point of my arrow. It made me more than simply happy. It made me euphoric.

"Stop, please." Another voice called out to me, but it was distant, a soft mumble that was almost indecipherable.

Do it, the harsh, cold whisper continued. *End him.*

A hand grasped me, and by his luck I stopped myself in time, bringing the point of the arrow to his neck, as I looked upon a terrified Meca. Silvertail, Segun, and Alag all looked at me with uncertainty, knowing that my decision was mine alone.

I stuck the arrow back in its quiver, then lowered down upon a shaken Cadon who jumped as I reached for the arrow buried in his shoulder. I had more hate in my heart for this child than anyone else I had come to know, whether Dwala, beast, or elf. More than Sir Calo, or the mountain giants, or even the accused mornowl who had stolen my sister. What he had done to Rose, what he had orchestrated with Nazda's former gang, whose slain faces I recognized from the night I first met Nazda in the black ring. Who seemed so welcoming that night, even with my disdain that I once had for their race.

With one foul yank and a painful screech from Cadon, I had the arrow in hand, the wooden shaft soaked in dark, red blood. He squeezed his shoulder, clutching at the gushing wound, at which point Segun rushed forward, tossing his sword to the ground, and without a minute to spare had sealed the wound using his talent. Segun smiled, helping up a quiet and apologetic-looking Cadon. Meca grabbed his hand, and before they or I could say anything, Silvertail spoke.

"These crimes are beyond them and those who attacked the city. I don't think that it wise to kill ones so young with their minds so easily warped. Still, a crime is a crime, and I think it fair that you remain behind and serve the houses of those who have lost anyone under the age of maturity as penance for this treachery. For although your lives will be spared, there were some who deserved life and received death who were not much older than you yourselves."

Cadon's eyebrows furrowed in anger, his lips quivering. Alag was furious at this display of ego. "Or would you rather die? Because I'm sure my people would have the greatest sympathy should I be the one burdened with the blood of such filth on my hands." Spit was coming from his mouth and I could tell he was unfathomably upset, but the boys got the point and Cadon, now eyeing Alag's sheathed sword, nodded his head in agreement.

"Now that that's settled," said Silvertail with a turn on his heel in the direction of the city, midway between securing his own weapon, when he stopped and positioned his sword on guard.

The tips of arrows, pulled by five more black-robed individuals with tattered masks that left some portions of their faces uncovered, were emerging from the brush into the clearing. I could see in the center of their half-formed ring, one with a mask that caused me to shudder with anger. I had seen it through the running gate around the purple ring, a feathered mask with hollowed eyes, a prominent beak, and plumage of fiery red. One standing to the left of the ostensible mornowl spoke who at this point I knew was nothing more than a fraud.

"Get them."

The voice was muffled, sounding both hoarse and harsh. I remembered how the ladies of the wood's masks made their voices deeper, helping to conceal their identity. Three of the black robed figures who towered over Segun, Alag, and I, circled around us and nudged us toward the thicket of brush in the direction of the city while another grabbed the lit torch that was pitched in the clearing, passing it to the one disguised as a mornowl, who led the way. Rain was pattering on the tops of the canopy, a few drops making it past to land on our distorted and confused faces.

Soon we were crossing into the clearing that led to the great stone bridge. The rain began picking up a little, speckling the dry ground like paint, but something odd was happening when the rain approached the torch. Upon nearing its flickering flames, the raindrops would dissolve in the air, leaving behind nothing but a tiny wisp of vapor. The only magic I knew to do anything of the sort was through sifting, for no talent could control both fire and water. This made my heart jump as my mind began to race. Creating a flame that could ever-burn without dying in rain was a feat that would take magic I'd only seen in sifting. For the first time my mind wasn't blanking or grasping for answers. In fact, every possible theory was being pushed aside in order for the answers to form a vivid picture that allowed for the truth to be easily seen, no matter how much I didn't want to see it. A master over animals, speaking to them to do their bidding, I thought, gritting my teeth in frustration. I wasn't sure. It was too farfetched. What cause would they have? The pots of powder, the same in the mountain trolls' keep and the same that were in her cottage. We were almost upon the stone bridge, the soft pecks of raindrops hitting the top of my head and the points of my shoulders.

"Alya?" I heard a voice call from a distance as I looked up to see Mira smiling gleefully, holding hand of none other than the one who had been feeding information to those who wanted nothing more than me to fall. The stone bridge was wrapped in a silver twine, ugly and ragged like rusted metal, glinting in the sun.

Mira started to come toward me but was stopped with a violent tug of the arm from Master Tali. Mira looked up at her with questioning eyes, obviously confused as to why she wasn't allowed to greet me, but I knew. For the first time Master Tali wasn't wearing long robes. Instead, she sported breastplates, gauntlets, and shin guards. In the wrappings of her braids were two long feathers of red and orange. Her eyes, however, remained unchanged as if she somehow thought that her secret was still safe.

"Meddling with traitors, I see," she said, brandishing a thin but sharp saber. Alag, taking offense, obviously feeling her words were meant towards him, retorted.

"What is the meaning of this, Tali? Speak to them. Tell them to free us. I agreed to let them leave the city in secret, what more do they want?" I couldn't believe that Alag knew that Master Tali was conspiring with these assassins and that he knew the Dwala were leaving the city—but from the terror in his eyes, he was just as confused by her appearance as the rest of us.

"She's betrayed us all." I muttered the words without thinking as I looked from Mira up at Master Tali, staring her daringly in the eyes. "She helped the warriors from the woods into the city. She helped orchestrate the placement of that fire powder that destroyed the Chamber of Light, the tower at Shiloh's School of Talents and—" I gasped. "It was you. You destroyed the judgment chambers in an attempt to end the council, and you poisoned the members of the courts and their families."

Segun and Alag were the only ones who seemed to be taking this by surprise, while Silvertail simply stared with the same daring at Master Tali who was now smiling. After a long pause and a giggle, she finally spoke.

"Very good, Alya. I daresay, as one of my brightest pupils, your deduction is uncanny. The bag I brought into the council meeting contained the powder, which I lit on my way out of the judgment chambers, and it was I who after visiting each respective courts member's house to appeal on behalf of the school, slipped poison into their stores of water. If the bomb I planted at the Tower of Light hadn't been lit early by lightning and exploded, I would have finished the council, you, and my sniveling sister's son at once, leaving the city at free rein and me as its leader."

Mira, having drawn everything together, tried to wrench away from her grasp, but Master Tali was too quick and grabbed Mira around her tiny neck, holding her tight. I struggled in the same manner but my cloaked captor, whose gripping hand was more massive than any of the warriors I had encountered, held me in place.

"—and strong willed as well. You and your sister have that in common. It wasn't easy getting her over the gate. When I awoke in my cottage, I thought I had failed and was discovered, but I heard you all talking and knew immediately that I had succeeded and you didn't suspect me." The tips of my finger were now digging into my palms, just a sample of the rage I felt for Master Tali. She seemed all too amused with herself and I was keen on wiping that smirk clear off of her face.

"Very well. Tie them up." The cloaked individuals roughly drove us to the ground, Master Tali shoving Mira to one who began wrapping rope around Mira's wrists. Mira pulled her hands, wanting to get away, but the black-robed assailant tackled her to the ground with his whole body on top of her, her frame spread awkwardly under their gruesome weight.

"Get off of her! You overgrown—" But my insults stopped as the black-robed individual, with great strength, shoved a knee in the crevice between Mira's neck and head, making a show of taking their time unwinding the rope slowly and cutting it with the sharp of their blade while Mira with watering eyes gasped for air.

"Please! She won't move again. Please." But they didn't budge, the lower part of their face visible under the chinked armor showing missing teeth and a swollen jaw. I watched Mira exhaustingly pull at his robes. Still he bore down, it sinking as Mira's breath slowed.

Like a hissing snake, an arrow came soaring from the trees and sliced into the head of the masked warrior, piercing the sheeted metal that covered the dome. Smoke trailed from its puncture as the sardonic abomination of a person keeled over on the ground, the helmet shifting slightly to reveal nearly his entire face. To my surprise, I found the young lieutenant who I had confronted in the Guerr's fort not too long ago. Mira hopped up just as the assailant who held me fell to the ground, writhing in pain, a searing arrow, the arrowhead still a bright red from the heat, lodged through their shoulder.

With one loud cry, I saw Rayloh, red curly hair and skin so tanned that he was almost unrecognizable, darting from the trees with an arrow ready for shooting. I couldn't believe it, as hot tears ran down my cheeks and joy erupted in heart, as our savior emerged like a long-lost hero returned to protect what's his. He shot without fear at Master Tali, who waved the arrow away like a bothersome fly, lodging it into the ground where it flickered with life, growing slowly into a small ember. Drawing her sword, she lunged toward Rayloh, who had yet to recess his bow. She was nearly upon his head when Silvertail, having overtaken his guard who lay strewn on the ground, blood draining from their back, blocked her falling weapon and forcing her to face him.

"Get across the bridge!" Silvertail yelled over his shoulder. I gathered up Mira, holding her hand and pulling her onward, followed closely by the lads. We were nearly upon the bridge where the embers from Rayloh's missed arrow were still burning, creeping slowly along the grass but well within control, when Alag's voice came booming from the middle of the ledge.

"You take orders from me," he spat, pointing two of his fingers at Rayloh and Segun. "I order the militia and Keldrock runs from no one." Rayloh and Segun stood for a moment, not knowing what to do, but I knew the oath they took and the punishment for breaking it. As we looked at each other with a mixture of regretful and ponderous eyes, another black-robed individual launched towards us, but Rayloh was ready. Segun, following suit, with his sword on guard, sailed forward in double combat with another black-robed individual, along with Alag.

Swords were clashing against loud battle cries and grunts of frustration, and through it all I could see it, with its hollowed eyes and colorful plumage, with a beak that up close and in the bright light of the sun appeared even more sharp and dangerous. It took a few steps with the torch still in hand, and slick, pointed feathers peeking from its sleeves over its hands, as its hollow eyes narrowed in on me. I shoved Mira forward, urging her to cross the bridge, but turned to face the bird-like human who peered down to what seemed to be the flickering flames on the ground and watched as they, just an slight inch off from the beginnings of the metal twine, collided with the ends, creating a tiny red spark. Within seconds, the sparks were traveling through the tangled mess of barbed metallic twine, making little pops as it went. With much gusto, the masked figure lodged the torch in the ground and made its way through the clatter of chaos towards the edgewoods. I turned to make sense of the riveting flame and metal wiring. Then, against the rain and the rising mist, I saw in the middle of the bridge five large pots that I would have assumed to be boulders had not I known better.

"Mira! Come back!" I shouted, my eyes still on the running sparks of fire that had now broken off into three separate sparks following their own line of metal twine.

She was a quarter of the way up the bridge, away from the ledge from where it began, and another quarter of the bridge away from the pots. I began panicking as the sparks moved faster. Mira was running now, her long hair flying behind her, which even in the wake of our ends—because I too was on the bridge now, sprinting toward her—made her look ever the more beautiful. I couldn't see the sparks anymore. Perhaps they went out, I thought, but I knew they hadn't, for they never had before. They didn't in the Chamber of Light or the watchtower at the school. They had burned in the judgment chambers, the flickering embers birthed from the explosions bringing death to the council members. Mira dove into my arms just as a jolt like I had never felt before sent me over the edge of the bridge which within seconds was collapsing, breaking Keldrock away from the rest of the world.

Chapter Twenty-Two

My ears were ringing. The air pushed against my face as my stomach bobbled in and out. My dress was frayed, and I could smell soot in my nostrils. Mira was falling, her eyes closed, just under my body. I pulled her in, fighting the wind and the force of gravity that was trying to drive her away from me. I clutched her head into my chest as stone fell down past us, breaking into the sides of the gorge. I looked down to see, to my horror, large geodes and jagged rock jutting out from rushing water. With one final glance at the kiss of destruction we would soon meet, I closed my eyes, gritting my teeth together in anticipation.

It felt like a lifetime was passing by, but I didn't want to open my eyes. I could feel something wrapped around me like a warm blanket. Am I in the afterlife? I thought. Will I soon be awaiting Olörun's judgment? I couldn't bear it anymore. I peeked at the bottom of the brutal gorge facing me, but I wasn't falling toward it anymore. I was moving away from it, the rushing water at the bottom appearing like nothing more than a rebellious stream. I still held tight to Mira as we lay strewn on a ledge. Mira's eyes were still closed, her face marred by soot and ash. I stroked her face as I tried to catch my breath, my head light and cloudy.

I looked up to my disbelief to see a bird with beautiful orange, gold, yellow, and red feathers like sun rays, a beak like a champion's shield, and talons that could meet any swords making short work of the warriors robed in black, some being skewered by its mighty talons, and others being tossed with its beating wings over the ledge into the rushing water and sharp rocks below. Silvertail, Rayloh, Segun, and Alag all lay on the ground, intact but unconscious from the bridge's explosion. The bird, having delivered a mighty blow to our enemies, reared its head and with one heart-filled rise of its chest let out a beautiful call that I hadn't heard since the veil fell. It rang out even through the stuffiness of my ears.

It beat its wings, its majestic neck craning up to the sky, its beautiful feathers cutting the air like fine sheets, the beads of rain glistening like diamonds against its vibrant plumage. My vision continued going in and out, the last glance of the mighty bird disappearing over the treetops in the eastern wood. I drifted off into darkness, the air now cool and sweet against the falling rain. The real mornowl had returned.

***

I awoke to the soft patting of cool hands against my face. I opened my eyes, the stars up above swirling about and starting to come into focus. Night had fallen and my head was aching terribly. I propped myself up on my elbows and embraced a tearful Mira, her face still dingy from the explosion of powders that destroyed the bridge. Segun was hovering over a wincing Silvertail, working on healing his arm, and Rayloh, seemingly having just awoken himself, sat on the ground slumped over. The remaining black-robed lay still, spread awkwardly in puddles of their own blood. The one that once gripped me was Czar Icar, his mask missing, showing his strong prominent jaw and bold eyes that even in death demonstrated that he lived for the hunt. Standing like an apparition just a few feet from the ledge was Alag, his long hair drifting elegantly in the wind, his skin like fine chocolate, radiant against the drifting stars overhead.

I looked around at the wet ground, wondering where the traitor Tali, who I would refuse to call Master again, had gone, but I found her not. I had never suspected her, and I tried not to think too much about why I hadn't—and if I had, how much pain and suffering would have been avoided. I looked out at the city as the last fumes of the dying fires had disappeared on the cusps of the winds. Just barely audible from such a great distance were the cheers of my people. Nothing linked us to them. Segun's parents, Madja, father, Sir Fueto, and the rest of my kind were all on the other side. There was no way across this giant moat.

I looked around at my sister, my allies, and comrades who had followed me out into the edgewoods who had been disconnected from their families just as I had. Their eyes were full of sorrow; their heads hung. With one deep breath I turned, facing the edgewoods, and looked into the mass of trees whispering with the sounds of calling animals and hooting night fowl. I looked at Mira who was standing up now as well, her hand sliding into mine. Together we took those first steps, then a few more. The sound of more feet joined us and soon everyone was at the very edge of the forest, half-covered by the casting shadows of the canopy. And as we took our first steps into the edgewoods, I saw in the brush the bright eyes slipping away of a familiar sight—its white foxy face disappearing into the brush as if pointing the way into the distant unknown.

END OF BOOK TWO

About the Author

M.C. Ray is a creative who has just made his premiere to the world through the writing of *The Unveiled*, the first book of a series. He is a Georgia native, born and raised in Stockbridge, Georgia, and has always had a passion for the arts, especially the power of story telling in all its forms.

"Creating a fantasy with characters that look like me is more than just about inclusion. In reality we are present, so why not in the magical, fantastical, and the alternative."

- M.C. Ray